THE
RUNAWAY
HEIRESS

EMMA ORCHARD

Allison & Busby Limited
11 Wardour Mews
London W1F 8AN
allisonandbusby.com

First published in Great Britain by Allison & Busby in 2023.

A CIP catalogue record for this book is available from
the British Library.

First Edition

ISBN 978-0-7490-2979-1

Typeset in 11/16 pt Sabon LT Pro by
Typo•glyphix, Burton-on-Trent, DE14 3HE.

By choosing this product, you help take care of the world's forests.
Learn more: www.fsc.org

Printed and bound by
CPI Group (UK) Ltd, Croydon, CR0 4YY

*Dedicating this book to my lovely family,
Luigi, Jamie and Annie, shouldn't be taken
as any sort of suggestion that I want them
to read it or, even worse, talk to me
about its contents. Ever.*

We are all fools in love

Pride and Prejudice – Jane Austen

CHAPTER ONE

A ragged cloud blotted out the sliver of moon. It was suddenly darker in the elegant square of fashionable houses, and Cassandra scurried down the shallow steps in front of her. Once at the bottom, she huddled in the shadows at the far end of the paved semi-basement area, panting. She was trespassing on some gentleman's private property, but that was the least of her concerns in this moment. Her heart was pounding in her chest, and she was dizzy with terror. It was good to stop running for a moment, to try to collect her thoughts. But she dared not relax, for there was no safety here – there was nothing at all to prevent her pursuers from finding her in this makeshift hiding place and dragging her away by force. There was not the least point screaming and hoping that passing strangers might come to her aid; the men who were chasing her had already demonstrated that they had a ready answer prepared for any passer-by who should question their actions. She had thought that the gentleman she had stumbled into a few hundred yards back might assist her, but her pursuers had caught up with her and told him some plausible tale, and he had shrugged, and gone on his careless way. She had barely escaped them then; only her desperation, her youthful speed and their drunken state allowed her to evade their grasp.

The streets of London in the dead of night were a perilous place for a woman alone, and she was well aware that in running out of her uncle's house at this hour she had forfeited any claim to respectability in the eyes of the world. There was no help to be found, only more danger. She was entirely alone. She must *think*.

There was a faint light inside the mansion, spilling out from a small, barred window and coming, she presumed, from the servants' quarters in the basement. What little she had seen of the house in her headlong flight did not suggest that it was currently occupied by its aristocratic owners, which was why she had made the snap decision to seek refuge here. Cassandra had noticed in a single desperate glance that the doorknocker had been taken down and the tall windows at street level and above were all securely shuttered. She supposed that the noble family who owned such a large and imposing building in the most exclusive part of Town were away. The Season was coming to an end, so it was reasonable to think that they had joined the rest of the polite world in some fashionable seaside resort, leaving a skeleton staff of servants to ensure the safety of their home. She was in danger from the servants too, of course – perhaps they would not molest her, but if one of them should have occasion to come out here, and saw her lurking where she had absolutely no business to be, they would undoubtedly raise a hue and cry that would attract the attention of her pursuers. And if a commotion should instead alert the patrolling Watch, she would be in no better position. She could surely expect no aid or sympathy from them. They might – she was ignorant of these matters, and hoped to remain so – apprehend her for vagrancy and lock her in some dreadful gaol, and if they should ascertain her identity they would merely return her to the care, for want of a worse word, of her uncle and guardian. And then she would be back where she'd started.

Cassandra stiffened as she heard voices, angry male voices, in the square above her. Her uncle, and . . . him. Clearly they had not given up seeking for her yet. Of course not: too much depended on finding her.

The best thing would be to gain entry to the mansion somehow, and hide there till daylight. The streets would be less dangerous then. It was not much of a plan, but it was all she had. If she could somehow attract the attention of the people in the house, so that they came out, she might perhaps slip inside while their backs were turned – how, though? – and be safe from her pursuers for a while. She could not think beyond that. She felt hot panic rising inside her, and pushed it down. Losing her head would not help. She must plan, and then she must act.

She crept towards the stairs that led up to the street – she had been huddling like a frightened animal in the darkest corner of the area – and strained to hear her uncle's voice. It was close, but if there was any chance of her desperate plan working it would need to be much closer.

The wait seemed interminable, but at last she could hear him cursing not far away. She judged that he was probably directly in front of the neighbouring house. She slipped back towards the basement door and picked up a wooden pail that had been left there; she had almost fallen over it a moment before, and that had given her the germ of an idea.

No time to hesitate. She flung the pail with all her strength against the lighted window and shrank back into the shadow of her former hiding place, close to the basement door but – she hoped – invisible. The wooden bucket clattered against the iron bars – a loud, shocking noise in the relative quiet of the deserted square – and she heard a shout of angry surprise from inside and, a moment later, the screeching of bolts as the door was unfastened. Meanwhile, a triumphant cry of 'Got her!' came from the pavement above, and heavy, urgent footsteps pounded towards her, then slowed a little as they descended the steps in the darkness. She had been counting on that: that they would follow the sound, confident that they had run her to earth at last.

The basement door was wrenched open, and a man emerged into the area. He was so close to her that she could have reached out and touched him. A servant, she supposed. He was an African man. Silhouetted against the light inside, he made an impressive figure; he was tall and powerfully built, and his posture was belligerent, his fists raised in front of him in what Cassandra imagined to be a boxer's stance. There was a woman close behind him, almost as tall and broad. A formidable pair, and their attention was not focused on her, but on the men who had just reached the bottom of the steps. 'Oi!' bellowed the manservant, moving nearer to the intruders, his fists still held ready for action. His companion, as bold as he was, followed him. 'What d'you mean by trespassing on a gentleman's property and making this racket?! If you've come to mill the ken, you'll have me to deal with, and you'll soon regret the day, my bully boys!'

'My good fellow . . .' began her uncle in the unctuous tones she so hated.

She did not stay to see how their altercation resolved itself; she edged closer and closer to the open door, still hidden in shadow and blessing her soft slippers for their silence, and then slid inside, entirely unobserved by any of the participants in the scene playing out behind her. It was dangerous – there could be others present in the basement rooms, and if anyone saw her now she was lost – but she was wagering everything on the chance that, if there had been anyone else there, they too would likely have been drawn outside by the commotion and the impulse to protect their master's property. It was a risk she was prepared to take. She had no choice.

Her gamble paid off: the stone-flagged corridor was deserted, and the room opening off it – a kitchen – appeared to be empty too. She did not stay to make sure, but penetrated deeper into the house, resolved to seek the upstairs quarters where she thought she might be safer from discovery.

The layout of a gentleman's town mansion generally followed a set pattern, and Cassandra had no difficulty finding the servants' staircase. She crept up it to the green baize door that must lead to the ground floor of the house, opening it a crack and poking her head cautiously around it. A grand entrance hall, paved in squares of black and white marble. A little chilly moonlight crept in from the large fanlight above the door, enough to see her surroundings. She thought for one awful moment that she saw a tall, motionless human figure, standing there in the alcove, watching her, and let out an exclamation of surprise that she muffled hastily with one ungloved hand. But she realised in the next second that it was a classical statue: a fine marble copy of the Apollo Belvedere, some part of her brain noted irrelevantly. She felt hysterical laughter bubbling inside her. Apollo could do her no harm, and just at this moment the prospect of being transformed into a tree as the nymph Daphne had been while he chased her was

14

not at all unattractive. No, it was living, breathing men she had to fear, not ancient gods.

She opened the door fully and slipped through it, closing it with agonising but necessary slowness behind her. She could hear no sounds of pursuit coming from below, and it did not seem to her, from what she had seen of him, that the burly servant who had accosted her uncle so confidently was the kind of man who would meekly allow two complete strangers to enter and search the building that was under his care. But still, it would be the highest degree of folly to stay here. She must find a more secluded place to hide. And do it very, very quietly. She crept forward. She was a criminal now, she supposed. A house-breaker. But she was committed to this course of action, and could not turn back. Which door should she choose . . . ?

CHAPTER TWO

Hal cursed as he struggled to insert the key in the lock. He could hardly blame the darkness for the difficulty he was having, for the midsummer dawn was just breaking over the square behind him, and he could see perfectly well. And yet he was damned if he could get the blasted key – which was large enough, in all conscience – into the confounded lock. He was, of course, drunk. Very, very drunk. Drunk, he reflected hazily, as a lord. Which, of course, he was. So that was perfectly in order.

At length he managed what should have been a simple task, and the door swung open in front of him. He entered. With exaggerated caution he closed the heavy front door quietly behind him and stood in the marble-tiled hall, swaying slightly on his feet and considering

16

what he should do next. Apollo Belvedere – evidence that his grandfather, like most of his generation, had in the previous century undertaken the Grand Tour and spent at least some of his money in the approved fashion – studiously ignored him, gazing off towards the library door with sightless eyes and outstretched marble arm, almost as if pointing the way. Perhaps the god of . . . all the things that he was god of, things that Hal couldn't quite recall at that precise moment, was disapproving of his owner's sadly inebriated condition, although, from what Hal recalled from his schooldays, all those Greek deities were what his friend Tom Wainfleet would call devilish smoky fellows.

'Not at all the thing!' said Hal with a crack of slightly wild laughter. The sound echoed in the hall, and all at once the big house seemed very empty. As it was, of course. He was not supposed to be coming home, but had returned on a whim, and most of the indoor servants had been given holiday. Some of them were still here, naturally; a house like this could never be left entirely unprotected. Hal's head groom, Jem Oldcastle, was somewhere in his private fastness, and presumably his wife, Kitty, too, but they were not expecting Hal's return tonight – this morning. Nobody was. Georgiana was in Brighton, Bastian was on a reading tour with some friends from Oxford, and the younger children were in Lyme Regis with Aunt Sophia, heaven help her.

After the trials of the Season, Hal had been looking forward to some peace and quiet with a fierce intensity, but now that he had finally obtained his wish he found the idea unaccountably depressing as he followed the direction of the statue's stony gaze and made his rather erratic way into his private sanctum and favourite room. The rest of the house, apart from his bedroom, would be done up in Holland covers, but he insisted that the library always be left ready for his use, and he was glad of it now. No doubt his sudden gloom would lift when he was in less chilly surroundings. Altogether too much marble in the hall: floor, wall panels and statues. Enough to make anyone blue-devilled.

He sighed with relief as he entered his library. That was better; much cosier. With the ease of long familiarity, he threaded his way between the furniture in the darkness and found the tinderbox that was always left ready in its accustomed place on the mantel. He fumbled a little as he attempted to light a candle by touch alone, but by the exercise of a prodigious concentration he achieved the feat in the end, and turned, momentarily dazzled, to pick up a candelabrum and light yet more.

He stopped. Something was wrong. He was not alone in the room.

There was a girl.

In his foxed state, Hal was not perhaps as surprised as he should be to find a perfectly strange young female in his library. Perfectly strange young females had, if truth be told, occasionally been a feature of his life in the years since he had left Eton. He certainly had no objection to them on principle. Especially not if they were pretty, which this one appeared to be, from what little he could see of her.

Vague thoughts that she might be some friend of his sister's flitted through his mind, but he retained enough sense somewhere in a dim recess of his brain to realise that that was nonsense; his sister Georgie was not here and, even if she had been, there was no earthly reason why one of her innumerable bosom bows should be huddled on his library sofa at – he squinted at the gold mantel clock, but it had stopped – some unconscionable hour of the morning.

Asleep. She was fast asleep, entirely unaware of his presence.

He moved a step or two nearer, and raised the candle to have a closer look at her as she slumbered. Yes, very pretty. The fair unknown was curled up on the big high-backed sofa, with one hand pillowing her cheek. She was wrapped in a voluminous black cloak, and against its darkness her vivid colouring stood out dramatically, even in the flickering candlelight. She had cropped hair of flaming red, and her short nose was scattered with the freckles that often accompanied such locks. Long lashes brushed her cheeks, and her skin was very pale. She had a heart-shaped face, and her pale pink mouth, which was slightly open as she slept, was rather appealing. 'Kissable' was the word that popped into Hal's fuddled brain. Yes, kissable. She looked to be about Georgie's age, it was true – perhaps eighteen or so. He could see a glimpse of very crumpled white muslin under the voluminous cloak, and small feet in dusty silk evening slippers peeped out from under the hem.

But what the devil was she doing in his library?

He must have made some sound, for suddenly her eyes sprang open – they were green, he noticed – and she looked at him blankly. And then screamed.

He swore, and dropped the candle, and the room was plunged into darkness.

CHAPTER THREE

Cassandra had not meant to fall asleep. The trouble was, there had been nothing else to do. She had opened the door and felt her way cautiously into the room. She had no means of making a light, and she would not in any case have dared to do so, afraid that it might show under the door, should the servants make a tour of the house to ensure that all was secure.

She did not need a candle to know that she was in a library. The scent of old paper and crumbling leather binding told her that, and there were few places in the world where Cassandra felt more comfortable than in a library. She felt better already, her spirits rising, though she was well aware that there could be no rational basis for her altered mood. She could not be sure that she had evaded capture, and even if she had indeed done so, she was now trapped in a strange house with nothing but the clothes she stood up in, a disturbingly light purse and the few possessions she had been able to cram into her reticule before she fled. These included her mother's pearls, and she supposed that she could pawn them, if she had the slightest idea how to go about such a thing. But she had come this far. She could at least sit down and contemplate her next move in comfort.

Edging forward gingerly, afraid of stumbling over pieces of furniture she could not see, she bumped her toes painfully on some hard object. Her hands found the back of a high-backed sofa, and she groped around it until she found the seat, and sank gratefully into the cushions. That was better.

Her mind remained stubbornly blank, inspiration refusing to make an appearance, and after a while she realised that she was lightheaded with thirst. There might very well be something to drink in a gentleman's library, she supposed. Alcohol, presumably, to which she was not in the least accustomed, but it would be better than nothing, and she had heard that it gave one courage. It certainly seemed to give her uncle courage, and as for *him* . . . She shuddered involuntarily, and pushed the thought resolutely from her mind.

She rose wearily, and resumed her careful progress around the room. Before long she found a desk, and upon it a heavy cut-crystal decanter. Her seeking hands found a glass beside it. This was good. But now she faced the problem of how to pour out liquid, in total darkness. She was bound to spill it, and it seemed grossly unfair to her unwitting host to make a disorder in his library. After a little thought, she set both decanter and glass down on the floor, and after some experimentation and some rather regrettable accidents, found that she was able, if she was very careful, to pour a dribble of the liquid into the glass; fortunately it was not a delicate stemmed wineglass but some sort of heavy bumper. She raised it to her lips, and took a doubtful sip. It tasted every whit as unpleasant as she had feared, and made her cough and splutter, but she felt a sort of warmth creeping down her throat, and after a few moments she decided that she did feel slightly better. She poured herself some more of whatever it was, and made her way back to the sofa, where she made herself comfortable again, and in a surprisingly short time she had drained the glass.

A substantial quantity of fine old smuggled French brandy was perhaps bound to have a powerful effect on a slight young lady of barely more than five feet, who had spent a most trying evening that had culminated in a headlong flight through the streets of London, and one, moreover, who had never had occasion to drink strong liquor before. It was not long before the glass slipped from her hand, and rolled unharmed and unseen across the Persian carpet. She did not feel it go; she was already asleep.

Cassandra woke with a start to find a tall figure looming over her with a candle, and saw no more.

She let out a scream in her shock, and the flame was extinguished. She heard a deep masculine voice utter some quite outrageous curses, and then before she could collect her scattered wits there was a scrape as the stranger employed a tinderbox, more curses, and a candle flared into life, and then another, until a candelabrum was fully lit. He held it up and stared down at her.

They looked at each other in tense silence for a few seconds. Cassandra saw a tall young man in dishevelled evening clothes, which looked as though they were the very height of fashion, but had undergone some ungentle treatment in the last few hours. His hair was dark and disordered, his eyes were a shockingly bright blue, and he was uncommonly handsome and very, very angry.

'What the devil,' he enunciated carefully, 'are you doing in my library?'

Her wits entirely deserted her. She could not think of a single word to say in response, but simply gazed at him in mute horror.

He looked down at her, frowning, and then his azure gaze seemed to find the glass, and the decanter. His face became even more thunderous, and he said, 'Have you been drinking my best brandy?'

'Yes,' she said in a small voice.

He sniffed. 'Have you been spilling my best brandy?'

'Just a little. I am most terribly sorry, sir. I could not see what I was about. I dared not look for a light.'

'I don't suppose you did. Are you a burglar? You

don't look at all like a burglar, I must say. But perhaps that is your . . . your . . .' He waved a graceful hand when it seemed that he was unable to retrieve the word he was seeking.

Cassandra was beginning to suspect that the handsome young man was, in fact, somewhat drunk. This was alarming news. Her recent experiences had given her no reason to trust men who were drunk, but then she had also learnt, to her cost, that they could be near as bad sober. The young man did not appear to have any immediate intention of molesting her in any way, and she was forced to acknowledge that his anger was quite justifiable, as she was undeniably trespassing in his house.

She said, 'I'm not a burglar. But truly I can see why my presence here can only appear rather odd to you.'

'Odd, you say? I'll wager it does!' He laughed, and dropped into the sofa beside her. She stiffened, but he did not move any closer to her, merely stretching out his long legs and crossing them at the ankle. Leaning back against the side of the sofa, he looked her up and down with his penetrating, disconcerting sky-blue stare, folded his arms and said, 'Go ahead.'

She knew that she owed him some sort of explanation. 'I was being chased. I hid near your basement door, and when your servants came out I slipped inside the house and came into this room to hide. And I drank your brandy. I'm sorry,' she said again. 'I know that it was an outrageous thing to do.'

'I expect you had your reasons,' he said vaguely. 'When was this?'

'About midnight, I think.'

'And why did my servants come out? Seems an odd thing for them to do, at midnight.'

'I threw a pail against the window.'

'Well, that explains it, then,' he said, apparently quite satisfied. But after a moment obviously spent in deep cogitation, he said, frowning again, 'Why were you out at midnight, heaving pails about, and who was chasing you? You're not a . . . a . . . are you?' He waved his hand again.

'No, I am not!' she said indignantly. 'Though,' she added with a small, woebegone sniff, 'I can see why you might think I am. I know that I should not have been roaming the streets at night, and believe me, sir, I would not have done so save for the direst necessity.'

'Oh well, dire necessity, obviously,' he said with a yawn. 'Didn't think you were. So if you're not a burglar and you're not a . . . can't think of a word appropriate for your ears, but anyway, you're not, why were you out and about at midnight, and who was chasing you? Doesn't seem at all the thing. Not that I mean to pry, of course.'

Cassandra sat huddled in her corner of the sofa, silently twisting the stuff of her cloak between her hands. The young man said suddenly, 'Do you have a name? Well, obviously you have a name, I'm not so drunk that I don't know that, but what is it?'

'I don't think I should say.'

'Have to call you something.'

'I don't see why.'

He puzzled over the logic of this for a while. 'I'm sure there must be a reason. I can't think of it just at this moment, granted.'

'Well, I won't tell you.'

His blue gaze swept over her again, and he grinned suddenly. 'Then I'll have to think of a name for you myself, mysterious and beautiful stranger. What kind of name would fit someone who creeps into houses at night and drinks people's old brandy and sleeps on their sofas?'

She said, 'I don't creep into *houses*. I don't make a habit of this sort of thing, you know.'

'So you say. Whether I am to believe you . . . Incognita, I could call you.'

She huffed. 'How ridiculous!'

'You think so? Not original, perhaps. Let me see, then . . .' he mused. 'I have it! I shall call you Biancaneve! That's perfect. Didn't she break into the cottage and steal people's food and fall asleep? Not brandy, but I dare say she would have nabbled theirs if they'd happened to have any to hand. I remember reading it to the children when they were small. Terrible example to set, of course, but as I recall they seemed to like it. I expect that's where you got the idea for your housebreaking from. Biancaneve, that's the ticket. Or Snow White, if you prefer.'

He scarcely looked old enough to have children, and certainly not children who were no longer small. He must have married extraordinarily young. She thought he was not yet thirty – perhaps seven or eight and twenty. She found herself asking curiously, 'Do you have many children?'

'Dozens,' he said gloomily. 'Well, not dozens, but five. Just seems like dozens sometimes. Especially the younger ones. They hunt in packs, you know.'

'I cannot believe you can possibly have five children. Your poor wife!'

'Oh, I don't have a wife, Snow White. Never have had.'

She gasped, and he looked at her in surprise, then grinned at her engagingly once more. 'What? Oh, you think . . . No, no, nothing of the kind. My life is quite complicated enough without that sort of nonsense. I'm their brother, and their guardian, for my sins. Bastian is twenty, Georgie – Georgiana – is eighteen, and the rest of them . . . fourteen and then twelve. Twins,' he explained in answer to her lifted brow.

'Goodness,' she said weakly.

'Yes,' he agreed with feeling. 'Although goodness has little to do with it, I assure you. They're terrors, apart from Bastian.'

It was absurd, but somehow she felt more comfortable with him now that she knew he had so many younger brothers and sisters; she did not know why it should be so. Perhaps, she thought suddenly, the fact that he had a sister of much her own age might make him more sympathetic to her plight.

'Are they here now? It seemed to me that the house was closed up.'

'They are not. It is. Just Jem Oldcastle and his wife, a couple of housemaids and coachmen somewhere, and me. And you, of course, Snow White.'

She shivered, suddenly aware of how vulnerable she was, for all practical purposes alone with him in his house like this, and all the evils of her situation came flooding back to her.

He was observant, for all his inebriation and the sleepy way he sprawled across the sofa. He said abruptly, 'I'm not in the habit of molesting young women, you know. Dash it all, not old women, either. Women. Girls. Anybody. Drunk or sober. Still not at all sure what you're doing here, but you're in no danger from me, I give you my word.'

'I only wish every man who calls himself a gentleman could say the same!' she blurted, unable to repress her bitterness.

His eyes darkened perceptibly, and he looked angry again, though not at her, and oddly formidable for a moment. Enunciating carefully, he said, 'I really think you should tell me, you know. I might be able to help.'

She buried her face in her hands, a sudden wave of weariness sweeping over her. 'I don't think anybody can help me.'

His voice was warm and reassuring as he said, 'Try

me. My sister's forever getting into scrapes. Or she was
– she's going to be engaged to be married. I expect she'll
still get into scrapes, mind you, but they won't be my
problem any more. Shouldn't wonder if I'll miss it, if
truth be told. So . . .'

Cassandra burst into tears.

CHAPTER FOUR

He did not appear in the least disconcerted. Perhaps he was used to weeping ladies. He found a large handkerchief, and handed it to her, and she sobbed convulsively into it for a while, as he sat at her side in silence. He did not attempt to touch her – she would not have welcomed it, however kindly it might have been meant – and he seemed to know instinctively that she needed the relief of tears.

Presently Cassandra blew her nose, and wiped her face, and felt some relief. She considered offering him his handkerchief back, but then looked at it, and thought better of the idea. She scrunched it into a ball, and clasped it tightly in her hands. He still said nothing, and after a while she said, 'I'll tell you.'

'Good. More brandy?'

She chuckled in a slightly watery fashion. 'No, thank you.'

'Probably just as well. I shan't either. Best to keep a clear head.' He seemed to be sobering up rapidly. It could be, she thought with a faint and fragile spark of hope, that with all his responsibilities he had experience of what was required in a crisis.

She took a deep breath. 'I am an orphan. My mother died when I was small, and my father early last year.' He appeared to be on the verge of speech, but she forestalled him. 'I do not say this to seek sympathy, but only so you should understand my situation. After my father's death, I had to go and live with my uncle. He is my father's half-brother and my trustee.'

'You have a fortune?'

'I do, and I cannot tell you how much I wish I did not!'

'That uncle of yours has designs on it?'

'Yes! I should have made my come-out last year, but my uncle put it off, saying it was too close to my father's death, which was true, of course. But this spring he produced a friend of his. A man his own age. I suspect they have agreed to divide my inheritance between them once I have been forced into marriage. He told me that I could make my come-out only if I agreed to be betrothed to his friend.'

'He didn't want you meeting any other men?'

'Exactly! I refused. He was very angry, and has grown angrier as I have maintained my resolve. He is

32

bad enough, but the friend he intends me to marry is much worse!'

'That's despicable. What a devilish ramshackle sort of fellow he must be. I take it your uncle is not a wealthy man?'

'I do not know, but I think not. I think he is supporting himself from my fortune. Of course, if I should marry anyone of my own choosing, he risks losing control of my money. And so he has hatched this scheme with his revolting friend.'

He looked at her, considering. 'Why now?' He saw that she did not understand him, and elaborated. 'Why did you flee tonight? What happened to make you take such . . . such sudden and frantic action?'

She said shakily, 'I have been locked in my room for several weeks, given my meals on a tray. I think he thought I would weaken. When I did not, he tried another tactic. He sent one of the maids up with a new gown for me – this gown – and said that he would whip me if I did not wear it and come down for dinner. I believed him. So I did.'

'Go on.' His voice was grim.

'The other man was there. They were both drunk, and grew drunker, and the way he looked at me made my skin crawl. At the end of the meal, my uncle simply walked out of the room and left us alone together.'

'My poor child,' he said, and he sounded perfectly sober now. 'I am so sorry. You need not tell me any more, if you do not wish to. I think I have heard enough.'

'I want to tell you. I have come too far to stop now. He tried to kiss me, up against the wall by the fireplace.' Tears were streaming unheeded down her face as she spoke. 'I struggled. I would not let him . . . I hit him.'

He made a noise of approval, and, emboldened somehow, she went on a little more strongly, 'I reached out my hand, I scarcely knew for what, and picked up a bronze figure from the mantel. I hit him with it. I do not suppose it can have been a hard blow, but it shocked him. He fell back; his head was bleeding . . .'

'And you ran.'

'I did. I had my reticule, with a few coins in it and my mother's pearls; I had been locked in my room so long, when I heard I was to be let out for a time I thought this might at last be my one chance to escape. There was a cloak in the hall – his, perhaps, I do not know. I seized it, and ran, and hid from them.'

'Did they follow you to this house?'

'They followed me into the square. I ran down and hid in the basement area, and when they heard the noise of the pail against the window bars they started down the stairs; they thought they had cornered me at last, I suppose. But your servant came out and argued with them.'

There was a smile in his voice. 'Yes, he would do that. I am sure they stood no chance of getting past him. He would knock them down and enjoy doing it. He used to be a prize fighter, you will not be surprised to hear. His life at present does not involve hitting nearly as many people as he would like.' His tone grew more serious

34

as he said, 'That was clever of you, to realise that Jem would think that they had caused the disturbance, and upbraid them, and that would give you the chance to slip inside.'

'I was desperate.'

'I perfectly understand why you should have been. Did he plant a facer on either of them, do you know?' he asked hopefully.

Despite her distress, she could not help but laugh at this. 'I did not stay to see!'

'Pity. Well, we can hope. I am sure they both deserve a taste of his home-brewed, and I expect it would have done you good to see it.'

'I wish he might have beaten them both to a pulp!' she said fiercely.

'Well, if he did not, perhaps he will find another occasion to do so. I would not mind helping him in the least.'

'But what is to become of me?' she said. 'I cannot go back. And they might have me arrested for assault. He was bleeding, I told you!'

'They won't do that,' said her companion confidently. It occurred to her that he still did not know her name, nor she his; how absurd. 'There's not a man alive who would care to explain to a constable – or anyone else – that a slip of a girl like you got the better of him. Least of all if you were to say why you did it. Set your mind at rest on that count.'

She could see the sense in his words, and she was a

little relieved. 'But where shall I go? I have almost no money, and I know no one in London.'

'You're safe here. Let me think of something.'

She could not imagine what scheme he could possibly devise that could help her in any way, but she did not have time to tell him so, for he said now, 'We can discuss all that in the morning. Well, later in the morning, for I daresay it is all of five by now. You need to go to bed. I'll show you to my room.'

CHAPTER FIVE

She recoiled from him, huddling as deep as she could in her corner of the sofa. She should have known it was wrong to trust him, to trust anyone, but she had no leisure to dwell on her disappointment that he was just like all the rest. 'No!' she croaked.

He frowned and said, 'Oh. No, I'm sorry, you misunderstand me. I told you I'm not that kind of fellow, I'm almost sure, but I can quite see that you have no reason to believe me. My bed is the only one that will be made up, because it always is. You can make yourself comfortable in there, and I'll get some sleep on the couch in my sitting room. I'd stay down here, but I thought you might not quite like being all alone upstairs. One of the servants might try to come in, and it would be damn-dashed awkward for you to explain.'

'I suppose that's true,' she said dubiously.

'You may lock the door, if you wish; there are two doors, and keys in both locks. In fact, it might be better if you did, then you can be secure that none of the maids will enter the room to clean it, or anything of that nature.'

'Do you normally lock your bedroom door?' she asked, and then blushed that she had had the temerity to ask such an intimate question. She imagined that a man might have all manner of reasons for doing so that he would not wish to disclose to a lady, least of all one to whom he had not even been formally introduced.

'I should say I do, when the twins are at home, and if you had met them you would understand why,' he said, not appearing to think that there was anything at all odd in the question. 'Not so much here, but in the country, there is simply no knowing what they might do. They put a live frog in my bed once.' He shuddered at the memory. 'And as for the things they've done to their governesses over the years . . .'

'Governesses in the plural?' she asked, very ready to be distracted from her troubles by this talk of a family life very different from her own.

'Governesses in multitudes. They never stayed long. They have a man now, a tutor, which seems to answer better – he's young, and has several brothers himself, so he is alive upon all suits and they don't play out their tricks on him as much. But we are wandering far from the point. You need to sleep.'

She did not demur, for as they had talked a wave of weariness had assailed her, and she could scarcely prevent herself from yawning in his face. They left the library, lighted by the candelabrum that he carried, and she followed him up the broad, sweeping stairs to the door he indicated. He plainly and rather reassuringly did not want to enter the room with her, and there was a moment of slight awkwardness as she waited for him to fetch another candle from somewhere and light it, then he handed the candelabrum to her, leaving it for her use.

'That's the necessary,' he said, indicating a door on the other side of the room, 'and I'll be in the sitting room through that other door. Lock this door to the hall and that one between us, and you will be entirely private. But I'll be close by, and if you call out I shall hear you. Goodnight, Snow White!' And with a punctilious, courtly bow, such as he might have made to her after they had danced together at Almack's, not that she'd ever been to Almack's, and which was quite ridiculous in the circumstances, he left her, closing the door firmly behind him.

She did as he said; she had little fear of him now, but it seemed sensible to be cautious, and he was quite correct when he said that it would be better not to run the risk of one of the servants stumbling upon her unawares. That would be a scene she was anxious to avoid, for how could she possibly explain her presence in their master's house?

It occurred to her suddenly that she was surely ruined: if anyone should learn that she had spent the night quite alone in the residence of a young, single, handsome and presumably extremely eligible man, she would have not a shred of reputation left. No doubt she should go into strong hysterics at the thought, but she really did not have the energy for the vapours at this particular moment. The problem of what in heaven's name she should do next to avoid destitution seemed far more pressing, and still no solution presented itself. Perhaps it would in the morning; she really was so very tired.

She was also in urgent need of a water closet, so she went through the door he had indicated, and found herself in a beautiful room chiefly equipped in marble and much more modern than any other she had ever seen. She made full use of it, much to her relief, and then returned to the bedroom and looked about her.

Despite her exhaustion, she must still be aware that it felt odd and somehow disturbing to find herself in a strange young man's – any man's – bedchamber. The room was decorated principally in very dark blue: wallpaper, curtains and bed-hangings all the same deep, rich colour, with touches of red, green and gold here and there in the Persian carpet and the paintings that hung close together on the walls. She was somehow surprised at what she saw; she had not, she realised, imagined her host to be someone who cared much for art, but clearly she had been mistaken, for the paintings and other fine objects had been chosen with a nice eye, and a congruity of taste that somehow spoke of an individual preference at work. And yet it remained a distinctly masculine room, despite the beautiful portrait – she thought it by the celebrated and newly knighted painter Sir Thomas Lawrence – that hung above the mantel. She raised her candelabrum in order to study it more closely. It featured a young woman in the simple Grecian fashions of some twenty years since, her luxuriant dark hair dressed very informally. She had a strong, beautiful face with a certain classic symmetry and high, sharp cheekbones that were very familiar, but it scarcely needed that detail to tell Cassandra that this was her host's mother. The man she had met tonight was quite recognisable in the small boy with the lustrous dark locks who stood at his mother's side in nankeen breeches and a frilled shirt, leaning against the lady's shoulder and clasping the outstretched hand of the chubby baby she held, presumably his brother Bastian.

She took off her cloak and slippers, and set down her shabby reticule on the table beside the bed. It seemed an intimate act to sleep in the stranger's bed, surrounded by his possessions, but it would be in the highest degree foolish to refuse to do so. She needed rest. She did not undress, for she could not well do so unaided, and she was certainly not going to call on Mr Whoever-He-Was to help her unfasten her gown and unlace her stays; the very idea put her to the blush. His big hands on her skin, his body so close to hers that she would feel his breath on her neck, the act of disrobing: what a shocking thought.

There were limits to the help that she could ask of him, however obliging he had been so far.

Cassandra sighed in the quiet room. She turned back the fresh linen sheets and clambered with a little difficulty into the high bed – it had plainly been designed for someone very much taller than she – and lay down in her stained and crumpled gown to sleep as best she could. Her weary mind was churning with all kinds of thoughts, and her pulse was racing, no doubt in reaction to all that she had endured this evening. Perhaps things would seem clearer and less confusing when she woke.

CHAPTER SIX

Hal used the second water closet that stood at the other end of the hall, and then took his candle into his sitting room, a chamber that he rarely entered these days but which had been his mother's special domain; he remembered coming home from school and spending time with her there when the twins were mere babies, and later. It had been a room full of cheerful chaos and children's laughter, not the barren, unused chamber it had become.

Pushing away a train of thought that threatened to become maudlin, he dragged off some of the Holland furniture covers that gave the room such a ghastly appearance, and piled them carelessly in a corner. Then he occupied himself in struggling out of his tight evening coat and waistcoat, and pulling the neckcloth, which had once been the snowy height of Corinthian fashion, and was now very much crumpled, from around his neck. He tossed the clothes on a chair, and stood in shirt and pantaloons, contemplating the satin sofa with something approaching dismay. It did not look in the least inviting and was certainly not designed to accommodate a man of his height for sleep. But sleep for a while he must, for he was in the devil of a coil and needed a clear head if he were to extricate himself from it, not to mention the lost girl who would presently be slumbering in his own big, comfortable bed. A bed that was certainly big enough for two, though he had never shared it with anybody, his domestic life being what it was, and would not be sharing it with her tonight. Even to think of doing so was sheerest folly. He might feel a twinge of interest in the prospect – he was only human, and it had been a while – but with the interest came a sense of shame, because the poor girl had been through enough, and it was surely the outside of enough for him to be thinking of her lustfully; would that not make him almost as bad as the ramshackle creature who had tried to lay his hands on her earlier in the evening? Obviously, it would.

He opened the door that led to the hall as quietly as he could and went in search of blankets and pillows. There was a linen press where such things were stored somewhere close by, he recalled – the twins had been particularly fond of hiding there when small, and jumping out at people in order to scare them out of their wits – and he might as well have what little comfort he could manage; the almost empty house felt chillier than it should, somehow, considering it was high summer.

Returning with an armful of bed linen, he arranged it as best he could on the inadequate sofa, peeled off his pantaloons, and settled down to attempt to sleep in his shirt and drawers.

It was every whit as disagreeable as he had feared. He lay with his knees drawn up awkwardly, trying very hard not to think about the soft mattress just a few feet away, and the girl who occupied it. The thought of the bed was tantalising enough, but the girl herself . . . He wondered if she would be asleep by now, her cheek pillowed on her hand and that kissable pink mouth slightly open, as he had seen her not long since. It was an odd thing, having seen her sleeping – strangely intimate and difficult to forget, considering that he did not even know her name. Snow White was all he could call her. It was all too easy to picture her vibrant red curls against the pristine linen of his pillow, and to imagine slipping in beside her and taking her in his arms. He was conveniently naked in this vision, and so was she, which was an enticing thought, and she would curl close to him, nestling into his embrace, craving his warmth and his touch, and she would make a soft little sound, too, that invited him to . . .

No, she would not. She would scream, and rightly so. Hal sighed deeply, and pulled the blanket more tightly around him, and wondered if he was going to get any sleep at all tonight, between the blasted sofa and the erotic visions that he could not seem to banish from his mind.

All at once, however, a most unwelcome thought struck him, one that drove thoughts of an amorous nature from his head – and other parts of him – entirely. He had compromised her, or she had compromised herself in his house, which amounted to the same thing. If anyone came to know that she had spent the night here, spent the night in his bed, for God's sake, her reputation would be utterly ruined. It seemed damned unfair to have ruined someone when he had behaved with perfect propriety from start to finish. He could not be held to account for his dashed unruly thoughts, since he had not acted on them. Hal had never ruined anyone before – any young women with whom he had had intimate relations had been thoroughly pre-ruined, which was an uncomfortable thought that he did not want to have to consider just at this moment – and he would have imagined previously that there would be more pleasure in it. His Snow White was a lady of quality, plainly, and he would be obliged to marry her. Honour demanded it. He sat up on the couch, and dropped his head into his hands; it was beginning to ache now, though whether he could blame the copious amounts of alcohol he had consumed or his current situation, he was unsure, and it scarcely mattered. Had he not reassured her a moment ago that he would think of something to remedy her desperate situation? He supposed sardonically that he had just done so.

Marriage. It would certainly solve all her problems in one fell swoop. Her uncle would hardly be able to refuse him – he was eminently eligible by anyone's standards – and the cursed mountebank who had tried to molest her would have no power over her any longer. Hal gained an odd sort of satisfaction from that thought.

But it was insane, and he was insane and drunker than he had realised for contemplating it for as much as a second. He was not, obviously, seriously contemplating it. That would be quite ridiculous. He did not even know her name, nor anything else about her, and while he hoped he could call himself a true gentleman, one who was always ready to do what he could to help anyone who should be in need, he scarcely owed Snow White that much, however wretched her position might be. It was not even as though he had the least desire to get married, or had ever entertained even for a moment any intention of doing so; with four younger brothers, he could hardly be said to lack for heirs. The last thing, the very last thing he needed in his life was to be setting up his nursery, when he already had so much responsibility on his shoulders. And it was a very large leap indeed from acknowledging that she appealed to him, and that he would very much like to be in bed with her now, to entertaining for so much as a second the prospect of offering her his hand in marriage and the protection of his ancient name.

At this point Hal groaned aloud, though there was no one there to hear it, attempting and failing to find a more comfortable spot on the sofa. One thing was for sure: when this ridiculous state of affairs was resolved, as surely it must be soon enough, he would take himself off to that discreet establishment he knew of in Russell Square and get himself thoroughly straightened out. It seemed he had a sudden strong fancy for a brave, diminutive redhead with freckles and luminous, expressive green eyes; very well, all tastes were catered for there. Anyone who wished and could afford to pay the staggeringly high charges could spend as long as he liked there – days, if he wished – indulging every fantasy that entered his head.

This train of thought was hardly conducive to slumber either, and between that and vain attempts to devise a plan that would leave the fair unknown safe from her predatory relative whilst also preserving her good name and his own, Hal passed a restless few hours.

He had fallen into an uneasy slumber when he was rudely wrenched from his dreams, some of which were decidedly pleasant and some of which were not, by a clatter that he knew signified the opening of the window and the shutters. A moment later he was being shaken somewhat roughly on the shoulder by a large, powerful, scarred hand. Any thought that Snow White had come seeking his company after all was swiftly discarded; Snow White had small, delicate hands, not great hairy fists the size of loaves of bread. Jem.

Hal groaned and stared up blearily at his servitor, who, he observed, was now standing over him with his meaty arms folded and an expression of mingled annoyance and concern on his battered features.

'What kind of coil have you got yourself into now?' Jem asked with a lamentable lack of the respect due to his noble employer. 'And who, may I be so bold as to ask, is in there?'

His master groaned again and said, 'A girl.'

'Well, I didn't think it was a monkey from Exeter 'Change. You has your standards. I realise it's a girl. What's she doing in there, though, and you out here?'

'Tell me you didn't . . . ?'

Jem shook his massive head. 'Locked, both of them. From the inside, I collect, or you and me will be having a dust-up.'

'Thank God for that, at any rate! Of course they're locked from the inside, and not because she has any reason to fear me. I hope you know me better than that, Jem; I told her to lock herself in so that she would feel safe. Sit down, man. I am in the devil of a fix, and I depend on you to help me out of it.'

Jem grunted and lowered himself carefully into a spindly gold-framed chair that creaked alarmingly. 'Wouldn't be the first time. Spit it out!'

CHAPTER SEVEN

Hal described the young lady's dire predicament and her flight, and saw an expression of profound disgust creeping across Jem's normally impassive face. Jem Oldcastle was, he well knew, despite his intimidating appearance and his taste for a good mill at a moment's notice or none, a man who had no tolerance at all to spare for those who ill-treated women or children; he had undergone too much in his own nightmare childhood to wish to see it repeated. When Hal related how the fugitive had managed to slip into the house while Jem's back was turned, he exclaimed in self-reproach, 'Bubbled by a gentry-mort! That I should live to see the day!'

'Never mind that,' said Hal. 'Obviously you're losing your touch – I expect it's your age – but tell me about the men who were chasing her, and what happened after she got past you.'

'Pair of swell coves,' was the dismissive answer. 'Stout one and a thin one. Dressed up to the nines. Shifty-looking, the both of them, and foxed besides. I thought they was area sneaks, naturally, come to mill the ken. Tried to tell me they was chasing a thief, or some such nonsense. Said she must've got into the house without me seeing. I said she hadn't. Course, I know now she had, but at the time I didn't. Bit of back and forth, offers to grease my palm, and my good fellow, is your master at home? His Lordship is not currently upon these here premises, I says. And even if he was, I wouldn't be fetching him to talk to a pair of queer 'uns what comes calling at midnight by way of the servants' entrance. Wanted to come into the house and search for her. Over your dead bodies, I said, for it won't be mine. After a while of this, they piked on the bean. And sorry I am that I let them do so, now I know what their lay was.'

'Did they say anything about coming back?'

'They did. They intimated their intentions of returning at a more convenient time, and seeking an urgent conference with my employer. Seek away, I said. He's not here, he's not expected, and he wouldn't see you if he was. I don't know who you are, I said, but I know who he is. A belted earl, that's who. And as for searching the crib, you go and find a constable or a runner, if you dare, and bring him back here and I'll tell him to his face the same as I'm telling you: no. Not a chance, cully.'

'That was well done. So even if they do return, they may be fobbed off easily enough. She is in no immediate danger from them.'

Jem grunted emphatic assent. 'Not while I has breath in my body. But who are they, and who's she?'

'I have not the least idea,' said Hal ruefully. 'She wouldn't tell me her name, only that she's in a desperate case, with hardly a penny in her pocket and not a stitch of clothing save what she's wearing. She has money, but no way of laying hands on it – that uncle of hers holds the purse strings good and tight.'

'What you need,' Jem opined, 'is some respectable mort you can stow her with while you puzzle out what to do with her.' Seeing his employer's doubtful expression, Jem said, 'You do know some respectable females. Surely. Along with the other kind.'

'Damn your insolence!' Hal said without heat. 'Of course I do. But if you can call to mind one who will take charge of an unknown and nameless young female that I deliver to her without any luggage at a moment's notice, I'd be interested to hear it. She'd be bound to think I was up to something damn havey-cavey – trying to give the girl a slip on the shoulder, or some such thing – and want nothing to do with her. Aunt Sophia would take her in, of course, if I explained, but she's not here. Or Louisa, for that matter. And in any case, it's not a long-term solution.'

Jem refrained from pointing out that his master was

hardly obliged to take on full responsibility for the current wellbeing and future happiness of a young lady met in such unconventional circumstances; he knew he would be wasting his breath, and besides, he agreed with him. To turn the chit out of doors now would be to condemn her to one of two fates: marriage to the man who had so importuned her, and from whom she had fled in terror, or a perilous life on the streets of London, where only one occupation could be open to her. It was not to be thought of.

The ill-assorted pair sat in gloomy silence for a moment, until Jem was struck with what seemed to him to be an inspiration. 'She could go as a governess! That's what gentry-morts do when the dibs ain't in tune. Your aunt could write her a . . . whatever they write for them, and then she'd be set for life. Governess to the Pendlebury brats – 'ighly respectable. And the young'uns have had so many ape-leaders, what's one more or less?' He perceived that his employer was looking less than overjoyed at the solution to all his difficulties that he had just discovered, and said, 'What's the objection?'

'You haven't seen her.'

'Doesn't look like a governess?'

A mental procession of all the numerous genteel females who had struggled, and for the most part struggled in vain, to instil some rudiments of knowledge and civilised behaviour into his younger siblings passed before Hal's vision now. They had none of them had huge green eyes, fiery curls and a mouth . . . 'No,' he said shortly. 'She looks about as much like a governess as you look like the Archbishop of Canterbury.'

'What does she look like, then?'

'Trouble.' Hal sighed, and elaborated. 'She's about Georgie's age, and she looks exactly like one of her friends. The kind of girl they're always trying to make me do the pretty to at Almack's.' This was perhaps not quite true, as Hal found himself almost entirely unable to distinguish any one of his sister's numerous bosom bows from another, while he was sure that his Snow White would stand out from them like a tiger lily in a vase of daffodils, but let that pass for now.

'That's mortal bad,' said Jem, sucking his teeth. 'If she's that sort and you can't think of any other plan, it's the parson's mousetrap for you, you know.'

'I am very well aware of it, thank you, Jem. Marriage seems a rather drastic answer to her difficulties, though.'

'Well, if you don't fancy her, you don't fancy her,' conceded Jem magnanimously, rubbing his nose.

'I didn't say that!' shot back Hal with sudden heat. Observing his servitor's rude grin, he said, 'Damn it, man, I've barely conversed with the chit for a half-hour. That's no basis for getting leg-shackled.'

'I suppose it isn't,' agreed Jem, 'Although I'd have taken my Kitty on within ten minutes of meeting her, and that's the truth. But the gentry do things different, of course. Stap me if I know what's to be done, then.'

But Hal was no longer listening. A germ of an idea was forming in his brain. Georgie's friends . . .

CHAPTER EIGHT

Hal said with sudden decision, 'I shall wake her up now. I have an idea and I need to discuss it with her. In private,' he added firmly, when Jem showed no sign of moving. 'Is there any food in the house? Stupid question – of course there is, with Kitty in residence. Could you ask her to make us some breakfast? We'll have to have it up here, mind, and she might as well bring it so I can talk to her. She needs to be in on the plan for it to work.'

Jem might not have much respect for his employer's wisdom, having known him from the cradle, but he had a boundless faith in his own wife's quick-wittedness, and so he had no fault to find with this scheme, and took himself off with alacrity.

Hal pulled on his pantaloons, waistcoat and coat,

and tidied himself as best he could; his neckcloth was far beyond redemption, so he had to go without it. He would be able to wash and change later.

He tapped on the door, and after a few seconds he heard an anxious little voice saying with an attempt at bravery that tugged at his heart, 'Yes? Who is it?'

'It's me. I hope you have managed to get some rest. Would you open the door and come out? I have an idea to put to you.'

He heard the key click in the lock, and the door opened, to reveal a woebegone maiden in a horribly crumpled muslin gown. There was some colour in her cheeks, and she appeared to have slept – *I'm glad someone did*, thought Hal drily – but his guest looked downcast. Clearly the apparent hopelessness of her situation was preying on her mind, and no wonder.

He removed the bedlinens from the sofa, dumping them unceremoniously on the floor, and indicated that she should sit there, while he took the chair that Jem had lately vacated. She sank into it, and they sat regarding each other and taking stock for the first time in daylight.

Cassandra saw a young man who was every bit as handsome as she had thought him in the candlelight, despite his dishevelment and a weariness that spoke of insufficient sleep at the end of a riotous evening. He was very tall and broad-shouldered, with the frame of an athlete, and those extraordinarily vivid blue eyes were just as striking now that she could see them more clearly. His dark, disordered locks tumbled over a broad forehead; he had strong bones in his face, distinct high cheekbones, a Roman nose and a firm chin, presently darkened with stubble, with a cleft in it.

For his part, Hal saw nothing to make him revise his previous opinion of the young lady's appearance, anxious though she undoubtedly was. She was tiny and delicate, but he did not dislike that in a woman. He had not imagined the size and brilliant green of her eyes, nor the scattering of freckles on her nose and cheeks, nor her flaming locks. She looked, if anything, even less like a governess than he had thought. And that mouth . . .

The silence in which they contemplated each other was becoming somewhat awkward; Hal saw a blush creeping into her cheeks, and would not have been surprised in the slightest to know that he too was colouring. He cleared his throat and said, 'I hope you were comfortable.' *In my bed.* Good God, that scarcely helped, he thought, and mentally cursed himself for a clumsy fool.

She flushed more rosily, but answered him readily enough. 'Yes, I slept well, thank you. I suppose I was exhausted. I have been awake for a little while, though, considering my situation.'

'And did you come to any conclusion?'

She shook her head despondently. 'No. I could think of nothing. But I cannot trespass on your hospitality any longer. Thank you for being so kind to me. I will go . . .'

Her voice was not perfectly steady as she said this, but she put her chin up courageously and met his eyes, and all at once Hal had a crazy impulse to take her in his arms and comfort her. Comfort her with kisses, to be precise. Quashing it ruthlessly, he said, 'There can be no question of that. You must see that no one who calls himself a gentleman would allow you to leave here with no money and no fixed destination in mind. Upon my honour, I cannot countenance it.'

Cassandra noticed idly that he sounded different this morning, presumably because he was now sober; he did not employ the slang words she had heard him utter, nor the curses, and somehow this made him seem older and more of a person to be reckoned with. But then she saw a flash of the careless boy of last night when he added with some heat, 'And as for letting you return to your uncle, I am da-dashed if I will, after what he put you through. I have a sister myself, you know.'

'Yes, you said you did,' she agreed listlessly.

'That's what I think I should do with you,' he said. 'Take you to Georgie.'

She stared at him in amazement. 'But . . . but even if Miss – I'm sorry, I don't know your name, it's quite ridiculous – even if your sister would be willing to receive me, how would that help? I have no clothes and no money, and how should I be introduced?'

He made himself more comfortable, stretching out his long legs in the tight pantaloons, and Cassandra averted her gaze hastily. 'There are several points to address there,' he said. 'First of all, I can assure you that Georgie will be very happy to see you. She's full of fun and gig, a dashed sight too much so on occasion, but she's got a warm heart; once you tell her what's happened to you, she'll be your stoutest supporter, you see if I'm not right. She will make no difficulty about lending you her clothes till you can get some of your own, I'm sure. In fact, there will be things of hers here that you can wear today. Because,' he said, eyeing her ruined muslin with strong disfavour, 'I am not taking you anywhere while you're wearing *that*.'

She opened her mouth to raise some objection, but he continued relentlessly, 'I will advance you money for a suitable wardrobe; I will keep an account and you can repay me when you are able. Oh, and I should tell you – she's not Miss anything.'

She did not understand him, and seeing this he said, 'Georgie. Lady Georgiana. Named for the late Duchess, who was a bosom bow of Mama's, but we almost always call her Georgie.'

Cassandra was not on intimate terms with any members of the aristocracy, and so did not know to which duchess he referred, but it scarcely mattered, and it was hardly the time to enquire. She did not understand why it should make things much worse that he was obviously a duke, earl or marquis, but somehow, absurdly, it did. 'I can't go and stay with a nobleman's sister and wear her clothes and let him – I mean you – spend money on me!' she almost wailed, perilously close to tears.

'You can, you know,' he said firmly. 'But I'm afraid you're going to have to tell me your name first. You can't go into society nameless, or under a false name. I am persuaded you can see that. Not at all the thing.'

CHAPTER NINE

'Go into society?' she spluttered. 'I can't go into society!'

'If you're staying with Georgie, you'll have to,' he said unanswerably. 'She's all the rage, Georgie is, never spends an evening at home. Anyway, going into society is the whole point. I can't precisely recall, but I think you said last night that you hadn't made your come-out, because that uncle of yours wouldn't allow it?'

'That's true,' she conceded. 'Papa intended me to make my debut last year, under the aegis of his cousin Mrs Thoroughgood. It was all arranged, but then he died . . .' She trailed off.

'I'm terribly sorry,' he said soberly. 'Believe me, I know what it is to lose your parents. But this cousin of yours – could you not enlist her help against your uncle? If your father was willing to entrust you to her for your come-out, I wager she isn't the sort of woman who would sit idly by while you're forced into marriage with a fortune-hunter twice your age!'

'She certainly wouldn't,' said Cassandra. 'She is a great admirer of the works of Mrs Godwin, and holds strong opinions about the position of women in society. But she's travelling in Europe. I don't know precisely where she will be by now. She set off before it was widely known that Napoleon had escaped from Elba, and I am sure her plans have been thrown into disarray. She wanted to take me with her, but my uncle would by no means allow it, though I did not know why at the time. And it was only after she left that he produced this friend and told me that I must marry him. I used to see her every week when she was in London, and stay with her sometimes. I see now that her presence restrained him from treating me as badly as he has done since she left. I haven't even been able to write to her! That is, I wrote, but I discovered recently that he was intercepting my letters and destroying them. He told me so – laughing at me, telling me I was entirely without a friend.'

Hal muffled a curse. 'There is no end to the fellow's villainy. But we will circumvent him, I promise you.'

'How?'

'That's why you need to tell me your name, now that I've told you mine.'

'You haven't. Just that you're a nobleman.'

He shook his head. 'It's not like me to be so scatter-brained.' He stood, and made her an elegant, courtly bow. 'Henry Pendlebury, at your service. Hal, to my friends. Lord Irlam, if we're being formal, Miss . . . ?'

She sighed, then rose from the sofa and dropped a correct curtsey. 'I do not suppose it can make the least difference, after all. I am Miss Hazeldon, my lord.' He was still looking at her expectantly, and she added, 'Cassandra.'

'I am delighted to make your acquaintance, Miss Hazeldon. Cassandra.' It was a pretty name, he mused, and suited her, but he thought it best not to say so at this juncture.

At that moment the door behind Hal opened, and a laden tray could be seen, and supporting it with no apparent effort was the woman Cassandra had seen last night. She was tall and buxom, with a high colour and an unruly mop of brown curls. The pair froze in their ridiculous attitudes for a moment, and then Hal sprang forward and took the tray from her. 'Capital!' he said. 'I'm starving. Kitty, if you will take the vase off that table and pull up the chairs, we can eat. Oh, yes – Kitty, this is Miss Hazeldon, who needs your help, and Miss Hazeldon, this is Mrs Oldcastle, who is both my groom's better half and my own old nurse. Kitty is entirely to be trusted, I promise you, and so, of course, is her husband, Jem. I have known them both since I was a child in short petticoats.'

Mrs Oldcastle ran a swift but comprehensively assessing glance over Cassandra as she whisked away the vase so that Hal was able to set down the heavy tray. She pulled the chairs forward to the small table and said, 'I'm glad to meet you, I'm sure, miss, though I'm sorry for the fix you find yourself in. Jem told me everything. But here's some breakfast for you both, and you must eat up while it's good and hot. I'm sure Master Hal – I'm sure His Lordship will think of a way to help you.'

'I have,' said Hal, already swallowing a mouthful of food. 'Kitty, thank you, this is just the ticket. Take a seat and I will explain. Come, Miss Hazeldon, I am sure you are ravenous.'

Kitty perched primly on the edge of the sofa, capable hands folded in her lap, and Cassandra murmured her thanks to them both and took her seat also, picking up her knife and fork. She was sure that a lady of truly refined sensibility would be too distressed at her perilous situation to have any thought for food, but she was excessively hungry, and the bacon, sausages and eggs set before her looked and smelt delicious. She fell on them, and Kitty was heard to emit a small sound of satisfaction.

There was a steaming pot of coffee on the tray, and Hal poured Cassandra a cup, and then served himself. 'It seems to me,' he said, after taking a deep draught, 'that your uncle has been very careful to keep you isolated – cancelling your come-out, stopping you from corresponding with your cousin, and locking you in your room in recent weeks.'

Kitty made an exclamation of disgust, and he said, 'Quite. Disgraceful behaviour. But it's worked, in so far as nobody knows you, or what he's up to, and so nobody can help you. I collect you did not reside in London when your father was alive?'

'No, we lived in Yorkshire, near Skipton, and all my friends are there. But my uncle came and brought me back to his house in London straight after my father's funeral, and I have not seen or spoken to any of my friends since. He would not even let my old nurse Polly remain with me, though she begged him; he turned her off along with most of the other servants, and she was obliged to go and stay with her brother in Leeds. I have written to Polly and to all of my friends, over and over again, but had no replies; I must think now that he has been destroying my letters to them too, and any that they might have sent me.' She said suddenly, 'And then I suppose if they thought I never replied to them, they might conclude that I no longer wish to maintain their acquaintance – they probably think I am entirely occupied with going to fashionable balls and parties and have no time for them any more.'

Both her interlocutors shook their heads sadly, seeing how distressed she was, and Hal said, 'You may write to them now, as many letters as you like, and I will frank them for you. The more people who know where you are and what you are doing, the better. My plan is to put it about that you met Georgie and Aunt Sophia at some watering-place a couple of years ago – Harrogate, that's the one – and that you have been corresponding ever since, and now she has invited you to come and spend the summer with her in Brighton.'

'My uncle will know that cannot be true, if he hears of it, or learns of my whereabouts,' she objected.

'He will, but no one else will think it at all out of the way, and he can hardly go around telling people that it's all a hum and you can't have been corresponding with Georgie because he's been locking you in your room and burning your letters! He's not some canting religious hypocrite type who'd do that sort of thing, is he? The kind of fellow who'd disapprove of Lady Georgiana Pendlebury and her frivolous ways on principle?'

'Hardly!' scoffed Cassandra. 'One of the reasons he toad-eats his horrid friend so is that he's a baronet. He doesn't understand why I am not in alt over the prospect of being Lady Delaney. If he met an earl or an earl's sister, I hate to think what he would do.'

'And I dare say he won't know but that you might really have met Lady Georgiana and Mrs Winterton in Harrogate years ago, miss, and somehow managed to contact them for help in your trouble,' interjected Kitty. 'He'd have to be a deal more careful how he went on if he thought you just might have powerful connections.'

'That's true,' said Hal. 'It all fits together – you could have been making for this particular house on purpose, after all. You understand that we want him to know that you're with us and that he can't touch you without creating a shocking bustle. You shall gloss over the details of your flight, and merely say, if anyone asks, that you have been living with your uncle but have now persuaded him that you should visit your friend in Brighton for an extended stay. Nothing could be more natural. And then I shouldn't wonder if that scoundrel of a friend of his just takes to his heels when the prospect of your fortune is no longer secure.'

'That would be excessively kind in you, and in your sister, and I can see that it might work,' said Cassandra slowly. 'I will not be beholden to you for money – what a shocking thing that would be – but I have an idea to avoid that. I cannot deny, either, that it would be very pleasant to spend time in Brighton and see something of the world at last. And I am sure you are right about his friend, and to be free of him would be a huge relief. But though I am very grateful, I must be aware that this is only a temporary answer, and not a permanent one. While he remains my guardian, for nearly another two years, I will be obliged always to go back to his house in the end. I cannot stay with your sister for two years!'

'I admit you can't. She's bound to be married before then, for one thing. But something might come up,' said Hal vaguely.

Kitty shot her former charge a sharp glance. Might it, indeed?! 'In the meantime, miss, you can write to your cousin, if you have an address for her,' she said comfortably, 'and I'm sure once she hears of your situation she'll come home from foreign parts just as soon as she is able, and then you will be much better placed, for you can live with her comfortably like respectable folk, and she can put a stop to all of this dreadful behaviour.'

Mrs Oldcastle was watching Hal all the while she said this, for she was most interested to see what his reaction might be. If he should show himself to be pleased to think that Miss Hazeldon would only be his charge for a short while, that would be natural, for he had enough responsibilities already without seeking new ones; if on the other hand he did not seem enthusiastic about the prospect of the young lady's imminent removal to heaven knows where, that would be only natural too, and would tell her something quite different.

Hal said without any noticeable degree of eagerness, 'That's perfectly true, Kitty, and a very good notion.'

Oh-ho! thought Mrs Oldcastle. *Stands the wind in that quarter?* But she was more than seven, and she only said aloud, 'How is the young lady to get to Brighton, Master Hal? For it's not at all proper for you to be taking her up in that nasty curricle of yours all that way, and don't you be thinking it.'

Hal had been thinking it. He could see through the tall windows that it was a fine day, and he could think of few things more pleasant than tooling his smart curricle and bays to Brighton with a pretty girl by his side. He was a fair whip, though he said so himself, and inevitably she would be impressed by his skill. She would look up at him with those big green eyes, eyes deep enough for a man to drown in, and bite her full lower lip and say . . . But it would not do, and he knew it. 'Of course not,' he said. 'I'm shocked that you could think such a thing of me, Kitty.'

She snorted, and appeared to be about to comment, and he went on hastily, 'Miss Hazeldon shall go in the travelling carriage with you beside her as her attendant, if you are willing to accompany us and stay in Brighton for a while, and I will ride alongside. I hope that fulfils your fine notions of propriety, Mrs Oldcastle?'

She sniffed and said, 'It will have to do, I suppose. But she can't travel in those clothes, Master Hal. If you don't mind me saying, miss, that gown looks as though you've slept in it.'

'I did,' said Cassandra, not in the least offended. 'I had no means of taking it off, you see, for I cannot reach all of the buttons at the back.'

Kitty tutted and said, 'You come along with me, miss, and you shall wash, and feel better, and in the meantime I will find something of Lady Georgiana's that I can alter for you. And you will need under-things, and a bonnet, and a valise, and bandboxes . . .' Miss Hazeldon found herself bustled from the room, and Hal, deserted, made for his bedroom, whistling an air, trying hard not to glance at the four-poster, with its crumpled sheets, and trying too to ignore the faint, elusive, feminine scent that his unexpected guest had left behind her.

CHAPTER TEN

Kitty rifled ruthlessly through Lady Georgiana's wardrobe, deaf to Cassandra's protests. 'She won't grudge it to you, miss, and that's a fact,' she said at last. 'And besides, as you can see for yourself, she's more gowns than she can ever wear. She's taken I don't know how many trunks with her, and you see how much is left, besides more down at the Castle, I shouldn't wonder. She's spoilt, and that's the truth, but she has a good heart for all that. I should hope all my children do, even the twins, terrors that they are, though I'll always say that Master Hal is the best of them, and I don't care who hears me say it. What that boy's had to put up with . . . But I shouldn't chatter when there's work to be done. Now, I mind I've seen her in a green spencer that would be just the thing for you, if I can find a gown to wear under it . . . There!'

Cassandra soon found herself standing in a borrowed gown, being measured and turned about this way and that. It seemed that Lady Georgiana was of similar dimensions to herself, apart from being several inches taller, and, as Kitty mumbled with a mouthful of pins, to take up a hem was nothing to a competent seamstress. 'I used to make her dresses when she was small, and shirts for the boys, too,' she said.

It was hard not to ask Kitty a thousand questions about the Pendleburys, and how they had come to lose both their parents while most of them were still in the nursery, but she knew that it was quite wrong to gossip with servants, and so she restrained herself. However, she could not prevent herself from saying, 'It is so very kind of Lord Irlam to have a care for my welfare. I do not know what would have become of me, if I had stumbled into another house than his.'

'I do,' said Kitty, 'for I'm well acquainted with the neighbours. You'd have come to no harm on the left, it's true, for a finer gentleman than Sir Richard you'll hardly meet anywhere, and as for Her Ladyship, she's a really kind young lady, with a smile and a word for everyone. But they're not in Town, and if you'd gone to the house on t'other side, well, I don't like to say, and I doubt you'd understand me if I did. Goings-on,' she said darkly. 'All sorts.'

'Oh,' said Cassandra weakly. 'How . . . shocking.'

'Shocking is what it is, miss. But by the operation of divine providence you came here, and I will take my

71

affidavy that His Lordship couldn't have been more decent to you when he found you, even if he did maybe have a drop taken.' Kitty peered at her sharply as she said this, and Cassandra found herself blushing, though she could not in truth have said why.

'He was a little angry, of course, when he first saw me in the library. But he was very kind and gentlemanly, even if he might have been rather . . . tired,' she said diplomatically.

'Tired!' snorted Kitty, spraying pins. 'Drunk is what he was, I'm sure of it. But it's no wonder, when you think of all he has on his shoulders, that he should want to let the cork out of the bottle when all the family are away. I think that's done, miss, and if you could just step out of it, we'll try an evening gown, and then you will have something to wear when you arrive, and no one will see anything odd. I'll stitch them both up in two shakes of a lamb's tail while you're getting washed, and put a couple of tiny tucks in the back of that spencer while I'm at it. And then I shall pack for the both of us – I'll take a couple more gowns for you that I can alter when we arrive – and we'll be all set to go as soon as the carriage is ready. Now let's see about linens, and shoes, and a bonnet . . .'

Some time later, Kitty conducted Cassandra to the drawing room, where she found her host awaiting her. Clearly he too had profited from the interval to perform his ablutions, and he had shaved, for the dark stubble no longer shadowed his strong chin. His glossy hair was immaculately arranged in artful disorder, not the genuine disorder she had seen previously, and he was wearing a form-fitting coat of blue cloth, riding breeches and very shiny top-boots. His linen was immaculate and snowy white, and he looked every inch the earl, assuming that earls were as a general rule not yet thirty and devastatingly handsome; Cassandra had never met one before, and so could not venture to say.

He smiled when he saw her, his blue eyes warm, and said, 'Miss Hazeldon! I am sure you must be feeling much better, and ready for our journey.'

'Mrs Oldcastle has been most kind,' she responded. 'I only hope your sister will not be excessively angry that her clothes have been altered to fit me. I do not know how I will be able to look her in the face when I meet her.'

'Not a bit of it,' he said soothingly. He did not think it appropriate to comment on her appearance, for it was bound to make her self-conscious, but he could not help but notice that Kitty had chosen a pristine white muslin gown – very obviously not the one she had arrived in – and a rich green spencer that became her greatly, to say nothing of the hat that matched it, a green bonnet with a deep poke, decorated with curling feathers dyed a bright azure blue. He could not recall that the bonnet had ever become Georgie half so well; it framed Cassandra's heart-shaped face to perfection, and the blue lining of the poke contrasted admirably with her sea-green eyes and fiery curls. She had blue gloves, too, and a reticule of the same shade, and her feet were clad in smart jean half-boots. Altogether she was complete to a shade, and he was once again sorry that she would not be riding beside him in his curricle. He would have been proud to have her next to him, no question. Perhaps he could take her driving once they were established in Brighton.

Cassandra found that she was disappointed that Lord Irlam did not see fit to commend her upon the transformation that she had undergone, but she mentally chastised herself for the shallow thought. What did it matter if he did not think that his sister's clothes became her? It signified not at all, as long as she presented a respectable appearance. Not at all. He was being so very kind to her, but only because he was a true gentleman, as Kitty, who knew him better than anyone, had said. He would have done the same for any stranger in difficulty. She should not read any more than that into his actions, and certainly should not be fishing for compliments, nor be cast down when she did not receive them. No doubt he was intimately acquainted with all the loveliest ladies in society, beside whom Cassandra, a little ginger dab of a miss from Yorkshire, must surely appear nothing out of the way.

Jem had brought down the valises and bandboxes that Kitty had considered appropriate for a young lady making a visit to fashionable Brighton, along with Kitty's own luggage, and a couple of bags that he had hastily packed for his master. The travelling carriage had been ordered up, and awaited their pleasure. It would have been normal practice for a lady of quality to have her conveyance brought round into the square so that she could enter it with due ceremony, but that had seemed unwise in this instance – there was no knowing who might be watching, and it was vital that Cassandra's unchaperoned stay under His Lordship's roof remained a secret from the world. So the short procession made its way through the house to the mews at the rear, Hal greeting his coachman and postilion cheerfully. Their eyes did not seem to dwell on Cassandra unduly, and she supposed that, if they troubled to wonder who she was, Kitty's presence was enough to dismiss any questions. The luggage was loaded up, and Hal handed Cassandra and Kitty into the chaise, swinging himself easily into the seat of a fine black horse that had whickered in greeting when it saw him. He saluted them with his whip through the carriage window, Jem raised one large hand in benediction, and then they were off, heading south, to what Cassandra could not help fearing would be a most uncertain reception.

CHAPTER ELEVEN

The carriage was luxurious and well-sprung, and could have carried in comfort far more than the two passengers it currently held. They travelled in silence for a while, weaving through the bustling, noisy London streets, and then Cassandra said a little hesitantly, 'Mrs Oldcastle, it was very kind of you to come. I am sorry to put you out.'

'It's not a trouble to me at all, miss. I shall be happy to see Brighton again. I always did like a bit of travelling. Staying in one place for too long don't suit me, and that's the truth.'

'I am sure I feel the same,' agreed Cassandra wistfully. 'I have always wanted to travel widely, and never had the opportunity. Now, I hope you will not think me a gossip, but if I am to pass as a friend of Lady Georgiana's, I think

I must know more about the family than I do. I suppose her to have some older lady to chaperone her in Brighton, and that lady will think it very strange if she sees that I am entirely unacquainted with the circumstances of her life and the members of her circle. I think Lord Irlam said that she was soon to be engaged to be married, and I have no notion even of the gentleman's name, which I surely would if we were intimate friends.'

'It's quite true, miss, and thank goodness you thought of it,' said Kitty easily. 'Let me see now, where shall I start? The Pendleburys are orphans, as you may have realised. Their father died more than six years ago in a hunting accident, a terrible thing, not long after his current lordship came of age, and Her Ladyship, she was that attached to her husband, she just wasted away a few months after. Influenza, they said it was, but it was a broken heart, miss, in my opinion. And so His Lordship had them all on his hands and him not much more than a boy himself. Master Bastian is very clever, a proper scholar from when he first learnt to read, and has never been no trouble to him; destined for Holy Orders, he is, and has done very well at Oxford, by all accounts. But the rest of them . . . Master Fred is fourteen now and army-mad; he seems to be settling down a bit now that he's at school and promised a cornetcy at sixteen if he behaves himself. But the twins are proper terrors – Jonathan and Hugh, they're called, and it's few who can tell them apart. And Lady Georgiana, she's as bad, in her own way. They're all good-hearted, I'm not saying

77

they're not, but they will be getting up to all manner of mischief.'

'Lord Irlam said they had put a frog in his bed,' said Cassandra, smiling. As an only child, she had had no such experiences, and found them fascinating – a life so very different from her own. No one had ever put a frog in her bed; there had been nobody to do so, and while she could not really regret that particular omission, she could see that it would be a fine thing to have such a close family about you rather than being, for all practical purposes, alone in the world.

'Frogs is the least of it, I assure you, miss. But if I was to tell you all the scrapes they've got themselves into, we shall be pulling up into Brighton before I'm done. The twins and Master Fred, they're in Lyme Regis with their Aunt Sophia, that's Mrs Winterton, her late ladyship's sister. She's a widow, you see, a proper nice lady, and her only son grown and doing well in the navy with a ship of his own. She's been a big help to His Lordship all these years, looking after the younger ones, though she can't control them, really, but then nobody can, not even His Lordship, if truth be told.'

'I must try to remember all these names,' said Cassandra. 'And who is Lady Georgiana's chaperone in Brighton, Mrs Oldcastle?'

'That's Lady Louisa Pendlebury, his late lordship's younger sister, and a lazier woman you never did meet. Wouldn't even set foot in Brighton unless His Lordship swore on his honour that the twins wouldn't be in the house with her. Precious little chaperoning she'll be doing, I'll be bound, more like lying on a sofa while she reads a novel, but it doesn't matter so much, you see, miss, because Lady Georgiana will be going about to parties and the like with her intended's mother and his married sister. The gentleman is Lord Lamington, his mother is Lady Lamington, and his sister is Mrs Somebody – I can't recall it, but I dare say His Lordship will put us in mind of it when we stop for a change of horses and a cup of coffee. The Dowager is some sort of cousin of her late ladyship's as well, you see, which makes it all the more proper that she should have charge of Lady Georgiana.'

'Do you think Lord Lamington might object to my presence?' asked Cassandra, dazed by all the names and tangled relationships with which she was being bombarded.

'Well, it's not as though he can be alone with Lady Georgiana anyway, is it, miss? So you can't be standing in his way,' said Kitty with robust common sense. 'There's bound to be at least his mother or his sister or Lady Louisa present, if she can put her book down for long enough to pay attention. And from all I hear he's proper besotted and will do more or less whatever she tells him, which would worry me if I were his mother, but it's not my place to say, of course. He's not a very young gentleman, if you were thinking that. I dare say he is all of one or two and thirty, but very handsome, so she tells me. I've never set eyes on him, myself.' She hesitated for a moment and then went on, 'Now that you know how things stand, I should probably warn you that Miss Georgiana may see your arrival as an opportunity.'

'What do you mean?' asked Cassandra uneasily.

'Well, from what I hear, Lady Lamington and her daughter are quite strict kind of ladies, and I dare say they will take their chaperonage seriously and not look too kindly on Miss Georgie slipping away where they can't see. Whereas she might think that you, being young, would be more sympathetic to her wanting to do what she ought not. I'm sure you wouldn't, miss, but she can be very persuasive, that girl can. She's been winding everyone around her little finger since before she could talk, being the only girl in the family.'

Cassandra considered this information, and thought she understood. 'You think Lady Georgiana might want to be alone with her fiancé, and expect me to aid her?'

'Well, it might be her fiancé, and it might not be,' said Kitty enigmatically, and then they were sweeping under an arch into an inn yard for the change of horses, and, even if Cassandra had felt able to enquire further, there was no time to do so just then.

CHAPTER TWELVE

Lord Irlam kept good horses on the road to Brighton – riding horses as well as the ones that pulled his chaise – so their journey was as swift as it could be, apart from a brief stop for a late nuncheon at the Chequers in Horley. He kept pace with them all the way, but when they pulled up for the last change he ordered tea and cakes for them and told them not to hurry over it; he was going to ride ahead, and see if he could not catch his sister at home and inform her of Cassandra's situation and her imminent arrival. Thus the servants could be alerted, a room prepared, and Miss Hazeldon might have a more comfortable arrival, just like any normal guest.

He enjoyed a fast ride into Brighton, going straight round to the stables and entering through the back of the house. The stately butler informed him that his sister was out, but that Lady Louisa was resting in the ladies' private sitting room. This was hardly news to him, as she did little else, so he grinned and thanked his retainer, and ran lightly up the stairs. He tapped at the door, and distinctly heard a gusty sigh, and an exclamation of 'What is it *now*?', which he took as permission to enter.

Lady Louisa Pendlebury was Hal's father's much younger sister. She was wealthy in her own right, and very handsome, and so had not lacked for suitors when she had first made her debut in society, but she had resolutely refused them all. She had told Hal once that every time a gentleman had proposed, she had looked at him, and then at the book she was currently reading, and asked herself which was the most interesting and which was mostly likely to offer her lasting pleasure and cause her the least trouble. As a result, she had remained unmarried. She appeared perfectly content with her single state, residing generally in a lovely house in Richmond, where she never had to exert herself in the least, as all the trouble of managing the household and ordering the servants was shouldered by Miss Spry, her energetic companion. Miss Spry – a lady of a literary bent, who was much addicted to modern poetry – was currently enjoying an extended walking tour in the Lake District; the very thought of accompanying her had filled Lady Louisa with sheer horror. Poems were all very well in their place, she said, but even thinking about looking at a mountain was quite exhausting enough.

She had only agreed to offer her nominal chaperonage to Lady Georgiana this summer on two strict conditions: that the twins remained some hundred and twenty miles away at all times; and that she was not called upon to actually do anything at all strenuous apart from sitting gambling with her cronies in the card room at dances and going for the occasional stately drive with her charge along the Steine in her barouche-landaulet. If anybody so much as mentioned sea-bathing, riding expeditions, picnics or archery in her presence, she said, she would have her maid pack immediately, and return to Richmond, where nobody ever pestered her and everything was ordered to her complete satisfaction. She was perfectly ready to attend social events if called upon to do so, but only if they seemed likely to amuse her. And she was not often at home to callers, unless they should be particularly beautiful, witty or interesting, which in her judgement so few people were.

She set down her book now, and allowed Hal to kiss her on the cheek. She was only a dozen or so years his senior, and they were profoundly attached to each other, though it was possible than a casual observer might not have guessed as much from the way they addressed each other.

'I find you in high beauty, Louisa,' said Hal. 'The sea air plainly agrees with you.'

She snorted. 'What do you want?' He met her gaze

– azure blue to azure blue – with an air of injured innocence, but she was not in the least deceived. 'In all my forty years, Hal Pendlebury, a man only paid me a compliment when he wanted something. And that ingenuous face did not deceive me when you were in the schoolroom, so it's hardly likely to do so now. Were we expecting you? I didn't think we were. I thought you'd scarcely left. It fatigues me even to think about it.'

'No, you weren't expecting me. I only left two days ago, and I was intending to go down to the country for a while, but something has happened unexpectedly, and so I was obliged to return.'

She looked at him with misgiving. 'I thought as much. I have an instinct for when people mean to try to make me do unpleasant things. Tell me instantly, is it the twins? Because I warn you . . .'

He raised his hand pacifically. 'It is not the twins. No member of the family has done anything that will put you to the least inconvenience – or at least, not as far as I am aware at this precise moment,' he added conscientiously, having been burnt before. 'It is merely that I am obliged to tell you something, and then you will have to issue a few orders to the servants. You need not do so much as rise from your couch.'

He swiftly recounted the tale of Cassandra's adventures, and of his plans for her reception. When he had finished, Lady Louisa shook her head. 'Unfortunate child, what an atrocious experience for her. I expect she's young and pretty, though – you need not trouble to tell me so. I have observed previously that young and pretty people find it much easier to gain help than others do. Well, you did quite right to bring her here, whoever she is. Her uncle can hardly snatch her from us without creating a great scandal, and I expect it will do her good to racket about the town with Georgie, if that's the sort of thing she enjoys. But what will you do with her at the end of the summer, if this cousin of hers doesn't come haring back to rescue her?'

'I don't know, Louisa. Let us cross that bridge when we come to it.'

'Hmm,' she said, regarding him shrewdly. 'I collect the carriage will be arriving shortly. You had better go and look for Georgie, and tell her she's supposed to be delighted to be receiving her dearest friend from Yorkshire. She's out promenading with Lamington – no, there's no need to look at me like that, his mother and sister are with them. All perfectly proper. Not that I think she'd be in any danger from him if they weren't present; if I were you, it'd be him I'd be worrying for.'

Hal said, 'Louisa, I have no time to talk of Georgie now. Thank you for understanding why I had to bring the poor girl here. I'll send Mrs Ward to you – I must change out of my dirt before I can show my face on the Brighton strut!' He was gone in an instant, calling for the housekeeper, and his aunt looked after him and shook her head once more, before returning to her novel and the adventures of another ill-treated orphan, a certain Miss Price.

CHAPTER THIRTEEN

Hal took off his riding clothes and washed away the dust of the road, arraying himself in the dove-grey pantaloons, tasselled hessians and swallow-tailed coat that were *de rigueur* for one of the most fashionable promenades in the kingdom.

He was impatient to find his sister and pour his tale into her ear, but he forced himself to stroll at a leisurely pace along the seafront, greeting the many acquaintances he saw on either hand and facing gentle teasing from some at his abrupt return when he had made his farewells a bare three days ago.

At last he spied Georgie, very smart in a new pink bonnet with an enormous poke and wearing an expression of saintly patience, walking arm in arm with Lord Lamington. They were not alone but, he was pleased to see, had the two older ladies close behind them; Louisa had not deceived him. He greeted them all, and was obliged to listen to several minutes of platitudes before he could say, 'I came in search of you, Georgiana, because a most extraordinary thing has happened, and I have a delightful surprise for you!'

His sister's blue eyes danced. 'Do you, Henry?' she said in dulcet tones. 'You know that I love surprises above all things; please tell me, without delay.' The siblings almost never addressed each other by their baptismal names, and to do so was a sign between them that something untoward was afoot, and that they should pay special attention.

He said, 'There has been some sad confusion in the date of Miss Hazeldon's visit, and she arrived in Town this morning, only to find our house closed up, and you absent. How distressing it must have been for her! But all was well, because by great good fortune I had dropped by to pick up some luggage I had forgotten, and once I understood her predicament I was able to escort her and her maid here. I am positive that I was right to assure her you would be just as glad to see her now, despite the fact that one of you has sadly mistaken the arrangements.'

'Oh, you are the best of brothers!' cried Georgie. 'My dear Miss Hazeldon! How I have longed to see her, for it has been an age! I declare it to have been months . . . years,' she amended hastily, on seeing a slight frown cross Hal's brow, 'since I set eyes on her. I am sure that the error is mine, for you know how shatter-brained I am. We must not delay, but return instantly, so that I can welcome her. Is Aunt Louisa aware of her arrival?'

'She is,' replied Hal, 'and I am sure she is exerting herself to make her welcome even now.'

A dimple peeped in Georgie's cheek, but she made no comment. Lady Lamington and her daughter were exclaiming at the news of the unexpected arrival, while Lamington's only contribution was to murmur agreement as he gazed adoringly at Georgie in what Hal considered to be a singularly foolish fashion, a slight smile hovering about his lips.

Lord Lamington was perhaps one or two and thirty, and there was little for anyone but the most captious critic to dislike in his appearance; he was tall and well built, and dressed very correctly as a gentleman of fashion, without any of the exaggerated fads and fancies of a tulip of the ton. He was generally considered handsome enough in the English or German style, if somewhat florid and gammony in appearance, like a large, glazed Cumberland ham in a starched cravat. He appeared to be of an amiable disposition, with pleasant if diffident manners. It was plain to anyone who made their acquaintance that his mother, at least – an imposing, lantern-jawed dowager of some fifty summers – considered him little less than perfect. But even his intimate friends would not have claimed that he was the possessor of any shining intellect or sparkling wit, and in public he was generally content to leave the fatigue of conversation and the arduous forming of opinions to his mother and his widowed sister; once he had ascertained what they thought on any subject, he could agree to it, and life went on very pleasantly as a result.

Lady Lamington was of a naturally censorious disposition, except where her son was concerned, and her life at present was a trial to her. The desire – nay, the Christian obligation – to set others on the path of correct conduct was one of her strongest impulses. Most of all she itched to correct her sadly unsteady, motherless young Pendlebury cousins, but this instinct fought a constant battle with her awareness that she needed, at present, to ingratiate herself with them, since they were both considerably richer and of higher social standing than herself. She was able to gain comfort from the fact that, once Lady Georgiana was safely married to her dear Jeremiah, things would be very different. Then, her sad flightiness could and would be checked, and possibly those wild young brothers of hers could also by slow degrees be taken in hand and the worst excesses of their behaviour curtailed. There would be a day, and soon, when she, Margaret Lamington, would come into her own, even though this was not that day. Yet.

But even a dowager is only flesh and blood, and she simply could not restrain herself now. She said, inflating her substantial bosom in disapproval, 'Surely, Irlam, I must have misunderstood you. You cannot have accompanied this young lady all the way from London in a closed conveyance! However noble your motives, duty compels me to declare that I cannot approve your actions, sir!' Her companions made faint clucking noises, presumably indicative of equal parts agreement and shock.

'Good heavens, ma'am, of course not!' said Hal in accents of the strongest disapprobation. 'I would hope you know better than to think I would contemplate such an improper course of action. No: Miss Hazeldon travelled in the carriage with her attendant, and I rode alongside.'

'Dear Miss Hazeldon,' sighed Georgie. 'Of course she would not countenance such a thing, even if Henry were imprudent enough to propose it. She has been very strictly reared.'

'Very,' said Hal firmly. 'These old Yorkshire families, you know . . .'

The thwarted dowager and her daughter were profuse in their apologies – they did not mean to suggest for a second – not the least intention in the world of implying – Lord Irlam would be so good as to forgive them – and even Lord Lamington felt impelled to add his voice to theirs, though he had not previously uttered a word on the matter, so that it seemed long before the siblings could extricate themselves from their company with many mutual professions of regard and turn towards home.

Georgie tucked her hand into her brother's arm, and said, smiling up at him, her dimples on full display now, 'Am I not the best of sisters? I do not think there can be another woman in Brighton who would have apprehended your meaning so quickly! Please tell me, brother dear, who on earth is Miss Hazeldon, and why am I to entertain her for a visit?'

For the third time that day, Hal was obliged to explain Cassandra's sad situation, her escape, and his discovery of her in his library. As he had known she would be, Georgie was full of warm sympathy for her, and furthermore inclined to see her as a heroine, declaring that it was all quite thrillingly like a novel. 'And while I am sure it was excessively unpleasant to have a horrid old man trying to kiss her, what an adventure! She can only have been a prey to the greatest apprehension when you appeared, and then to find you sympathetic, and disposed to help her! Why, it is the most romantic thing I ever heard. I am sure she sees you as her knight in shining armour!'

'Stow it, Georgie,' replied her loving brother briefly.

'How rude, when I am being an angel and helping your . . . your maiden in distress, and not minding in the least that you have given her half my wardrobe, I dare say. Oh, do not look so stern, I am only funning! You know I do not care in the least for such things when there is adventure to be had! Only tell me, though, is she enchantingly pretty? Somehow I feel sure that she must be,' she said innocently.

'I suppose you might describe her so,' replied Hal cautiously. He was far too wise to give Georgie his head for washing in such a fashion; if he revealed his true opinion of Cassandra's charms, he would never hear the last of it.

'A blonde?' hazarded Georgie. 'Angelic golden curls and large, sparkling blue eyes? Or a brunette, with melting brown eyes, like that girl you made such a cake of yourself over—'

'Neither,' said Hal, cutting her off hastily. 'She has short red curls, and green eyes, I believe. I barely took notice.'

'Oh, did you not? She sounds quite delightful, and only think how well we will complement each other, though I was resolved to like her even if she had had black hair like me. We are almost home, and I see that the carriage has drawn up outside the house, and she is getting out, so tell me quickly: what is her Christian name? I cannot be forever calling her Miss Hazeldon if she is my bosom friend.'

'Her name is Cassandra,' said Hal, trying not to linger over the syllables.

'What an excessively pretty name!' said Georgie, shooting him a mischievous glance, and then darted forward, crying, 'My dear Miss Hazeldon! Cassandra! I cannot tell you how delighted I am to see you at last! How I have missed you!'

CHAPTER FOURTEEN

Cassandra found herself enveloped in a scented embrace, and then drawn into the house and up a broad staircase to an elegantly appointed sitting room decorated in harmonious shades of blue, her companion chattering away to her all the while in the friendliest fashion. Clearly Lady Georgiana had been apprised of her situation, and had declared herself more than willing to help. In a bewilderingly short space of time, she found that her bonnet and spencer had been whisked away, refreshments had been ordered and delivered, and she was alone with three members of the Pendlebury family, who were regarding her with a variety of expressions from almost identical bright blue eyes.

They are all so very handsome, she could not help but think. Lord Irlam she had now seen in evening black, riding attire and a gentleman's fashionable day dress; it was impossible to say which became him the most, and best, perhaps, not to dwell on the subject. His sister and aunt resembled him greatly; Lady Georgiana was of medium height and very gracefully made, with an enchanting little face that sparkled with mischief, and abundant dark curls very stylishly dressed, while her aunt – who looked nothing whatsoever like any other aunt Cassandra had ever encountered – was built along magnificent, statuesque lines but shared the same striking colouring and lustrous black locks.

'Well!' said Lady Georgiana now. 'Miss Hazeldon, I am very glad to meet you. My brother has told me of your awful ordeal and how brave you have been, and of course I am very happy to help you in any way that I may. I trust you do not mind me calling you Cassandra, but it would seem odd if I did not do so, after all. I hope you will call me Georgie.'

'I am very grateful to you all,' she replied with a shy smile. 'I cannot possibly convey to you how much.'

Her hosts brushed aside her thanks, and Lady Louisa said, 'There was nothing else to be done, once my nephew found you in such desperate straits. I am only glad that by the sheerest chance you found yourself in his house, and not another man's. But it cannot be pleasant for you continually to speak of it before strangers, so let us not do so.'

There was nothing to be said after this, and so Cassandra found herself listening to Lady Georgiana's plans for her entertainment, which quite took her breath away. She was determined that Cassandra should accompany her everywhere, and adamant that such a plan necessitated a visit to her own exclusive modiste upon the very next morning. This put Cassandra in mind of something of great importance that she had had no opportunity to discuss with Lord Irlam upon any previous occasion. She said resolutely now, 'I can quite see the necessity of being suitably dressed, but I cannot countenance you paying for it, sir.'

'No indeed,' said Lady Louisa. 'Most improper. I shall discharge the bills, and you may pay me back when your affairs are set to rights.'

'That is most generous of you, ma'am, but I cannot allow it!' said Cassandra with some heat. 'Fortunately I am not quite destitute – I had my mother's pearls with me when I fled, and if you would engage to pawn them for me, Lord Irlam, I am sure that the sum raised will be sufficient to pay for any number of gowns.'

She was resolved upon the propriety of this course, and would have pledged the necklace herself if she had had the least idea how to do so, and at length he was obliged to agree, and promised to do so at the first opportunity upon the morrow.

Lady Georgiana had a dinner engagement; it was sure to be a very dull affair, she said frankly, with some relations of Lord Lamington's, and being scarcely acquainted with them she had not thought it proper to ask if Cassandra could be included in the party at such short notice. 'Quite right,' approved her aunt. 'It is not to be thought of. I dare say Miss Hazeldon is tired after all her exertions – I am tired myself, only thinking of them – and will not object to dining at home. Do you dine with us, Hal, or go out?'

'I will dine at home, Louisa,' he said. It seemed the least he could do.

The mantel clock chimed the hour, and Georgiana suddenly exclaimed, 'Goodness, I must go and dress, or I shall not be ready when the Lamingtons arrive to collect me! Come with me, Cassandra, and we can talk while I change, for I am sure the Lamingtons' dreary cousins dine far earlier than we do. Do not forget to tell me more about yourself, in case anyone should ask me where we are supposed to have met!'

As the door closed behind them, Lady Louisa said, frowning a little, 'I cannot believe that you intend to hock the child's jewels for her, Hal. What if someone should see you, or word should get about?'

'Of course I shan't do any such thing!' replied her nephew robustly. 'It would be all over Brighton within the hour that my pockets were to let, and if anyone should realise I was doing it on her behalf that would be even worse. I shall advance her a good sum, and tell her I have done it, but I will lock them up in my strongbox and keep them safe for her.'

'Good,' she said. 'I collect you saw the Lamingtons when you went to find Georgie?'

'I did, and a duller set of prosy bores I never met in my life.'

'I know!' sighed his aunt. 'They will insist upon visiting me, the pair of twittering hens, and of course I am obliged to receive them, for Georgie's sake, but I swear, Hal, I can scarcely keep awake. Do not grin at me like that! Do you know that Lamington intends – or rather I can only suppose that his mother intends, for you must know he lives under the cat's foot – that he and Georgie should reside with them when they are married?'

'By God, no, I did not know that!' he said, revolted. 'I can just imagine how it will be – all weak tea and moralising and reading books of sermons. I shouldn't think she could stomach it for a sennight, Louisa. I know I couldn't.'

His aunt shuddered. 'I should think not. What could be worse? I wonder you should be so keen on the match, Hal, really. It is not in the least my concern, but although I suppose it is respectable enough as marriages go, and they are our distant cousins, it is scarcely brilliant, and they are so exceedingly tedious! Georgie could surely do better.'

'I'm not especially keen on it. It's all Georgie. What a time I've had with her. You know some devilish ramshackle fellow had the temerity to ask for her hand right at the start of the Season when he'd hardly set eyes on her – a wastrel of a line officer with no means to support her, a fortune-hunter of the worst stamp?'

'I believe you told me something of it in one of your extremely tiresome letters,' she said, yawning shamelessly.

'Well, I sent him about his business quickly enough, and since then she has had quite a dozen offers; I swear, Louisa, it reached the point where Wilson would announce that a gentleman had called to see me, and I would say, "Another one come to offer for my sister?" and he would reply, his face perfectly straight, "I believe so, my lord, for he betrays all the signs of nervous agitation that I have come to recognise".'

'I don't doubt it; she is the hit of the Season,' his aunt said. 'But with so many to choose from, I don't see why you should plump for Lamington, of all men.'

'I didn't; she did! Obviously I gave none of them leave to address her before I had spoken to her first, however eligible they might be, and after I saw the way the wind was blowing I sat her down and told her that, since it seemed that every bachelor in London was beating a path to my door, it would be more convenient and far less fatiguing if she gave me notice of whether there was one she *would* accept, supposing he should ask. And she said Lamington.'

'It seems odd to me, you know, Hal.'

'It seemed devilish odd to me as well, and of course I asked her what was so special about him, for he appears to be a perfect booby, setting aside the impediment of his harridan of a mother, but she wouldn't give me a straight answer, no matter how much I pressed her. I told her there was no reason at all that she should be married in her first Season, but she was adamant it must be him. He then offered, of course, along with all the rest. I think it's the only time I've heard him speak more than four words together; he must have had it off by heart. And knowing she was determined to accept him, all I could do was refuse to announce it publicly and insist upon a long engagement, using her youth as an excuse.'

'She is very young. But has it occurred to you that she's up to something?'

'For God's sake, Louisa, do you take me for a slow-top?! Of course it has! In my experience, she's almost always up to something. But what am I to do, if she won't tell me anything? I don't suppose she has confided in you?'

'She has not. She is hardly ever at home, and when I try to talk to her, she turns the subject. Perhaps if she becomes friendly with your Miss Hazeldon, she might confide in her. They appear to be much of an age.'

Passing over whether Miss Hazeldon could be described as 'his' or not, Hal said, 'You may be right, although it does not sit well with me to be asking our guest to betray a confidence. It smacks of dishonour.'

'I dare say it does, and what of it? If you would sooner wait for Georgie to set the whole of Brighton by the ears and embroil herself – and all of us – in heaven knows what atrocious scrape, then please, do nothing. She is your charge, not mine!' Lady Louisa displayed quite unwonted vehemence as she spoke, and Hal sighed, acknowledging the truth of all she said, and told her that he would think on it while he was changing for dinner.

CHAPTER FIFTEEN

Lady Georgiana dragged Cassandra into her bedchamber, and rang for her maid, saying, 'I will merely have Phillips lay out my muslin and arrange my hair very simply, and then if you will help me do up my gown, we shall be able to have a comfortable coze.'

A short while later, Cassandra was fastening the last of the myriad of tiny pearl buttons that closed Georgiana's deep pink evening gown. It was a colour that became her greatly, and she told her so. Regarding herself in the cheval glass, Georgiana said, 'Yes, I think it does, though I wonder now if the embroidered rosebuds on the bodice are a little too *à la jeune fille*. I do not know what I can have been thinking – rosebuds for a debutante, how sadly trite. But it will certainly do well enough for Lamington's dreary cousins. I suppose I shall wear Mama's pearls, and they will all consider me to be a very correct young lady, as long as I do not actually *say* anything. What a dull evening it will be, and how I would rather stay here and make plans for your introduction into society. But tell me, Cassandra – or is it Cassie? Do your friends generally call you Cassie?'

'They do, although I have not spoken to any of them for many months. Your brother says that I should write immediately and explain why I have never received any of their letters, nor answered them.'

'Oh, you must certainly do so! Is there a young man, perhaps, who has been missing you sadly all this while? Not that you could correspond with him, of course, for that would not be proper.' Cassandra thought that there was a satirical note in her voice when she uttered the word 'proper', but she did not have time to reflect upon what it might mean, for Georgiana was still speaking. 'However, I dare say someone else may quite naturally pass on news of him to you, and vice versa, so you should definitely resume your correspondence as soon as possible.'

Cassandra murmured that she had only been seventeen when she had left Yorkshire. She was aware that this remark could hardly have been said to answer the question that she had been posed, and was hardly surprised when Georgiana said, 'Why, what has that to say to anything? I was at a dreary old school in Bath till earlier this year, and I assure you that I had a great many admirers for the whole time that I was there! But do tell! If we were truly intimate friends who have been corresponding regularly for the last age, you would surely have done so, you know. Come, Cassie!'

'There was a young man, but he . . .'

'I knew it! Tell all!' exclaimed Georgiana, sitting down on the bed beside her and bending to lace up her sandals. Cassandra could not help but notice that her white stockings had pink clocks that ran up as far as she could see, and was torn between thinking them very fast and wondering if the style might become her too, and where she might obtain some.

'His name is Matthew Welby, and he is the son of the squire in the village where my father's estate is situated. My estate now, I suppose, although I have not been allowed even to visit there since my father died.'

'And so you have not seen or heard of him in all that time? How terrible! Is he very handsome?'

Cassandra said, 'I could not say precisely . . . I suppose he is. I have known him since we were children, and his sister Emily was my greatest friend. We had always been used to do almost everything together, and we had spoken of marriage . . .'

'Oh ho!'

'But only teasing each other, you know? "If we were to be married, Cassie, we could travel all around Europe as you have always wanted. Just the three of us together. Imagine what fun we would have!" "Oh yes, Matthew, we could go to Rome!" That manner of thing. Nothing more than that.'

'I understand,' said Georgiana, sticking out her dainty feet and wiggling them thoughtfully. 'Do you like these sandals? I'm not sure . . . But were you in love with him – are you in love with him now?'

'No,' confessed Cassandra. 'But I do miss him, and would like to see him again. But then, that is true of all my friends.' She did not say that she was having the greatest difficulty in calling the precise arrangement of Matthew Welby's regular features to mind, and that when Georgie had asked if he were handsome, her instinctive reaction had been to say, *Not near as handsome as your brother!*

'Perhaps when you write to your dearest friend Emily and tell her that you are in Brighton, you will find that he rushes to your side at once, to declare his love and sweep you away with him to be married!' said Georgie, her eyes sparkling.

Cassandra thought that that was extremely unlikely, but said only, 'But I'm not at all sure I want him to.'

'Oh. Well, I dare say we will find you another suitor, then, perhaps one more eligible. Now I am more or less engaged, you know,' Georgiana said naively, 'there are any number of young men who are at a loose end, and would be quite ready to fall in love with you, I should think. I will see if I can call one to mind.'

Slightly alarmed, Cassandra said, 'I think I would prefer it if you did not, although I am grateful that you should think of it, of course. If any young man were to offer for me – not that I am saying that I think anybody would, or that I want them to in the least, you understand

103

– I should have to explain my whole awkward situation to him, and I dare say it might give him or his family a disgust of me, that I have such dreadful relations as my uncle.'

'I am sure everyone has dreadful relations,' said Georgiana consolingly. 'I know we do. My youngest brothers are absolute monsters. And you can hardly be blamed for your uncle being so horrid, or having such horrid friends, I am sure. Oh, look at the time! I must go to my dull party, or they will be cross with me. I am sure Lady Lamington disapproves of me dreadfully already. Only tell me quickly, where did we meet, and where did you live? In case someone should ask me.'

'Your brother suggested we might have met in Harrogate, taking the waters, and he was quite right, for I grew up in the countryside near Skipton, not far away, and I have often been in Harrogate.'

'How clever Hal can be when he tries! I went there some years ago with Aunt Sophia, when she had persuaded herself that she was of a bilious habit – though I would rather blame living with the twins, as I am sure they are enough to make anyone bilious – and someone told her that she should take the waters. They were excessively nasty, I recall. Yes, that will do very well,' said Georgiana, and she seized up her reticule and shawl, and in a moment she was gone, running down the stairs in a most unladylike fashion and crying, 'I am coming! I am so sorry to be late!'

CHAPTER SIXTEEN

Cassandra did not know where her own chamber might be located, for there had been such a bustle since her arrival that nobody had thought to tell her, but as she came out of Georgiana's room and stood hesitating on the landing, Kitty emerged from the rear of the house and led her away, saying, 'You have very little time to change, miss, but I am sure I know that Lady Georgiana is to blame for detaining you. How that girl does rattle on!'

Cassandra submitted to being undressed and stepped out of her gown. She washed, and Kitty helped her put on the evening gown that she had altered for her that morning. It was an unusual shade of blue – not the bright blue that she was coming to associate with the Pendlebury eyes, but rather darker and more muted – and she could imagine that it had become Lady Georgiana excessively. But Kitty stood back in satisfaction and said, 'There! I do think you look well in that, miss, if you don't mind me saying so! It proper brings out the green of your eyes. It's as well your hair is so short, for I'm no hand at dressing a lady's hair, and that flighty maid of Lady Georgiana's is that disobliging I can't tell you. But we don't need her. I laid out a pair of sandals for you and a shawl, and I'm to show you to the dining room when you're ready.'

She put on the sandals – like the boots she had worn today, they were slightly too large for her, but nothing to signify – draped the paisley shawl around her elbows in the approved fashion, and took up her shabby reticule. It was still heavy with her mother's pearls; she must give them to Lord Irlam this evening. She followed Mrs Oldcastle down the grand staircase to a small but charming room on the ground floor, where she found His Lordship and his aunt awaiting her.

He was still wearing the elegant attire she had last seen him in, and she had no fault to find with his appearance. Lady Louisa had changed into a splendid gown of rich red silk, which set off her pale complexion and dark curls to perfection; clearly her laziness did not attend to matters of fashion. Cassandra felt ridiculously tiny and insignificant next to her tall, impressive hosts, but they both smiled at her kindly, and Lord Irlam pulled out her chair so that she might sit, then did the same for his aunt.

It was an enjoyable dinner; she did not care to think how long it was since she had dined in such congenial company. Her uncle had commanded that she eat all her meals in her chamber even when she was not locked in, and he had not taken the least interest in her until his friend and co-conspirator had made an appearance. Then she had been obliged to wear gowns that he had bought for her, and dine with him, and with his friend, and she had soon wished herself back in her lonely room, for she had not cared in the least for the nature of their conversation, nor for the way they attempted to force wine on her. This evening was very different; she was given a glass of wine as a matter of course, but nobody insisted that she drink it, nor ridiculed her when she did not. She took a few cautious sips, since she was under no pressure to do so, and found it pleasant enough. Lady Louisa talked of the novels she had been reading, and Cassandra had read a few of them too, as had Lord Irlam, rather surprisingly, and so the conversation flowed pleasantly, until she was astonished to find that it was time for the ladies to withdraw from the table.

Hal had ascertained that Cassandra had never visited Brighton before, and he had suggested that they might go for a short drive after dinner, so that she could see something of the town; his aunt complained at the thought of the exertion, but assented, and he assured them that he would not linger long in solitary state, but would join them in a few minutes, so that they could set off before the evening became too advanced.

He sat back in his chair and considered. It had been a long day, with hours of riding in the heat, on top of a night of very little sleep and too much claret, but he found that he was not tired, but possessed with a restless energy. He was looking forward to driving out with Cassandra – with Louisa at her side to satisfy the proprieties, of course, which could not be helped – but he would rather have taken her dancing. He had long thought the assemblies at the Old Ship and the Castle Inn dull affairs, but that had been . . . before. He could picture her piquant heart-shaped face, flushed with activity and the pleasure of movement, green eyes sparkling. She had had a dreadful time, but she had begun to relax tonight, he thought, and he would like to see her really enjoying herself as any girl of her age should. They might even waltz – he would take her in his arms, holding her close as the dance permitted, and she would look up at him, and smile . . .

He had liked to see her in the blue gown tonight; it was modest enough, as befitted a young lady in her first Season, but as was the current mode it had small puff sleeves that left her arms almost entirely bare once she had removed her gloves to eat. Its almost sombre colour set off her pale skin, which had a fine golden down upon it and a scattering of freckles. She had worn no jewellery, and in his estimation she had not needed any.

Although he could imagine her in emeralds, old emeralds the colour of her fine eyes. He would give her the emeralds, and then later he would remove them, the tips of his fingers just caressing her bare skin. Obviously they were quite alone, in this scenario, and the room had a bed, or at least a decent-sized couch, in it. His imagination was not troubling itself any further than that with the interior decorations. As his fingers brushed her throat, she would sigh, a soft, intimate sound, and perhaps whisper his name. Not 'my lord', but Hal. Yes, Hal . . . The fine golden hairs on her arms would stand on end and she would shiver with delicious anticipation as he trailed butterfly kisses down her neck, and across her shoulders. She had a mole on her left shoulder, he had noticed – one that looked very much like the beauty spots his grandmother's generation had used to adorn their faces and décolletages. He wondered if she thought it a blemish, and was self-conscious about it, wishing it gone; he did not, not in the least. He liked it, and wondered if she had others, and where they might be. The thought was arousing. The one he could see was just above the neckline of her gown, and he would press his lips to it, and then . . .

Hal drained his glass, and set it down firmly. He would compose himself, and then go to collect the ladies, and take them out for the evening drive that he had suggested. He would sit forward in the barouche, of course, and Cassandra and Louisa would be opposite him, so he would have ample opportunity to feast his eyes on that damn tantalising mole, and be tormented by the unsettling thoughts it stirred in him. He sighed, and went to get his hat.

CHAPTER SEVENTEEN

The drive that Lord Irlam had suggested enabled Cassandra to understand a little of the town's layout, and she was glad of it in the following days, which passed in a disorientating whirl of activity. Late the next morning, after Lady Georgiana's maid had with a sulky air trimmed her hair into a more fashionable crop, her hostess took her to visit her preferred Brighton modiste, and in an astonishingly brief space of time she found herself the owner of a bewildering number of gowns for day and evening, pelisses, spencers and even a riding habit. They seemed to do nothing but shop for several days, and Cassandra also acquired sandals, slippers, half-boots, shawls, an evening cloak, reticules, silk stockings, under-things, night-rails, a parasol and bonnets. As she contemplated a particularly lovely and outrageously expensive silk bonnet with curling green feathers, she consoled herself with the thought that at least she was not beholden to her hosts for money, if for so much else. She had handed over her pearls to Lord Irlam that first evening, and he had returned the next day with a reassuring smile and a quite extraordinarily large roll of notes. She had asked him to keep it locked away safely for her, and he had agreed to do so, leaving her with enough to pay her bills when they should arrive and have something in her reticule for pin money besides.

Lady Georgiana proved not to be an early riser, so Cassandra had time on the first morning of her visit to write letters to her cousin. She penned several identical notes to Mrs Thoroughgood, to be sent to the various European cities she might be expected to visit. It seemed to Cassandra that that lady, however adventurous she might be, would hardly have stayed long in France after Bonaparte's triumphant, if brief, return there in April; probably she would have pushed on to Italy, which had been in any case her destination. She supposed it was just possible that she might have decided to travel back to Paris or even Brussels after the dramatic events that had culminated in the Emperor's defeat and overthrow, so she addressed two of her notes to the *poste restante* in those cities. But it was far more likely that she would be in Venice, Florence or Rome, perhaps even Naples by now. Cassandra wasted a little time in daydreaming of all the sights her cousin would have seen, and which she might have seen too if she had been allowed to accompany her as they had wished. Now that the Corsican despot was cast down at last – one could only assume that his captors would be considerably more careful to secure his person this time – the whole of Europe and beyond was open to intrepid British travellers, and Cassandra could think of nothing she would enjoy more than to be one of them. But this was not possible at the moment, and so she returned to her task, firmly repressing thoughts of warm, scented evenings on elegant stone terraces overlooking mighty Vesuvius, and tours of the most interesting excavations at Pompeii.

It was an odd experience, she found, writing the first letter, and then so many copies. It was no pleasant thing to set down in ink what she had undergone while in her uncle's house, and supposedly in his care; the writing of it so many times affected her, and she was glad to pass on to the more cheerful part of her news, and briefly describe her current situation and the identity of her hosts. She thought it unwise to reveal on paper exactly how she had come to be in their company – the tale of that night and her strange, memorable encounter with Lord Irlam in his library – but merely described Lady Georgiana as her kind friend, and mentioned her brother only in passing. When she returned, her cousin would no doubt ask exactly how such a visit had come about, and Cassandra would have no choice but to tell her. It would be no easy task, but there was no need to think of it now. Even if Mrs Thoroughgood received one of her letters without undue delay and returned immediately, it would surely be many weeks at best before she could arrive.

Later that afternoon, before she changed for dinner, she sat down to write to her friends in Yorkshire: another challenge, she found, as again she was unsure how much to tell them. It was her first hot impulse to denounce her uncle and his friend in the strongest possible terms, in words that would scorch the paper, but her better sense counselled caution. If spicy rumours began swirling around her name, it would be her reputation that suffered more than his, she feared, society being what it was. And so she wrote to Emily Welby, telling her only that her uncle had prevented her come-out and not allowed her to correspond with anyone. She could not help but say this, as she supposed – hoped – that Emily and her other friends had written to her after her departure, at least for a while, and must have been hurt and puzzled when they received no answer. She was sure that Emily would pass on news to her brother Matthew, and she was glad of it, for things had passed between them that would always linger in her memory, even if she chose not to share them with Lady Georgiana, for fear she would be shocked.

Cassandra found it odd and unsettling to think of her friends at home now, and to speculate on what changes there might have been in their lives in the long months since she had seen them. It would be the height of foolishness to picture them necessarily still in exactly the same places, doing exactly the same things as they had done before, for it was even possible that Emily was married by now, to some person entirely unknown to her, though she was reasonably confident that Matthew would not be. She could only imagine, though, that her friend and former teacher Kate Moreton was still living in York with her grandmother, still teaching Italian and singing, as she had done for several years, and so she wrote to her there. Kate had already been four and twenty when Cassandra had bade her a sad farewell, and since she had escaped matrimony so long, and to Cassandra's knowledge previously refused at least one respectable offer for her hand, it seemed unlikely that her circumstances could greatly have changed in the intervening time.

This train of thought was melancholy, as it led her to wonder if she would ever see the Welbys and Kate again, let alone her home. Writing to Polly, her old nurse, was worse, as she did not want to worry her and knew she would fret over her news, however she tried to sugar-coat it, even though she was comfortably settled in Leeds with her widowed brother, a prosperous manufacturer. The thought that Polly, who was no longer young and had been almost a second mother to her, had been forced to go without news of her charge for so long was perhaps the cruellest thing her uncle had done, among his many heartless actions. She sniffed dolefully, and wiped away a fugitive tear with one inky finger.

Cassandra was forced to take herself to task – it was ridiculous and inconsistent, she upbraided herself, at one moment to be pining for European travel, and the next to be feeling homesick for the old faces from her childhood, and the hills and dales of Yorkshire. She was, most unexpectedly, in Brighton, centre of the fashionable world, and she should be grateful, and enjoy the pleasures that it offered her. A few days ago she had been facing a most uncertain, even terrifying future, and, if in truth this was still the case, at least her immediate prospects were considerably brighter than they had been. Cassandra resolved to try to put aside her anxieties and immerse herself in the whirl of gaiety that surrounded her; she could not help but recognise that, after the Pendleburys had received her into their home so kindly, and exerted themselves to make her welcome and keep her safe, it would be the height of ingratitude to show them a sad or worried face. What more could they possibly have done for her? Nothing, in truth, and she must not repay them by being a gloomy guest.

She set aside her pen. She had other friends to write to, and other of her father's servants to enquire after, but she would do it tomorrow. It would not do to sink into despondency when she had so much to be grateful for.

CHAPTER EIGHTEEN

Lord Irlam had said that his sister was the height of fashion, and never spent an evening at home, and Cassandra soon learnt that this was entirely true. The mantelpiece in Lady Louisa's sitting room was barely visible beneath stacks of snowy-white, gilt-edged invitations; there could scarcely be an event held by the more exclusive sections of Brighton society to which Lady Georgiana was not invited, and Cassandra, as her bosom friend, soon found herself included as a matter of course. It seemed that nobody saw the least reason to question the presence of Miss Hazeldon from Yorkshire; she supposed that the acceptance of the Pendleburys was guarantee enough of her birth and breeding. And so she began to relax a little. She would scarcely have been human had she not found herself enjoying the balls, theatre visits, subscription assemblies, *fêtes champêtres* and al fresco breakfasts that filled her days, especially since she had been so starved of society ever since her father's death, and most recently kept a virtual prisoner. It had been an unnatural, lonely life for a young lady, and once she had overcome her initial self-consciousness she began to revel in her new freedom, and the new experiences and fresh acquaintances it brought her.

Her circumstances inevitably led her into a great deal of intimacy with the Pendleburys. Something that she began to find puzzling, as she saw more of it, was Lady Georgiana's relationship with Lord Lamington. She had learnt that their engagement had not yet been officially announced to the world, for reasons that had not been disclosed to her, but it seemed to her that the whole of society was perfectly aware that a match was to be made between them; it could scarcely be otherwise, when Lord Lamington's attentions were so very marked. Yet his mode of courtship was a curious one. It was true that, on each social occasion that the group of cousins attended, His Lordship could be observed by anybody who cared to watch him to have not much to say for himself, but this could not be taken by any rational observer as a sign of indifference. On the contrary, he seemed perfectly content merely to gaze adoringly and wordlessly at Lady Georgiana, only breaking off occasionally to agree vigorously with anything that his beloved might chance to say. Sometimes, Cassandra noticed, her new friend would entirely contradict herself within the space of a few short moments, saying, as it might be, that it was a very hot day, and then immediately after that there was a distinct chill in the air, and His Lordship could be relied upon to approve both statements equally fervently. Cassandra knew Georgiana to be somewhat capricious, but not to this extent; she began to suspect that she made these topsy-turvy statements because she was deliberately pushing her suitor to see how far he would go – the words entered her mind with a slight shock, but once they were there she could not dismiss them – in idiocy.

After this idea had occurred to her, she could not help but observe that, while Lord Lamington's feelings were plain for all to see, Lady Georgiana's were far less clear. Perhaps she was too well-bred, thought Cassandra somewhat doubtfully, to betray the affection that she surely felt for the man she intended to marry. Perhaps she would consider it unladylike to appear to reciprocate his sentiments in an obvious way. Yet there did not seem to be an answering warmth in those brilliant blue eyes when they rested on her suitor. Not only did she fail to seek out his company, it seemed at times as though she positively avoided him. And sometimes, indeed, she spoke to him with an edge of impatience in her voice, although he appeared to be entirely unconscious of it.

Cassandra reflected that she was not well acquainted with the habits of such an exalted level of society, and perhaps she had been naïve in assuming that this was a love match – perhaps it was no such thing, but instead an alliance arranged between the families, one which His Lordship accepted with great complaisance, but Georgiana with considerably less enthusiasm. It could be that this was how such things were generally ordered among the nobility, and a mutual affection was not considered necessary or even desirable. But if that were the case, then one of the prime movers behind the marriage must surely have been Lord Irlam, the head of his family, and as the days passed she became aware – she could hardly say how – that her host had no great opinion of his brother-in-law to be, and, much like his sister, avoided his company if at all possible.

She was confirmed in this suspicion on one memorable occasion, at a private ball in a grand country house some short distance outside Brighton. The glittering white ballroom was oppressively warm, the scent of hothouse flowers almost overwhelming, and Georgie, radiant in pink silk and silver gauze, was dancing and flirting outrageously with one of her other admirers, a dashing young military gentleman. Lamington stood to one side watching her, not betraying the least token of jealousy, that small smile ever-present on his blank but undeniably amiable face, and Cassandra was sure she heard her own dancing partner, Lord Irlam, mutter, 'Blockhead!' explosively to himself, a few inches above her ear.

She was so much startled that she lost her place and stumbled a little in her dance, and his foot caught in the flounce of her gown, and tore it. They were obliged to retire in confusion from the dancefloor, and he escorted her directly into an antechamber near the ballroom, so that she might inspect the damage.

'I'm sorry, Miss Hazeldon,' he said ruefully, as she sat herself in a satin chair, and extracted a needle and a skein of fine white thread, which she had prudently brought with her, from her reticule in order to repair the tear.

She looked up at him, leaving off threading her needle for a moment. 'You have no cause to apologise, my lord,' she said. 'I was the one who misstepped so clumsily, and so the fault was mine. You could scarcely help but catch your foot in my gown.'

'That is true, of course,' he replied, throwing himself down in a chair opposite hers and stretching out his long, black-clad legs in his habitual manner. 'But still you should not take the blame, for I am sure that you only stumbled because you were surprised by my somewhat incautious utterance. You need not trouble to deny it; I know you heard me, and I have a shrewd suspicion that you know to whom I was referring. It seems to me that you have a very quick understanding, and I think you cannot fail to be aware of my feelings for the gentleman in question.'

So complimented, Cassandra found herself quite unable to pretend that she did not apprehend his meaning, and in a sudden regrettable burst of curiosity said, 'It has sometimes appeared to me that Lady Georgiana does not feel towards His Lordship . . .' She broke off, aware of the impropriety of what she had been about to say – what business was any of it of hers? – and moreover of the intimacy of the conversation, and of their being alone together, as they had not been, she now realised, since the morning they had first met. She felt herself blush hotly, and lowered her eyes to her needlework, but that was no help, for in order to complete her task she would be obliged to lift her skirts so that she could reach the damaged flounce, exposing her petticoat to his sight, and as she flushed she found herself conscious of his intent regard, even though she dared not meet his gaze. She was quite unable to ply her needle with a steady hand, and so did nothing.

He did not refer to her indiscreet utterance. 'Let me help you,' he said instead, and before she could reply he had risen and set his chair down close by her, and his long fingers were lifting the hem of her gown, raising the torn white muslin and smoothing it out, placing it beneath her hands. Her trembling hands.

He was so very near, and her nostrils were filled with the scent of him: the spicy soap he used, clean linen, and beneath it all something that was indefinably masculine and essentially him. It reminded her, it must remind her, of his bedroom, and the night she had spent in his bed, among his possessions, and suddenly her mouth was dry, and her heart was pounding hard and fast in her breast. She wondered what she would see in his face if she raised her eyes to his, but before she could do so he let out some exclamation, and forced back his chair, leaping hastily to his feet and striding across the room to stand by the window.

His broad back was to her as he spoke in somewhat clipped, terse fashion. 'I think you should do your mending without loss of time, Miss Hazeldon, rather than dallying over it, so that we can return to the ballroom before we are missed. It will not do to set malicious tongues wagging, you know.'

Cassandra murmured some confused words of assent, and bent her head again, drawing the fabric together all anyhow and setting clumsy, uneven stitches that would have to be unpicked later – Kitty would be shocked at the sight of them – but would be invisible to the casual glance, and at least should serve to hold the tear for the rest of the evening. The air in the small room seemed hot, electric, charged with things unspoken, with actions not taken, but if he could ignore it and speak so coldly, so could she, and so it was just a moment before she bit off her thread, and said quietly, 'I am done, sir. You are quite right to reproach me. Let us return.'

She rose, put away her sewing materials in her reticule and shook out her skirts as he turned towards her, crossing the room to her side. She forced herself not to react to his nearness, and thought she had succeeded, but she could not control the expression in her eyes, nor the instinctive way her body yearned towards him. If he only might not perceive it!

'Snow White, my Snow White . . .' he whispered, 'oh, Cassandra, forgive me for speaking harshly to you . . .' and he took her in his arms.

CHAPTER NINETEEN

Hal was in a state of heightened irritation, the evening of the ball. He had been out of sorts for days. While he might choose to blame his tension upon his increasing conviction, firstly that Lord Lamington was one of the stupidest human beings he had ever had the misfortune to encounter, and secondly that Georgie had not the least intention of marrying the utter booby, but was playing some other sort of deep and probably dangerous game entirely, he knew at the back of his mind that this was hardly true. He cared for his sister – of course he did – and his ingrained habit of responsibility for all his younger siblings would hardly allow him to regard the prospect of her creating some dreadful scandal (from which, furthermore, he was bound to have to extricate her) with indifference, but after all he should be well accustomed by now to her particular brand of chaos. And in justice to her, even her worst escapades had – so far – paled into insignificance beside the twins' truly terrifying adventures. Georgie, at least, had never yet attempted to stow away on board a navy vessel and run away to the wars. He was reasonably confident that he was awake upon all suits and would be able to deal with whatever mischief she could devise in the way of rash behaviour or unsuitable flirtations.

No. This time his restlessness and inability to sleep could be laid to another cause entirely. It was Cassandra who had him tossing and turning at night, Cassandra whose face haunted his unquiet dreams, dreams of a nature that he would be sorry indeed to be obliged to describe to anyone. He found himself aware, always, of precisely where she was in the house, and when she was absent at some damn tea party or on some shopping expedition he could not settle to any activity, but would inevitably end up forcing himself to go for a long, punishing ride, in an attempt to distract himself, which never did the least good, or, worse, wandering aimlessly about the streets of Brighton in the pathetic hope that he might encounter her party, and be invited to join it, so that he could linger at her side.

Hal did not blame her for his sad condition; he had been reared by his father, best of men, never to delude himself for a second that any woman of any station in life was responsible for the feelings of lust that she might happen to inspire in him, with or without her knowledge.

He had been brought up to believe that a decent man was obliged to acknowledge that he was accountable for his own impulses. These wild imaginings that the sight, the very thought of Cassandra roused in him might seem stronger and more persistent than any he had entertained since he was a schoolboy, but he must wrestle them into submission – Christ, there was an image he could do without! – none the less. No, he knew that the problem was his to deal with and his alone, and he also knew that there was only one way in which the erotic fantasies that troubled his nights – and, if truth be told, his days – could be transformed into reality: by marrying her. And that was a step he was by no means keen to take at this stage of his life. Even if she were willing, and he had no reason to think her so. She had a dozen ardent admirers already, curse them for the importunate puppies that they were, and he could not flatter himself that she looked on him, Hal Pendlebury, with any more favour than she did on the spottiest and most incoherent youth who sought her hand at every dance. And then again, if she did care at all for him, pleasant and distracting though the thought was, where could it lead but marriage?

His uncontrollable thoughts had led him back to marriage again, it seemed, and to the thought of her as his bride in his bedchamber – here, in Town, at the Castle; damn it, any bedchamber with a good big bed in it – turning to smile at him over her shoulder as he brushed the tiny red curls and the soft skin of her neck with his fingers and commenced undoing a line of tiny buttons so that he could slip off her gown and . . . Hell and the devil confound his cursed imagination! Perhaps he should take up daily sea-bathing to cool his heated thoughts. He certainly needed to do something, and the idea of seeking out another woman was oddly distasteful to him. In his wildest moments he found himself actually wondering if he should call a physician and have himself bled, but then his natural good sense reasserted itself, and he could only laugh at himself, and try, without any notable degree of success, to turn his thoughts in another direction.

It was in this febrile state that Hal attended the Windlesham ball. He meant to comport himself with perfect correctness, and thus demonstrate to his own satisfaction that the fever of desire that sometimes threatened to overmaster him was a mere passing fancy, a summer whim, which could, with proper manly resolution, be suppressed and, in due course, forgotten. Or laughed at. Ha. In pursuit of this laudable aim, he danced with all the ladies of rank, both married and unmarried, who were presented to him, until, after being bored almost into insensibility by, what seemed to him, their inane chatter and unwelcome attempts at flirtation, he suddenly realised that to neglect to ask Miss Hazeldon to dance could in itself cause gossip. She was after all a guest in his house, his sister's intimate friend as far as the world knew, and in common courtesy he must take her out for one dance, if no more. It would be ridiculous and unbecoming if his secret obsession with her (or at least he very much hoped it was secret, and he would be wise not dwell on that now) led him to treat her with rudeness. That would never do.

He approached her, and somehow the crowd of Cassandra's young admirers – his rivals! Pah! – melted away; had Hal but known it, the expression upon his face was, briefly, murderous, and discretion seemed the better part of valour to most of them. He asked; he was accepted. In fact, Miss Hazeldon, whose dance card was rarely empty, had already been engaged for the dance that was about to begin, but she did not seem in that instant to recall it, and her poor swain did not feel equal to the task of informing his supplanter of his prior claim, since His Lordship – so very tall and well built, so very fierce in aspect, blue eyes positively blazing – looked in that moment ready to throw out a challenge to pistols at dawn, or something equally alarming.

Lord Irlam had himself well under restraint, he thought, as he and Miss Hazeldon took their place in the ballroom. It was hardly his fault, was it, if the dance he had chosen, entirely at random, happened to be a waltz? He had not designed it so, and if he could not control himself merely because he was holding her in his arms, in a perfectly proper fashion and surrounded by a multitude of other persons, he might as well take himself straight off to Bedlam and be done with it. The waltz had, it was true, in ancient times – some five years ago – been considered fast, but it was, as most sensible, modern people now acknowledged, an entirely acceptable dance, with nothing in the least lascivious about it. Why, he had not an hour since danced it with Lady Lavinia Trumpington – a woman considered by the haut ton to be both attractive and charming – and, when she had pressed her substantial (and substantially naked) embonpoint against his chest and smiled coyly up at him, not one indecorous thought had crossed his mind. He had been as one sculpted out of ice. It was a test of his new resolve, dancing the waltz with Cassandra; so be it, he welcomed the challenge.

He was a fool. He realised that a few short moments later. Lady Lavinia Fiddlesticks. Cassandra, unlike her predecessor, danced entirely correctly, and would not dream, clearly, of insinuating herself closely into his embrace, nor of ensuring that every available inch of her frame was connected to every inch of his, as if glued there. But she was, undeniably, in his arms, and it seemed that that was sufficient to overwhelm him, and send all his good intentions to perdition. Her head just topped his chin, her fiery curls tickled it occasionally, and as they turned about the ballroom together he was lost. He was not, he thought, holding her particularly close, but by God it was both close enough – close enough to affect him in a most regrettable fashion – and at the same time nowhere near close enough for his liking. At that moment, it seemed to Hal's heightened senses that however tightly he might hold her, however intimately he might embrace her, it could never be sufficient. Perhaps those censorious persons who had decried the waltz as scandalous and indecent had been right all along – perhaps it merely depended on the identity of one's partner.

Desperately seeking distraction, Hal glanced over Miss Hazeldon's shoulder, and at once beheld the nauseating spectacle of his sister's accepted suitor looking on with apparent approbation and a preposterous and sickly little smirk while Georgie made sheep's eyes at her current waltzing partner: one of her more ineligible and rackety admirers, of course, young Captain Hart. At once it was all too much, and he blurted out the first word that came into his head: 'Blockhead!'

His incautious utterance set in motion a chain of events that led, as though some capricious fate or mischievous deity had designed it so to torment him, to the situation in which he found himself five minutes later. He was alone in a small private room with Cassandra. That was delicious torture in itself, but in his unutterable folly he must lift up the hem of her gown and offer it to her, the soft fabric sliding between his fingers, tempting him with the thought of how much more arousing it would be to touch her bare skin, to press his lips to hers. He so very nearly kissed her then, but with an enormous effort of will he tore himself away, and spoke unforgivably coldly to her. But his self-control was an illusion; a moment later he was standing intoxicatingly close to her once more, both of them suddenly breathless, and their eyes locked, a spark sprang instantly to roaring life between them, and all his noble resolutions were swept away in a tide of pure need.

He might have spoken; he had no idea what he said. Her name, perhaps. An apology, maybe. But then she was in his arms, and his lips found hers.

CHAPTER TWENTY

They fell back against the panelled door as they embraced, and Cassandra found herself lifted entirely from her feet and locked in Lord Irlam's arms. If she had been in a condition to think, she would surely have been shocked at his boldness, and all the more shocked at her own failure to push him away. But she was in no state for rational thought; she could only feel.

He had seized hold of her so masterfully – but had he, in truth? Was it not possible that she had moved instinctively, eagerly to meet him, had flung herself into his embrace? She could no longer tell, and it did not seem to matter in that moment – yet his kiss was not insistent or demanding, not at first. His lips brushed tentatively across hers, wordlessly seeking permission, and it was only when she gave it, when she opened her mouth to him, that he increased the pressure, as did she, and in a moment they were devouring each other with an equal wild hunger, their tongues tangling and their bodies straining together, close as they could be while fully clothed.

He cupped her face in both of his big hands, and she slipped her arms about him and clung to his broad, muscular back. So much shorter and slighter as she was, she might have felt overwhelmed by his size and strength, but she did not, or if she did, she welcomed the fierce, unfamiliar sensations he aroused in her. He was pushing her urgently against the door, pressing the length of his hard body against hers, and she was pressing back, thrusting her breasts up against his chest, feeling – just one sensation among a tidal wave of physical pleasure – her suddenly erect nipples abrading the fabric of her chemise, a delicious friction, but one that made her want more. More of him, more of his touch.

Perhaps he could read her mind, or perhaps their bodies were speaking to each other, in a language older and more powerful than mere words. His right hand released her face now, and began caressing her bare neck and shoulders, stroking her, making her shiver at the contact of flesh to flesh, promising her the greater intimacy that she craved. And then, yes, he was cupping her breast, his hand curling to hold it, warm, possessive, wonderful. His thumb and forefinger sought out her taut nipple beneath the layers of flimsy fabric, and found its hardness, encircling it and squeezing it gently, and she moaned, open mouth to open mouth, and drew his full lower lip between her teeth, and bit it, not so gently. He increased the pressure of his fingers, tugging and twisting, obedient to her wordless command, and she drew his lip into her hot mouth, and sucked on it, while his other hand tangled itself in her hair, and she still clung to him.

Her hips and her mound were pressed against the tight muscles of his abdomen, and she could feel his member hard against her thigh through the silk and muslin that covered them both, the extent of his desire for her perfectly evident. Once again some tiny, irrelevant part of her knew she should be shocked, should shrink away, but she had not the smallest wish to do so, however perilous her situation. In that moment, she did not care what happened next.

Cassandra was later to think that their embrace could only have had one delicious, scandalous conclusion, if it had not been for the sudden rattle of the doorknob at her back. Lord Irlam dragged his lips reluctantly from hers, and found her ear, and whispered very softly in it, 'Hush! Not a sound.' His breath tickled her sensitive skin, and she had to stifle a gasp at the sudden frisson it created. He did not seem to be in the least alarmed or even distracted by the threatened intrusion, but instead took her earlobe between his lips, and began sucking on it, all the while continuing to caress her breast as assiduously as before. She closed her eyes, and clamped her lips together to smother the moan of pleasure that threatened to escape her.

Whoever was trying to enter the room from the corridor now pushed the door impatiently, but Hal and Cassandra were still pressed against it with all their weight, and he did not relax the tension of his body, nor move away from her so much as an inch. On the contrary, he placed one hand flat against the panel, leaning into it, and into her, and they remained in their close embrace as the door shook in its frame, but did not yield, and at last the unknown intruder gave up, and – it seemed – moved away.

'They could still be there – don't move!' he hissed into her ear, and she nodded mutely. His lips were at her throat now, and as they stood in charged silence he traced tiny, tantalising butterfly kisses down her neck and across her shoulder, until he came to the large mole just above her neckline, and pressed his lips to it with passionate intensity. Cassandra threw back her head and gave herself up to the sensations of his mouth and hands and the hot pressure of his body against hers.

After what might have been a long while or just a brief moment, he sighed, and raised his head, and said in what seemed to her a jarringly matter-of-fact voice, 'I think we should be safe now. And we really should return to the ballroom. Though Christ knows I would greatly prefer to stay here, with you.'

It was as if someone had emptied a pitcher of cold water over her head. How could he speak so calmly, appear so unaffected, when his body still gave him the lie? She found herself incapable of reply, but merely stood in his arms, lips parted, her chest rising and falling rapidly. It was over, it seemed. Whatever it had been, it was over. She slid her hands reluctantly from his back, and as if her movement had broken the last lingering remnants of the spell, he released her instantly, and stepped away from her, running his hands through his glossy dark hair.

With their physical contact removed, all the thoughts that the flaring passion between them had been holding at bay came rushing in. Cassandra raised her hands to her hot cheeks and blurted out, 'My God, what was I thinking?'

'The fault was mine,' he said curtly, his face a shuttered blank to her, betraying no emotion that she could discern. 'I seized you in my arms, took unforgivable advantage of our proximity.'

'Did you?'

'I must think that I did, though I confess I can scarcely recall doing so. But I did not plan it – please believe that much, at least. I am no practised seducer of maidens.'

Her brain roiled with contradictory thoughts. It would have been in one way comforting to think that she had fallen prey to an experienced philanderer – it might be shaming, but at least it would relieve her of all responsibility for what had just taken place. She would merely have been one in a long line of women unable to resist Lord Irlam's charms. And those charms were undeniable. She supposed it might still be true that he was a practised seducer, despite his denial – it was not to be expected that notorious rakes went about informing their victims of their untrustworthy characters. Libertines, she had to presume, did not advertise their base natures; at least, not to the women who were their dupes. Of course they would claim that each time was the first time, that their principles had been no match for the superior attractions of their victims.

But this was the meanest sophistry. Even if His Lordship had been Casanova himself at the height of his powers, she could hardly claim to have been mesmerised into his arms. Whether he was habitually licentious or not, whether he was a liar or an honest man, it made little matter. She had been as willing a participant as he.

'I do not know, sir, whether you might be an habitual rake. I am glad to say that I have no experience of such persons. But I do know, and am obliged to own to you, that I was as culpable as you. I wish my conscience would allow me to deny any share of the responsibility for . . . for what just happened. But you must know in your heart that I wanted . . . that as much as you did. I am aware it was very wrong.' The honest admission cost her something to make; she was distressed now, and her voice trembled as she spoke.

Some indefinable emotion flared in his bright blue eyes, and he said softly, 'I must know in my heart . . . ? I suppose that it is true. Yes, I do know that you wanted it. That you wanted me.'

A great scalding wave passed over her, and Cassandra felt herself flush hotly. Again she would have liked to deceive herself, to label it as shame, but she knew it was not. He had named her desire, and he was right. She had wanted him. She did want him. If he reached out for her once more, even now, would she not gladly be enfolded in his arms again, gladly feel his hands and lips on her body, gladly touch him? She knew the answer.

Fortunately – she told herself she was glad of it – she was not to be tested. 'You really are an extraordinary girl, Cassandra Hazeldon,' he said, when she did not speak. 'We are to share the blame, then, if blame there can be for something so delightful, and just now I think that has to suffice. We have a more pressing problem – how to remove ourselves from this room without being seen and causing the most fearful scandal.'

CHAPTER TWENTY-ONE

They could not leave the room together, that was plain. If Hal were to be seen alone, it would make no matter; if Cassandra were to be seen alone, it might raise a few eyebrows, the world being so much more censorious where unmarried women were concerned. But if they were to be seen together, it would mean certain disgrace, the destruction of her reputation.

Hal opened the door, very cautiously, and peered around it. The corridor was empty, deserted, and the scrape of fiddles and hum of chatter still came from the nearby ballroom. Perhaps only ten minutes had passed since they had left it. Such a short time, to shake the foundations of a man's world.

He eased out into the passageway and forced himself to stand casually, naturally, smoothing – he hoped – any trace of what had just occurred from his face. He strolled away, acting the part of a man entirely at his ease, even slightly bored. Such dull affairs, these country-house balls, though naturally one does one's duty. He was not accustomed to dissembling, and he found it hard, very hard, to arrange his features in a mask of indifference, while his body still tingled from her touch and every inch of him still craved satisfaction.

While he sauntered lazily along, under the blank eyes of the numerous busts of classical personages – Venus, a leering Cupid, Bacchus – that stood in niches on either side, and Cassandra watched him go, peering around the door, he felt a kind of delirium possess him. Had he followed only his strong inclination, he would have turned back, made damn sure that the door was locked, and drawn her down on the sofa, he had noticed that there was a sofa, and finished what they had started. Time would have passed: minutes, aeons. Planets would have collided, shooting stars trailed flame across the sky. And in the aftermath of ecstasy – mutual ecstasy, obviously, he wasn't an animal – he would have whispered in her beautiful little ear, as she lay flushed and panting in his arms, 'I think, do you not, Miss Hazeldon, that we should be married without loss of time?' And she would, of course, have murmured yes, oh yes, and looked at him with those huge green eyes, eyes a man could drown in, and he would have kissed her very tenderly, and then . . .

And then a few months of dizzy bliss – he could

be reasonably sure of that, he thought – followed no doubt, as night followed day, by an announcement that his wife was in an interesting condition, and before they knew it they'd be knee-deep in babies, napkins, wet-nurses, croup, epidemic colds, septic sore throats, influenza . . . He remembered a particularly dark and harrowing winter not long after his mother's death, when it had seemed all too likely that the twins would follow her into her grave. The doctors' grim faces, and Kitty, who never cried, weeping silently throughout one bitterly cold night, when their lives hung in the balance. He recalled all too well the aching helplessness he had felt at two and twenty: his conviction that he could never hold his fractured family together, that he could never be equal to the task that had devolved upon him. But he had done it – with a great deal of help and a pinch of luck, somehow he had done it. Had got them all this far. And now, now that at last he had a little breathing space, a little time and freedom, he was seriously contemplating putting himself through all that again? That, and worse, for there was childbed to be considered, and all the terrifying risks that that entailed. One day, perhaps, these things must be faced, one day when he was older and more able to bear it all, but now?

Madness. Insanity. Bedlam beckoned. His cell was without doubt being prepared for him even now, with a nice, snug strait-waistcoat standing ready. He kept on walking.

The corridor ran along the narrower side of the ballroom, and from it two doors led inside – one some yards away, and one quite close by. Lord Irlam had made for the further door, and as he reached it he did turn at last, and nod almost imperceptibly at Cassandra, his handsome face quite expressionless, before he opened it and stepped inside, nothing in the least furtive or suspicious about his demeanour.

She let a few agonisingly slow minutes drag by, and then left the room in her turn, and stood in front of a pier glass in the passage. If anyone should come out and observe her now, they might believe that she had slipped out to check on her appearance, to make sure that the exertions of the dance had not left their mark on her. The exertions of the dance! She was almost afraid to meet her own eyes in the mirror, but she must.

A stranger probably would see nothing amiss. Her fiery curls were somewhat disarranged – was it any wonder? – but they were cropped so short that it was an easy enough matter to run her fingers through them and restore their artful disorder. Her gown was creased – well might it be – but she shook out the folds as well as she could. Her eyes were bright, her cheeks pink, but so might any young lady show herself after an hour or two of vigorous dancing. His lips had left no mark on her pale skin, though it was still flushed and tingling at the memory of his touch. She would pass muster, she supposed. She squared her shoulders and took a deep breath, resolved to enter the ballroom with head held high, quite as nonchalantly as His Lordship had.

She was not to have the opportunity to do so.

CHAPTER TWENTY-TWO

Her hand was on the doorknob when she heard a voice at her back calling archly, 'Cassie! How providential to find you here!'

She turned, to see Lady Georgiana approaching her. She too was flushed and bright-eyed, and her face held an expression that Cassandra recognised all too well from the mirror: an explosive mixture of defiance, shame and the lingering dregs of pleasure. *I have a secret*, those blue eyes said. *And as I perceive, so do you!*

'Have you mended your gown?' asked Georgiana blandly. 'I saw you tear it. I have never known my brother be so sadly clumsy. It is most unlike him.'

'Yes,' Cassandra said, as steadily as she could manage. 'Yes, I have mended it, and it will do for now.'

'In fact, I think you will recall that I very kindly helped

you mend it, is it not so? It was for that reason that I left the ballroom a mere moment after you did. And now we shall return together.' As she spoke, she took Cassandra's arm in a most friendly fashion, and pressed it warmly, and together they entered the room, and stood watching the dancers for a moment, as a set drew to a close. No one was close enough to overhear their conversation, and Georgiana said softly, her eyes sparkling, 'I shall not ask you where you have been this age, dear Cassie, and you shall not ask me where I have been. And so everything has arranged itself famously.'

Cassandra was about to say, *Your brother at least must know that we were not together all this time!* But she checked herself. Her friend might suspect that she had been alone with Lord Irlam, and might divine the amorous nature of their encounter, but she could scarcely know for sure, unless Cassandra herself was so foolish as to tell her. And for her own part, she had no idea with whom Georgiana had spent a snatched, illicit few minutes, except for a strong conviction that it was not poor Lord Lamington. Perhaps her companion was in truth entirely innocent – perhaps she, the undoubtedly guilty one, sought dishonourably to besmirch the reputation of another in order to lessen her own culpability. She felt that she could no longer reliably distinguish right from wrong, and suddenly she longed passionately for this evening to be over. Would it never end?

At that moment, two young gentlemen, their starched

shirt points sadly wilting in the oppressive heat of the ballroom, approached the ladies, and reminded them with a little diffidence that they were promised for the next country dance. And so after a little inconsequential conversation they all took their places in the figure, and Cassandra smiled rather wanly at Georgiana at her side, and was answered with an audacious wink, before the music struck up again, and they began to go through the motions of the reel.

Lord Irlam was not dancing. Nor had he observed that his sister had, most curiously, accompanied Cassandra when she had re-entered the room, so his suspicions were not aroused as to Georgie's conduct. It was entirely possible that in that moment he was unaware that he had such a thing as a sister. He was standing at one side, aloof from the throng, alone, his arms folded, with a formidable and entirely unconscious scowl upon his face. This evening was proving to be quite interminable. He was pleased – pleased, dammit! – to see that Cassandra had so completely recovered her poise and was smiling engagingly up at the blinking idiot who was her partner, as they twirled and twisted about. Obviously, their embrace had meant little to her, if she could recover so easily from it and look with apparent favour on another man, if one could even call him a man. Whereas he – he, Hal Pendlebury, a man of some experience, dash it all, a man of the world, had been shaken to the foundations of his being, merely by a simple amorous episode with a debutante that had lasted a bare five minutes and surely meant nothing. If she could forget it with such insulting readiness, why, so could he! He should find another woman to dance and flirt with – he was sure Lady Lavinia would be more than willing. Well, perhaps not Lady Lavinia – it would be approaching blasphemy to hold her in his arms where Cassandra had so lately been, to touch her hand with the fingers that had so lately caressed— but somebody. Anybody!

But Christ, he did not want so much as to look at another woman, let alone dance with one. Her lips had been so soft, her mouth as kissable as he had imagined. A hundred times more kissable even than he had dreamt, and he had been dreaming of her for weeks. There had been no awkwardness, no hesitation: their bodies had moulded together as if nature had designed them to be joined, and when he had found her erect nipple with his instinctive fingers and she had bitten and sucked his lip so fiercely in response he had known with utter certainty that the jolt of pure pleasure that shook him to his core was mutual.

When he had whispered in her ear and kissed his way down her lovely neck to find the mole that had so enticed him from the first time he had seen it, she had thrown back her head, closed her eyes and surrendered herself to him. The vision of her face then, softened with desire, her lips parted and swollen from his kisses, was burnt on his brain. He believed, he could only believe, that it had meant as much to her as it had to him. She had confessed as much, looked him in the face and said so, with an honesty that had taken his breath away, and which he thought he would never forget. It was grossly unfair, hideously unjust to blame her now because she was able by sheer effort of will to recover her composure and face the world with the appearance of unconcern. It was necessary that she should, that they both should, in order that no one should notice anything amiss. He too must put what happened from his mind completely, and treat her with well-bred courtesy, and nothing more. They must not be alone together again. That was to be avoided at all cost. There could be no repetition of tonight and, even though he now knew just how glorious they could be together, he dared no longer indulge himself with visions of undressing her, of his caresses finding her secret places, of his mouth exploring her and bringing her . . .

Hal bit his lip unconsciously at the thought, and his tooth unfailingly found the tender place where she had bitten him in her passion a bare few minutes ago, and that same searing jolt of electricity raced through him once again. Once again in an instant he was hard; he thought he gasped aloud. Good God, what was he to do? He knew that this was folly, that it must surely lead to marriage and all that that entailed, but the sensations she aroused in him were overwhelming, too strong to be denied. He was on fire with wanting her. And she, she felt the same . . . It was a kind of madness that possessed them both. And he feared it was too strong for him.

At last the ball came to a close, as all balls must, the

147

elegant company – now considerably more dishevelled than it had been several hours earlier – dispersing under the light of the full summer moon to the drawn-up rank of carriages, sore-footed, yawning, weary. The Pendlebury party soon found itself snugly seated in His Lordship's comfortable travelling chaise. Lord Irlam was oblivious, such was his preoccupation, to the fact that his sister cunningly engineered how they arranged themselves, so that she sat beside her aunt in the positions of greatest ease and honour, while Hal and Cassandra faced them. There seemed nothing in the least odd in this to him – where else were they to sit? – but Cassandra found Georgiana's insistence suspicious, after all that had occurred earlier, and shot her a sharp look under her lashes. She was met with a lazy smile, and a catlike little yawn, which Georgiana covered with a kid-gloved hand. 'I do not know when I have been so excessively fatigued after an evening's dancing. If you will arrange the rugs around us more securely, Hal, I am sure I will sleep. Louisa is already nodding.'

It was true; although Lady Louisa had spent most of the evening in the card room with her particular cronies, and had never set her elegantly clad foot upon the dance floor, her eyes were almost closed, and she returned no other response to her niece than something between a snore and a snort. Hal obediently tucked the thick travelling rugs about his aunt and sister, and Georgiana emitted a satisfied sound and snuggled into hers, sighing, 'I hope you will be very quiet, dear ones, and let me rest . . . But you are sadly lacking in courtesy to Cassie, and I am sure she too must be cold after the dreadful heat inside.'

Cassandra murmured that she was not, not in the least, but His Lordship was already arranging the folds of soft wool about her. Their eyes met, and held, and she saw that his were gleaming in the moonlight. Under the pretext of arranging the blanket more neatly about her, his hand slipped deftly under it, and found hers. He leant back against the velvet squabs as the coach rumbled between the gates of the estate and out into the road, but he did not release her, and she did not try to pull away. She should, she knew, but . . . she did not. What harm could there be, in simply holding hands?

They did not speak. Lady Louisa was soundly asleep, and Georgiana appeared to be, snuggling against her aunt's soft shoulder like a kitten in a basket. The carriage was of the most modern design, and the suspension ensured as smooth a ride as could be had, but Cassandra could not have said that she was comfortable. And she certainly did not feel at all inclined to sleep. His nearness made that impossible, and his hand in hers, warm through the thin kid leather. He was not wearing his own gloves, and she was acutely conscious of his touch. It was, she thought, addictive. And it reminded her, it must remind her, of what they had shared such a short while ago.

Then his clasp was withdrawn, and she had no time to consider if she was glad or sorry, because she felt his fingers working, unfastening the tiny buttons on her gloves, moving up from wrist to elbow. She stirred in her seat, but he whispered, 'Ssshhh!' and she was still. She felt the tips of his fingers softly, very softly tracing the crease of her elbow, and pushing down the glove to bare her arm. The most delicate of touches, as his fingers ran slowly down the tender flesh of her inner forearm to her wrist, where her pulse pounded hard in her veins. He caressed it for a second, and then one finger, just one, moved on, pushing under the tight leather to find her palm and draw lazy circles on it, still very gently. She closed her fingers around his – she had been passive under his touch till then, though her breath was coming short and her whole body seemed sensitised. With the leather-clad pads of her fingers, she stroked him in return, rubbing over his knuckles and up towards the back of his hand. They were both breathless now.

The carriage juddered a little as one of the wheels found a pothole, and out on the box the sleepy coachman smothered a curse. Lord Irlam withdrew his finger from her palm with tantalising slowness, but before she could feel bereft his touch was climbing her arm, stroking the smooth flesh, passing her elbow now and exploring the softness of her upper arm where it lay so close to her breast. He reached the edge of her sleeve, and traced its path around her limb, and then his finger was pushing under the hem, seeking entrance, where the flesh was even more sensitive.

One of their companions made some small sound, and moved restlessly in her seat, and Cassandra froze, unconsciously stiffening and pressing Lord Irlam's hand between her arm and her body, trapping it there. The back of his hand was warm against the side of her breast through her gown and chemise. Another bump in the uneven road drove them closer together with a lurch, and his hand brushed her nipple, taut as it was. She whimpered softly.

'My God!' he breathed, the faintest whisper. 'My God, if we were alone . . .'

But they were not, and the journey was not a long one, and so soon – too soon – they were rattling over the cobbled streets of Brighton, and drawing up outside the door. He withdrew his hand from her, clasping her palm for a fleeting moment as he let her go, and then Lady Louisa and Georgiana were waking – if Georgiana had indeed ever been asleep, Cassandra had some while since ceased to care – and all was disorientating motion. Cassandra drew her light evening cloak about her with her fully gloved hand, concealing the undone, dishevelled glove in the silken folds, and accepted Hal's aid as he helped her from the carriage. A few moments of bustle, a chorus of goodnight, and she was mounting the stairs to her bed. Her lonely, empty bed.

CHAPTER TWENTY-THREE

Hal rose the following morning in a mood of cheerfulness quite foreign to him of late. He had come to a decision, sometime during the early hours, when he had risen from his lonely bed and paced up and down in an effort to take stock of the situation. It was preposterous, he had realised, to torment himself so, and to give way to Gothic imaginings of death and disaster. Clearly, he could not banish Cassandra from his mind; what had passed between them last night had made that obvious to him. It had been little enough, in all conscience – a kiss, a passionate embrace, a few breathless, silent moments in the darkness of his carriage. And yet every second of it was engraved upon his mind, and the thrill of it had far overtopped any of his most fevered imaginings in the nights that had led up to it. Very well. She was a young lady of birth and breeding, and although he was not very well acquainted with her – once again the image of her closing her eyes as he caressed her obtruded into his thoughts, and was ruthlessly suppressed – he had to admit that he admired her very much. It was not just her beauty and her physical allure that captivated him. She was brave and funny, and devastatingly honest, and her company was pleasing to him. Extremely so. His aunt liked her. *Christ, Hal, is that the best you can do? Your aunt likes her!* Well, why not? Louisa was a shrewd enough judge of character, for all her indolent ways.

He would woo her. Properly woo her, with conversation. In a civilised fashion. No more pushing her up against doors, at least for now. Circumspectly, so as not to cause a bustle, but in a gentlemanly way. Promenades, curricle rides, dancing. Definitely dancing. He lusted after her, he had acknowledged that, but there was no need to fancy himself in love with her, or any such nonsense. Love was irrelevant. He would woo her, and if all proceeded smoothly, he would in due course ask her for her hand, and she would accept – was he not eligible? He was highly eligible by anyone's standards. He was no duke, but dukes were scarcely to be found in these modern times. He had been described as handsome, though his younger siblings were pleased to mock him mercilessly and tell him that his nose was too big, his cleft chin perfectly ridiculous. (At this point, Hal found himself in front of the cheval glass in his chamber, twisting his head in uncharacteristic anxiety from side to side in attempt to assess the truth or otherwise of their cruel words. But the curtains were still drawn, and it was too dark to say). No doubt she would overlook his nose, even his chin, assuming they did not positively repulse her – they had hardly seemed to repulse her last night, after all.

Yes, he would woo her in form, and she would accept, probably, no, of course she would, and they would be married, quite quickly – why wait? – and then he could, by God he could . . . Hal returned to his bed at this stage in his deliberations, and spent a heated few minutes in contemplation of their wedding night, and then, tension relieved for a while, he slept the sleep of the resolute.

He woke in the same frame of mind. He had a plan, and really he could not see what could possibly go wrong with it. It was ridiculous to assume that marriage inevitably and swiftly led to children; it was the nineteenth century, for heaven's sake, and there were ways and means of preventing such things. He was well enough versed in these matters already. Most men desired an heir above all things; he, at present, did not. Very well. No need to make a Cheltenham tragedy of it.

And as for the rest of the problems that beset them, even if her atrocious uncle and his scoundrelly co-conspirator were to show themselves – as it seemed likely they would at some point – he would face them down and drive them off in disarray, and Cassandra would be pleasingly grateful. What had Georgie said that first day – that he was Miss Hazeldon's knight in shining armour? Well, so he was. Earl. Earl in shining armour.

Hal breakfasted alone, the ladies still being abed after their dissipation on the previous evening. He assuaged his disappointment at not seeing Cassandra in copious quantities of coffee, ham and eggs, and then went for an invigorating ride in the brisk sea air. Encountering a few friends as he rode, he repaired with them to one of Brighton's many inns, and enjoyed a few bouts of fisticuffs, where, being handy with his fives and in a mood to brook no opposition, he carried all before him. The day was shaping up delightfully, the sun was shining, and after a light nuncheon he would no doubt have the opportunity to begin his campaign, by asking Cassandra if she would care to go for a drive with him – alone – in the afternoon.

She looked quite adorable at the table in Pomona-green muslin, as she toyed with a hothouse peach that had been sent down from the Castle, and Hal flattered himself that she was quite as conscious of his presence, and of what had passed between them, as he was. There was slight flush across her cheeks, which fluctuated in intensity but never left her, and sometimes she raised her eyes to his, and then looked away hastily, and sometimes it was his turn to capture her gaze and then look down, and altogether it was both devilishly awkward and unaccountably exciting.

The party retired to the drawing room, and the ladies

took up their books and needlework, Cassandra poking unenthusiastically at a piece of embroidery. Hal did not know why women must always be sewing. He wanted to seize the dratted thing from her grasp and fling it across the room, and pull her to her feet . . . He did not do so. He knew he would have to muster a passable air of nonchalance, in order to ask her for her company on a drive without stirring any suspicions in the all-too-acute brains of his female relatives, and he was just formulating the words when Wilson entered the room, and took a card on a silver salver over to Lady Louisa, bowing correctly as he offered it to her.

She set down her book with a martyred sigh – was there never to be a moment's peace? – and picked it up, scrutinising it through the lorgnette she had lately affected. 'Mr Matthew Welby? Who the devil is Mr Matthew Welby?'

Hal was just about to say that he had not the least idea, and that he wished the fellow at perdition, whoever he was, when he observed with a shock of disagreeable sensation the galvanising effect that this announcement had had upon the two younger ladies. Georgiana was looking up from her stitchery with an expression of sparkling interest, and as for Cassie, her eyes were shining like stars, as she exclaimed, 'Matthew, here! Oh, I cannot believe it to be true!'

She turned to Lady Louisa and said animatedly, 'I think I told you when I arrived here, ma'am, that my uncle had been preventing me from corresponding with my friends from Yorkshire. Lord Irlam was kind enough to frank my letters, and I wrote to several of them, but have as yet had no response. Mr Welby is the brother of my great friend Emily, and we grew up together. May he be admitted? I am all impatience to see him.'

Lady Louisa nodded to the butler, who bowed and withdrew, and, with a regretful glance at her discarded novel, sat back to await her unexpected visitor, while Hal seethed in frustration. Georgiana darted a quizzing look at Cassandra and said teasingly, 'It seems that this young gentleman is very eager to see you, Cassie! He must have posted down here directly, as soon as his sister received your letter and he learnt of your whereabouts. How very interesting and romantic it all is, and how glad I am that Hal brought you to stay with us! I am sure you will agree, brother dear?'

Hal was on his feet, and had flung himself over to the window, from where he gazed down sightlessly at the busy street, his thoughts in turmoil. Just at that moment, his cloud castles – so recently constructed – tottering on their foundations, he was heartily wishing that he had never laid eyes on Miss Hazeldon. He felt a sharp, stabbing pain in the region of his third waistcoat button, which he recognised as that cruellest of rapiers, jealousy. 'Of course!' he said tersely over his shoulder.

At that moment the door opened once again, and the butler announced Mr Welby, and withdrew. An angelically fair youth stood on the threshold, flushing slightly under the scrutiny of three handsome, well-dressed persons who were all complete strangers to him: Lady Louisa, lorgnette raised, statuesque, mildly curious; Lady Georgiana, her piquant little face alive with mischievous enquiry; Lord Irlam, tall, dark and intimidating, his finely sculpted features drawn together, scowling with what appeared to be, but surely could not be, barely suppressed rage.

Mr Welby visibly gulped, and seemed momentarily bereft of words, and Cassandra stepped forward to greet him. 'Matthew – Mr Welby! What a wonderful surprise it is to see you here.'

Is it? thought Lord Irlam savagely, grinding his teeth. *Is it, indeed?!*

Cassandra took her friend's arm and drew him forward. 'Lady Louisa, may I present Mr Welby? Matthew, this is Lady Louisa Pendlebury, and her niece Lady Georgiana, who have been so kind to me. I could not tell all that has passed in my letter to Emily, but I will do so now you are here. And this is Lord Irlam.'

Lady Louisa extended a languid hand, professing herself pleased to meet him, and Mr Welby bowed over it gracefully, and then turned to greet Lady Georgiana, who was regarding him with strong approbation, as any young lady well might. He was a very handsome young gentleman, of average height and slim build, perfectly proportioned. Nature, and the barber's art, had blessed him with a head of tumbled golden curls, which fell carelessly across an alabaster brow. His profile was classical, and his eyes a fine, clear grey, set under delicately arching brows. His manners were good, and his face, now that he had recovered his composure, showed intelligence, and a gleam of fugitive humour. He was dressed, not perhaps in the height of dandiacal fashion, but with propriety and good taste, in a coat of fine corbeau cloth and the pantaloons and hessians proper for a morning call in Brighton. All in all, he distinctly resembled an angel of the Renaissance period, updated and costumed to suit a nice modern taste. Hal, forced by common courtesy to shake his hand and murmur some highly unconvincing words of welcome, conceived an instant, violent loathing for him, and could happily have pitched him right out of the elegant sash window, possibly without pausing long enough to open it.

The party seated themselves, and Mr Welby said, 'I must apologise, ma'am, Lord Irlam, for intruding on you in this fashion, but when Miss Hazeldon's letter arrived we were so very glad to see it, after hearing nothing from her for this age, that I felt I had to come in person, and make sure that all is well.' His voice was low, a little husky, with a touch of warm Yorkshire in it, and even Lady Louisa, who had not the least interest in young gentlemen, however handsome they might be, found it undeniably pleasing to the ear, and sat somewhat straighter. For Hal, it was otherwise.

'I must explain, Miss Hazeldon – and I apologise to you all for speaking of persons with whom you cannot be acquainted, which cannot fail to be tedious for you . . .'

Lady Louisa and Georgiana murmured, 'Not in the least,' while Hal ground his teeth and said nothing.

'My sister has not read your letter, and hence not replied to it, for she and my father are from home; they have been in Brussels, as so many people are just now, with a party of friends. My mother's delicate health naturally did not permit of her undertaking such a journey. But we have been so very worried about you that Emily left strict instructions – if by chance some communication should arrive from you, we should open it without delay. Of course I recognised your hand in a second when the letter came at long last. And we were greatly shocked and surprised to read that your uncle had been keeping all your correspondence from you. For I can assure you that Emily has written to you a hundred times, I dare say, since you were obliged to leave us.'

'And I have written as many letters to her, or more, and now I know for certain that not a one of them has reached her. I am forced to admit,' said Cassandra, smiling a little mistily, 'that I did wonder rather at not hearing a word back from any of my friends, once I was able to write to you all at last. But then I told myself that it was foolish and wrong to expect everybody to be sitting at home as I had left you, like marionettes with the strings cut. My life has been very tedious since my uncle brought me to London, and I have not mixed in society at all until I came to Brighton, but I expect it has been quite different for you. Brussels! Have they been there long – were they there for the battle?'

'Yes, and we would have been in a fever of apprehension had we known, but of course all was over and victory announced before we had had chance to worry for their safety. They have written the most striking descriptions . . . but this is beside the point. You understand now, I trust, why you have not heard from Emily, and Miss Otley too, if you have attempted to write to her, for she and all her family accompanied my father to the continent. And I know you would have been anxious for a word from Miss Moreton, also, and can have received none. If you have been cut off from all communication, you will not have heard of the change in her circumstances.'

'Kate?' said Cassandra in sudden anxiety. 'I hope she is well. Her I really did believe still fixed in York with her grandmother. I hope there is nothing amiss.'

'No, indeed. She too left us, not long after your departure, and went to live in Berkshire with her grandfather, the Reverend Mr Waltham, who was gravely unwell, and has since died.' The company murmured polite regrets, appropriate for the death of a complete stranger, but Mr Welby had not done. 'That was a sad event for her, but Miss Moreton is now married, and has a new-born child. She is Lady Silverwood – she married Sir Benedict Silverwood last summer.'

'Why, how extraordinary!' broke in Lady Georgiana. 'I know her – I have met her in London, at least, this past Season, and so have you, Hal. A tall lady, dark, very beautiful in the Italian style. It was quite the

161

sensation of last year, Sir Benedict having suffered so many tragedies previously, and finding happiness at last. He is quite besotted with her, and she with him, and they have a little boy now, I believe. I had no idea that she was a friend of yours, Cassie, or I could have given you her direction.'

'Kate, married and a mother! And to Sir Benedict, whom she . . . It is wonderful news, I had not the least idea . . . I have missed so much, it seems, of my dearest friends' lives, and all the while they must have thought me so rude, so neglectful,' said Cassandra, and a tear made its slow way down her cheek. It was obvious that she was greatly distressed, and Mr Welby made haste to reassure her that no one had been in the least offended; all her old companions knew her well enough to dismiss any such thoughts entirely from their minds. 'Nobody was angry, Cassandra, but we have been terribly worried. My father even went so far as to write to your uncle, although he is barely acquainted with him, asking for news of you, but he received no reply. And so we feared something was terribly wrong.'

'And you were right,' said Lady Louisa grimly. Cassandra was overset, and asked her new friends to explain what had happened, and they did so, even to her flight and her appearance in Lord Irlam's library. Cassandra's hand crept out as they spoke, and Mr Welby's found it, and clasped it reassuringly, and she clung to him.

Hal saw it, for he missed nothing where Cassandra

was concerned, and his instinctive reaction was jealous fury – what was this puppy to her? – but then he felt ashamed, some better part of him being glad that she had a friend, someone she had known since childhood, who could offer comfort when she was upset, where he could not, or could not yet. These new feelings, however one chose to label them, were very confusing, he was finding. His innate honesty compelled him to admit that this Welby did not seem to be a bad sort of fellow, though there was no need for him to be so damnably handsome. *His* nose was not too large, Hal reflected gloomily. *His* nose was bloody perfect.

Refreshment was ordered up, and consumed, and tea seemed to work its customary magic on Cassandra, for she brightened a little, and apologised for her weakness, though her friends were united in assuring her that it was quite natural to be so affected, and no apology was necessary. Mr Welby then became aware that he had stayed far too long for a visit of ceremony, and although his hosts reassured him that it did not signify in the least, he was punctilious, and took his leave, but not before Lady Louisa had invited him to dine that evening, and he had accepted. He still had a great deal to tell Cassandra, he said with a speaking look as he departed.

CHAPTER TWENTY-FOUR

Cassandra, to nobody's great surprise, could not think of settling to her needlework once Mr Welby had left, but pleaded the headache, and went to lie down upon her bed with the curtains drawn and a handkerchief soaked in Lady Louisa's lavender water pressed to her heated brow. Her head was pounding, true enough, and it would have been delicious to close her eyes and forget her worries in sleep, but her thoughts were whirling madly, and she would do well to try to order them before the evening.

She was very glad to see Matthew. It might appear remarkable to outsiders that he had set aside his daily avocations and rushed to see her as soon as he had read her letter, but she wasted no time on this; of course he had. There was a bond between them that no separation of time and location could break, and it was immensely frustrating that propriety insisted that they could not be alone to open their hearts to each other; even as indulgent a hostess as Lady Louisa would, without question, never allow it.

His news had set her in turmoil, and made her realise, if she had needed the reminder, that there was no going back; the life that she had had in Yorkshire before her father died no longer existed. She must acknowledge herself guilty of folly, for she had written to her friends thinking in a childish way that they would be able to save her, if they only knew of her plight. But they could not, and though she was happy that she would be able to correspond with them, perhaps even to see Kate, now that she was fixed in the south, and meet her new husband and child, her situation was not materially altered. She had no alternative but to await her cousin's return, and trust that that lady would be able to face her uncle down and put an end to his so-called guardianship.

It was possible, of course, that Matthew, now he knew all that she had been through, might offer marriage as a solution. It was something they had talked of often enough. Her uncle would never agree to it, and would make life as difficult as he could, but Matthew's parents and sister would be delighted by the match, for they had always liked her, and her fortune and her snug little estate would sit very nicely along his. No doubt Matthew's mother had urged him to hurry to see her with that very idea in mind. And then she could go back to Yorkshire, and try to pick up the threads of her old life, as Mrs Welby instead of Miss Hazeldon. They could live in her old home, Polly could come and join them if she wished to do so, and everyone would be so delighted for them. Oh, despite what she had said to Lady Georgiana on the subject, there was much to be said for it.

But there were several excellent and compelling reasons why this idea, so superficially attractive, was a bad one. One of those reasons was six feet tall and broad-shouldered, and if he entered her chamber now – she had a sufficiently vivid imagination, and it was perfectly adequate to the task of picturing that – would she not forget her headache and all her woes and surrender herself eagerly to his embrace? Well, she would. Last night had proved that. Even in her distress, her body still tingled at the memory of his touch, and longed for more.

It did not seem sensible to marry one man while feeling that way about another. She could look for no such passion with Matthew, much as she loved him; she was uniquely qualified to make the comparison, and his kisses and caresses – clumsy, unpractised and understandably hesitant as they had been – had never roused a fraction of the tumultuous feelings in her that Lord Irlam's finger stroking her palm, running up the inside of her bare arm, tweaking her nipple, my God, that most of all, had set raging in her.

Of course, she reflected glumly, she had no idea of His Lordship's intentions towards her. He might have been yielding to a momentary impulse last night (and then in the carriage, yielding to it again), or his intentions might be thoroughly and deliberately dishonourable. Despite his words of denial, he might be entirely without scruple, and aim to seduce her. Obviously, that would be terrible.

It would be terrible. All a young lady had – even a young lady of fortune – was her reputation, and once that was lost, her case was desperate. Cassandra had been very lucky indeed, she knew, to survive her flight and subsequent night spent in Lord Irlam's town house without a breath of scandal.

But it had not been luck, had it? Her safety, her honour and her present comfortable situation were all due to His Lordship's care and consideration for her. *He* had made sure her reputation remained undamaged; he had given up his bed to her, showed her every sign of tender care and consideration, brought her here and introduced her to his family and to the society in which they moved. He had kept her safe. It would be odd, to say the least, if after doing all that he now decided that he would abuse her trust and make her his mistress. He might have done that before, or attempted to, without involving his aunt and his sister in the matter.

The only difference, she was forced to admit, was that in London she had behaved as a correct young lady, one deserving of his protection. Whereas last night, in his arms, she had been a shameless wanton. And in case her actions hadn't been enough, in case he hadn't noticed her lack of maidenly reserve, she had pointed out to him in actual words her equal culpability in what had happened. A young lady of unblemished virtue, assuming she ever found herself in such a shocking situation, which she never would, tiresome creature, would surely have lied through her teeth, and said it was all his fault. Because he was a Man. Which responsibility – was she truly the stupidest girl who had ever lived? – he would have been perfectly willing to accept, for had he not said as much himself?

So probably he did intend to seduce her, rather than offer marriage. Of course he didn't want to marry her – why should he? And that was perfectly fine – not that she would let him seduce her, obviously, not even slightly – because she hardly knew him, and certainly didn't want to marry him at all either. Or marry anybody. She would go and live with Mrs Thoroughgood, just as soon as she returned, and take up Good Works, and get a pug, and die miserable, probably quite soon. And only the pug would be sorry.

CHAPTER TWENTY-FIVE

Cassandra, her imaginary pug trotting at her heels, wheezing slightly but unseen by any save herself, was a little heavy-eyed and silent that evening, but if anyone noticed her sad condition they were not discourteous enough to say so. They had other guests than Mr Welby – Lady Louisa's crony Lord Carston, Lord Irlam's friend Mr Wainfleet and his sister Mrs Hungerford and her husband. The presence of these persons not admitted to the secret forced the conversation onto more neutral topics, which was probably fortunate. They spoke of the sublime beauties of Yorkshire and the English Lakes, where Miss Spry was no doubt wandering lonely as a cloud as they spoke, and the news from abroad, and the soirée that Lady Louisa was to hold in two days' time. All of the other guests had naturally been invited to this event, and Mr Welby was soon assured that he too would be very welcome to attend; it would have been uncivil to do otherwise, and besides, everyone – apart perhaps from Hal – was disposed to be very pleased with him, and happy to admit him to their company.

Matthew took Cassandra in to dinner, as they, and Pug, were of the lowest rank, and was able to find a moment to whisper, 'I have other most important things to tell you, and I am sure you find yourself in the same case! We may have a chance to converse properly at the party, do you think, Cass?'

Cassandra could only nod, conscious of eyes upon them, and they had no further opportunity for private speech. The dinner was a merry one – Lord Carston, a handsome widower in the forties, was an acknowledged wit, and kept the table amused with his well-informed account of the latest follies of the Regent, which fortunately he, a father of daughters, was wise enough to edit ruthlessly so that it was suitable for the ears of the two young ladies. It was a pleasant evening, then, and in such elegant and refined company Cassandra found it impossible to dwell upon her fears for her future; inevitably, in such circumstances, they appeared exaggerated, even Gothic.

The next day, therefore, she felt somewhat better, though her heart lurched in her chest when Lord Irlam invited her to drive with him in his curricle. If Lady Georgiana shot her a significant glance when he proffered this suggestion, she was able to ignore it easily enough.

It was perfectly correct for a young lady to be driven thus by a gentleman, and she would be on high alert for any words or actions suggestive of seduction. However, she scarcely thought that His Lordship, whatever his intentions might be, would make any improper advances in an open vehicle, on the main and most fashionable thoroughfares of Brighton, with his tiger up behind.

And he did not. He drove very well, and looked very handsome and imposing in his many-caped driving coat, though she thought his blue and yellow striped waistcoat surprisingly garish. Both conscious of the presence of His Lordship's diminutive manservant at their backs, they conversed lightly on indifferent subjects, and in any case they were often held up in the press of traffic, being greeted by acquaintances who had also chosen to take the air in their open carriages that fine afternoon. It was in no sense at all a private interview, and when it was done Cassandra was no closer to divining His Lordship's intentions towards her than she had been before it.

As for Hal, he was quite unable to ascertain what was going through Cassandra's mind. He thought that she did not look happy; there were shadows under her eyes, and he sensed that she was troubled. It hurt him to see it, more than he liked to admit to himself, and he wished he had the right to take her in his arms and ask her what the matter was, and kiss away her frown, and make her smile again. But at least it did not seem – and he must take comfort from this, even if it was not a very laudable emotion to be experiencing – that the appearance of Mr Bloody Perfect Welby had instantly banished all care from her heart, even though she had undoubtedly been confoundedly pleased to see him. It was a puzzle. If Welby had been her accepted admirer in Yorkshire, if they had cared for each other, there was nothing stopping him, surely, from renewing his suit now, and offering for her hand in honourable solution to all her difficulties. But perhaps, Hal reflected with sudden dismay, it was merely that he had not yet had the opportunity to do so. Perhaps that was why she seemed so melancholy – because nothing was resolved. The two of them had had no chance to be alone since the fellow's arrival, and perhaps he intended to propose to her at the party. *That would be just my luck*, he thought savagely, *to be obliged to toast – in champagne that I myself have paid for, or will, when the bill comes – the engagement, to another man, of the woman I, the woman I . . .* This thought he left deliberately unfinished.

Hal too had no prospect of being alone with Cassandra, particularly not with the house in an uproar with the preparations for the soirée, and maids and footmen in every nook and cranny, dusting, sweeping, staggering about moving furniture, then moving it back again as Louisa and Georgie gave conflicting instructions. It was plain that there was to be no repetition of the events of two nights ago, and nor could he even speak of them, supposing by some astonishing chance he found himself alone with her for two minutes. It would be outrageous, and outrageously vulgar, to remind the lady of the intimacies that had passed between them. What would she think of him if he did so? What did she think of him now? He had no idea. She might be waiting for him to declare himself, and wondering why he delayed; conversely, she might shudder at the idea – his ridiculous nose? His preposterous chin? Something else? – and simply regret a summer evening's madness. It was hardly his fault that he had had no chance to woo her as he had planned, and by slow degrees ascertain how she was disposed towards him. He had thought that there would be plenty of time, but it seemed to him in his fevered state that there was not. What he *should* do was offer for her immediately, if he could contrive a way to do it, before the other fellow was able to do so. Perhaps there were others among her ranks of admirers who aspired to her hand, and meant to throw their hats in the ring at the party. Perhaps they could form an orderly queue.

He resolved to claim the first available dance – it could not be the very first dance, that would be too pointed, but soon after that. He was the host of the party, and she a guest in the house, so it would merely seem as though he were paying her a pretty compliment. And then somehow he would find a way to take her aside, and make his declaration. Before anyone else had a chance to do so. He had no idea whether his offer would be welcome, nor what her answer would be. But he had to try.

If Hal had been in a perfectly balanced state of mind – which, emphatically, he was not – he might have reflected that there was something a little odd about the way in which he was behaving as the fateful evening drew near. When he had so recently taken the decision to woo Miss Hazeldon and then to ask for her hand, he had told himself that it was merely a practical solution to the situation in which he found himself: he desired her with an intensity he had never previously experienced; she was eligible in every respect; he enjoyed her company; he would presumably be obliged at some point to marry someone. This could not be described as a cold-blooded decision, as God knows his blood was heated enough, but it was one that did not seem to take account of anything resembling feelings. Not Miss Hazeldon's, which he could not know, but also not his own. He did not admit that he possessed any.

And yet . . . if his intended bride should happen to be in love with another, and therefore did not favour his suit, it must be no great matter, not as long as his tender emotions were uninvolved. It would be a blow, of course, to his pride and to the lustful impulses with which he was presently struggling, but surely no more than that. He was not a vain sort of a fellow, a coxcomb who could not handle rejection, and nor was he a libertine who carelessly indulged his every amorous impulse. Therefore the prospect of failure ought not to be so very distressing, nor should it occupy his thoughts to the exclusion of all else. And yet, somehow, it was, it did.

CHAPTER TWENTY-SIX

When they had visited the modiste together soon after Cassandra's arrival in Brighton, Georgiana had made sure that Cassandra commanded the perfect gown for the party that was to be the highlight of their summer. It was silk, which Miss Hazeldon confessed that she had never worn before, and it was not a pale pastel shade but a deep sea-green, with a gauze overdress dyed the same rich colour, and trimmings at neck, sleeve and hem in ribbon of the same hue. She had no jewellery to wear, her pearls still being in pawn, but Lady Louisa had lent her a beautiful and curiously wrought pendant studded with pearls and emeralds, and it looked very well, depending from a length of the green ribbon. She had another yard of the green gauze draped about her elbows as a shawl, and a bright embroidered reticule and golden Grecian sandals to complete the ensemble.

They stood together to await the arrival of the first guests, and Georgiana, radiant in celestial blue embroidered with silver, regarded Cassandra with satisfaction as she said, 'Louisa, do you not think that Cassandra looks very well? That jewel of yours complements the gown perfectly.'

'Yes,' said Louisa, 'you're quite right, Georgie.' She smiled at Cassandra and said gently, 'I have observed before that if one is conscious of appearing to best advantage, one can more easily face the world with courage. I know you have had a most trying time these last few years, my dear, and there is still much to concern you, but you do look quite delightful, and I hope you allow yourself to have an enjoyable evening. You have friends about you, you know. You are no longer alone.'

It was most unlike Lady Louisa to speak so seriously, or at such length, and Cassandra felt a lump rise in her throat at such evidence of kindness, and could do no more than nod, and smile gratefully at her hostess. Her confusion was hardly lessened when Lord Irlam said abruptly, 'My aunt is quite correct, both in regard to our concern for you, and your appearance. You look quite lovely, Miss Hazeldon.'

She was startled by his words and by the tone in which they were uttered, and her eyes darted to meet his, but the first arrivals were admitted at that point, and she had no leisure to reflect on what they might signify. It was as well that she did not observe the sequel to Lord Irlam's words: Lady Louisa's lifted eyebrow, and Georgiana's significant nod and mischievous smile in response.

Matthew arrived promptly, and claimed her hand for the first dance, and she was torn between the comfort that his presence brought her, and the fear that he might be intending to seize the opportunity to make her an offer of marriage. She had resolved that she would not, could not accept him, but their relationship was such that he would inevitably ask her why, and she did not wish to share her jumbled feelings for Lord Irlam with him. It was all too new, too raw, to be put into words, especially when she remained unsure both of her own emotions, and of His Lordship's intentions towards her. He had told her she looked lovely, but what did that really mean? The fact that her appearance was pleasing to him could hardly be news to her after what had so recently and scandalously passed between them, gratifying though she must still find his compliment.

Mr Welby did not make Miss Hazeldon an offer while they twirled about the floor, but he asked her for the supper dance, and when she tried to joke rather wanly that they would set tongues wagging if they were seen to favour each other's company too much, he replied stoutly, 'Well, and what would be wrong with that, Cassie?', which hardly reassured her.

She was next claimed by one of her youthful admirers, an inarticulate boy little older than herself, and then it came time to dance with Lord Irlam.

He took her gloved hand in his, and she would scarcely have been human if she had not been reminded forcibly of the last time he had held it. His intent expression told her that this was a consciousness they shared. They moved through the figure in silence, but their eyes caught and held, as they moved apart and together, and Cassandra found herself in a very curious state of mind. The music seemed to fade, and so too did her awareness of the presence of others. She no longer questioned her own feelings, or laboured to describe them to herself; she was sure that, whatever she felt, he felt too. His eyes, his whole body told her so. The merest touch of his hand sent thrills of sensation racing up her fingers to every part of her, and she knew, suddenly and fiercely, that it was the same for him. He was smiling down at her now, and she felt her lips curve in response. If this was lust, or something altogether more, she did not know, but it was magical.

The dance ended, and by common consent they moved to the side of the floor. He did not release her hand. He said, 'Miss Hazeldon – Cassandra – I must—'

Before he could finish speaking, his butler appeared at his elbow, and said, his voice low but his normally impassive face expressive of some strong emotion, 'My lord?'

His master turned, letting her hand drop from his, and said with suppressed feeling, 'Wilson! What the devil do you mean—?' But he checked himself, for the man was plainly suffering from considerable agitation, and had interrupted only because he felt he had no choice.

His Lordship continued in a lower voice, 'I'm sorry. Whatever is the matter?'

Wilson's gaze inexplicably strayed to Cassandra's face, and then slid away, as if he could not bring himself to meet her eyes, and the warm sensations that had been tingling through her veins began to dissipate, to be replaced by a creeping cold assurance that something was very wrong, something that concerned her closely.

'I'm sorry, my lord, miss, but we have . . . intruders. Two persons who insist that they require urgent speech with you. I have told them – as they can surely see for themselves – that you are otherwise engaged, and unable to meet with them this evening. I offered, much as it went against the grain, my lord, an appointment with you tomorrow morning, at their earliest convenience. But they were adamant that it must be tonight. They seem quite prepared to cause a scene if you do not come, and if I instruct the footmen to eject them by force, that too will draw attention.'

The butler's voice was as low as it well could be, but something about the urgency of his speech and the clear discomfort he was experiencing were beginning to attract attention: just a faint stir of curiosity from those guests who happened to be standing nearby.

Lord Irlam sighed. 'I suppose I shall accompany you, then, Wilson, to deal with these mysterious and very ill-bred visitors.' He turned to her, and smiled down at her, his bright blue eyes intent. 'Please excuse me, Miss Hazeldon; I assure you I will be back directly.'

Wilson looked even more uncomfortable as he said, 'Forgive me, my lord, for not making myself clear. They are not mysterious; they have announced their identities and asked that I made them known to you. They are a Mr Millington, who says he is Miss Hazeldon's uncle and guardian, and a Sir Jasper Delaney, who claims to be her affianced husband.'

CHAPTER TWENTY-SEVEN

Cassandra could not prevent a gasp from escaping her, and Lord Irlam reached out, as if by instinct, and took her hand again, clasping it firmly. Even through her horror at Wilson's words, she became aware of a growing buzz of excited conversation around her and a sensation of being watched by avid eyes. She thought that to pull her hand from his grasp by force would make things worse, cause more gossip, and in truth she did not want him to release her. She felt a desperate need for the comfort he could give her.

His Lordship's face was grim and his voice cold as he said, 'Really? Well, I have been eager to make the acquaintance of these gentlemen for quite a while, although I could wish it had been in less public circumstances.' He squeezed her hand reassuringly, and tucked it through his arm, saying in an altered tone, 'Shall we go and confront them, Miss Hazeldon, or would you prefer if I dispose of them alone? I wish to do whatever you would like best. I am only sorry that they should have come to spoil your pleasure in this fashion, at the most inconvenient moment possible.'

She clung to his sleeve without speaking for a heartbeat, and then said with resolution, 'I will come with you. It would be cowardly to do otherwise. I must face my uncle one day, and it might as well be now.'

'Very well, my dear, it shall be as you wish. No one could ever accuse you of cowardice.' Lord Irlam gave her a reassuring smile, and she tried to match it, without any notable success. He said warmly, 'Be assured that I will not allow them to insult you, whatever their intentions may be. Where are they, Wilson?'

'In the hall, my lord. I regret to say that they do not appear to be entirely sober, and have already attracted an unpleasant degree of notice. Sir Jasper has most unfortunately recognised various gentlemen among your guests whom he claims as acquaintances, and attempted to accost them.'

'I see. We will go to them, Wilson, but you need not accompany us. Do you seek out my aunt and my sister, man, and Lord Carston too if he should happen to be nearby, and explain to them swiftly what has occurred.' The butler bowed, and left them, and Lord Irlam steered her through the throng, ignoring the very lively curiosity that could be seen springing to life on many faces on either side. They passed through the double doors of the ballroom into the entrance hall, and Cassandra could not repress a shudder when she saw the two men who awaited them. Her companion felt it, and tightened his hold on her.

They were much as they had been when she had seen them last: both dressed in evening clothes and both evidently, as Wilson had warned, to varying degrees inebriated. Her uncle was a stocky, oleaginous little man in his fifties, who still retained the remnants of good looks, though drink and dissipation had rendered them coarse and blurred. His colour was high and his eyes roamed about the room uneasily. His taller companion was cadaverously lean, indefinably disreputable-looking, and perhaps labouring slightly less under the influence of strong spirits. He caught sight of her first, and cried out in accents both implausibly affectionate and unnecessarily loud, 'My dear Miss Hazeldon – Cassandra, my love! I have been so anxious about you!'

Ignoring him entirely, the Earl stepped forward with Cassandra still on his arm and addressed her uncle in arctic tones, 'I am Irlam. Millington, perhaps we would be more comfortable in my study, without so many . . . observers?' It was perfectly true that the hall was by no means empty; four tall, liveried footmen stood by the door as if carved from tree trunks, and a quite surprising number of party guests who ought to have known better appeared to have followed Hal and Cassandra quite shamelessly from the ballroom, without any reason

183

whatsoever to do so, and now crowded behind them in expectant silence, as at a play. Among them, Hal gained a fleeting glimpse of the Lamington ladies, their faces an unattractive mixture of avidity and nascent disapproval. This was just the sort of scene that the gorgon would most enjoy, was his fleeting thought.

Mr Millington blustered, his words a trifle slurred, 'I am sure it would suit you, Lord Irlam, to confront me in private, but there is not the least necessity to do so. Unhand my niece instantly, sir, and return her to my care, and we will be on our way and leave you to your party.'

'Miss Hazeldon, sir, is residing under my roof as a guest of my aunt, Lady Louisa Pendlebury, your "care" having proved so very far from satisfactory. Are you really sure you wish to have this conversation in public? I am quite willing to do so, but then I have nothing to fear from general scrutiny. It might well be otherwise for you.'

Millington's face grew quite scarlet, and he began to splutter indignantly. 'You have not the leas' right to address me in such a way! The chit is my ward, and under my protection. I have arranged a fine match for her with m'friend Sir Jasper. Lady Delaney, she will be, and you have no business interfering!'

'There's no need to cause a scene, old fellow,' said Sir Jasper smoothly. 'I'm sure Irlam don't want that either. Not in his interests at all, whatever he may say to the contrary. Be a good girl, Cassandra, and come with us now. We can be married directly – I have a licence in my pocket – and all this unnecessary bustle will soon be forgotten.'

Cassandra said in a low but very clear voice and tones of utter certainty, 'I shall not come with you. I would far sooner drown myself than marry you.'

Some of the interested spectators were heard to gasp at this. There was an ugly expression on Delaney's face now, all attempts at suavity abandoned, and his teeth were bared in something approaching a snarl. 'I daresay you might, but I think you shall have me all the same, my girl!'

'Miss Hazeldon is not your girl, Delaney, and I give you my word she never will be. You shall not address her so in my house.'

'Is she yours, then? I think you should be damned grateful, wench, that I'm still prepared to wed you. You may play the innocent, but I know very well that you spent the—'

He was not to have the opportunity to complete this sentence, for as he started to speak Hal released Cassandra and sprang forward like a panther, and his punishing right found Delaney's chin, and dashed him to the floor. Various persons about the room were heard to let out small cheers of 'Huzzah!' and 'Well landed, Irlam!'

Lady Louisa and Georgiana had arrived just in time to witness the blow, and they pushed their way unceremoniously through the throng to Cassandra's side, and put their arms about her.

Lord Irlam turned on Millington with an expression of barely suppressed rage, his fists still clenched, his knuckles showing white. The older man visibly cowered from him, and cringed towards his companion, who was unable to offer him any protection, since he lay groaning on the marble floor. Hal's lip curled in an aristocratic sneer, and he said contemptuously, 'You have no need to be apprehensive, sir. Once we have corrected the many misapprehensions under which you are labouring, you are quite at liberty to leave, unmolested, although God knows it is more than you deserve.'

Millington made no response, merely blinking at Hal stupidly as he said, 'There is no engagement between Miss Hazeldon and your friend. There never has been. I wish to make this quite clear in front of all these witnesses.' Here he waved a hand at the crowd of people who stood watching him in rapt silence. 'This young lady agreed to no such contract, and your disgraceful attempts to force her into it by holding her prisoner have all failed, for she was brave enough to resist you. Your attempts to see her compromised and thus blackmail her into marriage have also failed, for she was most fortunately able to seek the protection of my family. She has no longer any need of your rather dubious guardianship, and I am sure would much prefer never to set eyes on you again. Am I correct in my assumption, Miss Hazeldon?'

'You are indeed, my lord,' said Cassandra, as she stood supported by the two taller ladies. Her voice wobbled a little, but after all she had endured she felt it important to say her piece. 'Every word that you have uttered is entirely accurate. I have been most cruelly treated by one related to me by blood, who should have been my protector, but I have met with nothing but kindness and consideration from you, and from Lady Louisa and Lady Georgiana. I can only apologise for the disturbance that your chivalrous concern for my safety has brought to your door.'

'There is no need to apologise. Nothing that has happened has been in the least your fault, and though I must regret the distress that this unhappy scene has caused you, I can never regret the fact that you sought safety with my family. I believe no gentleman worthy of the name could do other than to exert himself to protect a young lady in such a situation.'

There were murmurs of agreement from the crowd, and one or two excitable persons showed a disposition to burst into applause. Lord Irlam did not regard them, though, and they were soon hushed by their neighbours, for he was not done speaking. 'No woman of sensibility could accept an offer made to her by such a creature as that . . .' Here Lord Irlam indicated with a disdainful hand Sir Jasper, who had risen to his knees and now crouched upon the floor. 'His reputation is well known, and I may add that in the unlikely event of it entering your head to challenge me, Delaney, and finding seconds willing to assist you, you will find me arriving at any meeting armed not with pistols, but with a horsewhip.'

There was a buzz of appreciation, and one lady was heard to cry 'Bravo!', but still Lord Irlam had not said all he meant to. 'I think we have endured enough of Sir Jasper's company. William . . .' The head footman leapt like a startled deer to hear himself addressed, and sprang to attention. 'Remove this person. Do not trouble to be too gentle about it.' The four liveried servants moved forward with a will, closing around their prey, and Sir Jasper, uneasily eyeing their number and their impressive height, allowed himself to be ejected without any further protest. Hal had not ordered Mr Millington's removal, and so he was left unmolested; he looked as though he very much wished to leave, but could find no easy way of doing so. For the moment, nobody paid him the least attention.

The door closed, and Hal turned to Cassandra, and smiled at her, and her heart turned over at the expression she saw in his eyes. 'Miss Hazeldon, the timing is all awry, and the occasion far more public than I would have wished, but perhaps it is as well that there should be no ambiguity here, nor any speculation afterwards about why I say what I am about to say. I do not speak now because I have compromised you, nor to protect your reputation, for your reputation is unblemished. You have faced your trials with enormous bravery, and I have come to admire you more ardently than I can well express. In my eyes, you are a heroine. Will you do me the great honour of granting me your hand in marriage, Cassandra?'

CHAPTER TWENTY-EIGHT

S ilence. The tension in the room was palpable. The
dozens of persons present held their breath, and
some of them clutched their companions by the hand
or sleeve in a convulsive grip as they awaited Miss
Hazeldon's answer.

She knew she must give it without delay – there was
no time to consider the very flattering things he had said
about her, and whether he had truly meant them, nor
why he should speak if he did not – and so she met his
eyes and said steadily, 'I thank you for your very kind
offer. I am sure I do you no honour, quite the contrary,
but . . . Yes. Yes, my lord, I will gladly marry you.'

There was a collective release of breath, and now
several people did burst into applause and choruses
of congratulation. Several ladies of sensibility were

observed to be crying quite openly, and some gentlemen of a romantic disposition dashed away a manly tear or two. It was such a very satisfying conclusion to the dramatic events that had just unrolled before them.

Hal and Cassandra had no attention to spare for their audience. He strode forward and took her gloved hand in his, raising it to his lips and kissing it. They remained thus joined, their eyes locked, saying nothing aloud, and Georgiana was obliged to recall them to their surroundings by tugging on her brother's arm, laughing at him and shaking him a little when he did not respond immediately, so that she and her aunt were able to proffer their congratulations. When they had done so, others felt emboldened to surge forward, and all was confusion for a while.

It was Lord Carston who managed to restore order at last. With a significant glance at Hal, he had Mr Millington escorted into the study by a courteous but firm footman, and with great tact he personally shepherded the guests back into the ballroom, and instructed the musicians to strike up again. Although most of the older guests preferred to stand chattering, some, at least, of the younger persons present took to the floor, following Lady Georgiana's example. Once again the evening took on the appearance of a civilised soirée in a gentleman's house, instead of a theatrical performance in the French manner.

Lady Louisa remained in the hall with the couple, and said with quite unwonted decision, 'Hal, Carston was quite right to have Cassandra's uncle kept apart from our guests – you must go to speak with Millington directly, and make sure you have his explicit agreement to your marriage. Make him set it down in writing. I hardly think he can stand against you after the public nature of what has just taken place, but do you make sure of it. Overawe him with talk of lawyers and marriage settlements, and your rights as Cassandra's husband. Hint at bribery if necessary, to sweeten the pill. He should be kept separate from Delaney, so that they do not concoct any more mischief between them; Delaney can do nothing on his own, I believe. He will be shunned now, I should think, and will not dare show his face in society.'

'It is much less than he deserves,' said Hal grimly. But his countenance softened as he looked down at Cassandra again. 'I'm sorry, my dear, that I am obliged to desert you. I would wish to have private speech with you, and explain why I declared myself in so flamboyant a fashion. I had not intended . . . but we cannot speak now. I must go to your uncle, as Louisa says. Perhaps we can share an engagement dance in a short while, and be toasted by our guests in the proper form. I know you can only be exhausted, and thoroughly sick of the public gaze, but it is vital that we convert this party into a celebration, and carry the thing off with flair.'

'Of course we must,' replied Louisa. 'If we show embarrassed faces, the polite world will say we have private reasons to be ashamed. We shall be quite imperturbable. And to that end, Cassandra, come and rest a moment in my sitting room, and drink a restorative glass of wine with me. Hal, do you collect us when you are ready, and we will face down all the world, and make them dance to our tune.'

Lord Irlam nodded and left them, and they retired upstairs. When they were alone together, Louisa raised her glass to Cassandra, and said a little drily, 'Congratulations on your engagement, my dear girl. I have congratulated you before, but I believe you might not have been fully attending.'

Cassandra looked down at her wine, and then shook her head and took a healthy swig of it. 'My head is spinning already – what difference can a little wine make? I thank you for your kindness, ma'am, but I am sure you are excessively angry none the less. This cannot be the marriage you wanted for your nephew.'

Lady Louisa shrugged. 'Oh, I am never angry; it is so fatiguing. I like you, child, and I think you may do very well together.' She hesitated for a second and them went on abruptly, 'I am no matchmaker, Cassandra. I am opposed to the very notion of it. I resisted all attempts by my parents and other well-meaning persons to arrange a suitable alliance for me quite against my own inclinations twenty years ago, and Hal's father was one of my strongest supporters then. Do not be thinking that I have ever had some duke's daughter in mind for him; I may have many faults, but I am not a hypocrite.

'But I own myself surprised at how quickly this has all come about. I was aware, of course, that Hal was attracted to you already when he brought you here – I am not blind – but I had thought him firmly resolved against marriage for several years yet. It was not until earlier this evening, when he complimented you upon your appearance in extremely warm terms, and Georgiana sent me *such* a look, that I realised that his intentions might be serious. Had you, in fact, reason to expect a declaration from him?'

Her companion coloured, and said, 'Yes – no! I thought perhaps he admired me . . . but I did not know any more than that. I cannot think he meant to ask me to marry him this evening; on reflection I am forced to believe he did so because of the hideous scene my uncle and that horrid man created between them. I was so happy when he hit him! And I must always be grateful to Lord Irlam for dealing with them so splendidly.'

'That's all very well, Cassandra, but it's hardly enough. I should not pry – I never pry – but I hope your feelings for my nephew are considerably warmer than mere gratitude. No!' She raised a languid hand. 'Do not tell me. Forget I spoke. I don't *want* to know people's secrets. You will find a way to work things out between the two of you. And in justice to him, I do not think Hal could well do anything other than what he did. It is a very melancholy truth that, if that little drama had ended merely with the ejection of Delaney, people would have gone away whispering about you, and you know how rumours spread. It is monstrously unfair, but your reputation would have been damaged, probably beyond repair, and I shudder to think what you would have done then, alone in the world as you are, heiress or no heiress. They will not say such things now, and if they do, you need not regard them. You will be a Pendlebury.'

'I will . . .' said Cassandra slowly. She had not had leisure to think, to consider the great position in which it seemed she would shortly find herself. She had been at first preoccupied with her own affairs, and then all too suddenly and intensely aware of Hal Pendlebury as a man, a man who looked on her with desire blazing in his blue eyes, rather than an earl and head of a great family. She was about to say that she hoped Lady Louisa did not think she had in any way engineered this, when she became aware that her hostess was making some very curious noises.

'My dear,' she gasped, 'please tell me you saw Delaney's face when Hal's fist caught him! And his stupefied expression when he crashed to the floor! And amid the astonished silence, a few cheers. I might have cheered myself!'

'And then my uncle,' gasped Cassandra, 'when he shrank away from Lord Irlam, fearing he was about to hit him too? Did you see?'

Lady Louisa set down her glass and mimed, with surprising accuracy, Mr Millington's cringing aspect, throwing up her hands in supplication and rolling her eyes, and Cassandra too found release from the tension of the evening in helpless laughter at the sight.

At length Lady Louisa said, mopping her eyes, 'As a woman and a rational person, one deplores violence, naturally, and should not condone such primitive masculine action. But to witness it was wonderful, and I must confess, fond as I am of Hal, I have never liked the ridiculous boy so well as I did then.'

Cassandra could only murmur confused assent. Her companion said, 'You know, my thought in that instant was that his father would have been proud of him; I wished he could have been there to see it. And I felt so all the more when he made his declaration. There was a magnificence about him, in that moment. He really did seem to know his own mind. Perhaps you will be the making of him, Cassandra Hazeldon!'

CHAPTER TWENTY-NINE

Cassandra stood on the terrace of the Castle and looked out on the rolling lawns below her. She was alone, and she welcomed the solitude. Lord Irlam – Henry, but nobody ever called him that, Hal, her husband, her husband – had left her a few moments ago, murmuring that he had a small matter to attend to and would return very quickly. He had asked if she were cold, if she would prefer to remain indoors, but she had said with perfect truth that it was a lovely evening, and that she would await him out here.

The sun was setting in a fiery haze to her right, silhouetting looming Gothic towers and battlements against the burning sky. She had heard the Pendleburys speak casually of the Castle, their ancestral home, but she had not realised until today that it really was a castle, a proper castle from a children's story, and a substantial one. The only similar structure with which she had previously been familiar was that at Skipton, near her childhood home, and this was much grander and more intimidating. Her first sight of it today had been astonishing, as Hal had driven up the avenue of trees and it had loomed larger and larger on the hill it commanded. She felt its presence behind her as an almost physical weight – hundreds of years of history, and she now, preposterously, its mistress.

But the sky ahead of her was still a soft blue, and if she ignored the huge, imposing building at her back, the scene was peaceful, soothing: regular, well-tended lawns sloping down to a small lake, with waterfowl swimming upon it, and a little Grecian folly, a charming classical temple, built on a slight rise above it. The lake was set against a backdrop of woods still green with summer, and reflected the trees in its silver mirror. It had rained earlier, a sudden fierce shower lashing the mullioned windows while she was dressing for dinner, but the storm clouds had vanished as quickly as they had appeared, and now the air was still, and every leaf and flower was tipped with liquid silver. There was a cobweb stretching between two rose bushes in the flowerbed below her, and tiny diamond droplets trembled on the threads, much more beautiful, she thought, than the jewels at her throat.

They had travelled into Hampshire by curricle, leaving Brighton directly after their wedding breakfast. The brief ceremony itself and the celebration after it were a blur to her now, as were the hectic days that had preceded it. The drive was the first time they had been alone in weeks, since they had kissed so passionately at the Windlesham ball, but of course they were not really alone, not with Hal's tiger up behind them and sixty miles to cover. The past month or so had been a whirl of frenetic activity, and as Cassandra looked back over it now her impressions were bright, noisy, fractured. Ever since the night of Lady Louisa's party, when Hal had been forced to declare himself, she had not, it seemed to her, had so much as a single moment for quiet reflection. She felt slightly dazed – she supposed it was natural. At the start of the summer, she had been a virtual prisoner in her uncle's house, seeing no one but him, his stony-faced servants, and the man he intended her to marry. Her days had been spent in almost nun-like seclusion, her evenings – but she would not dwell upon them. Not tonight. Then she had escaped and found herself in Brighton, every day full of breakfasts, balls and parties. And now . . . now this.

If she had previously reflected upon the matter, she would have imagined that an old aristocratic family, one that had long owned and dominated huge swathes of England, would be very grand, very cold, very high in the instep. Nobody could describe the Pendleburys as that. But it seemed to her that, for all their casual, charming, informal manners and their endless teasing of each other, there was steel beneath the silk; they were formidable when they united in a single purpose. And their purpose over the last weeks had been to organise a wedding – no, more than that, to arrange a marriage, in a very deliberately public fashion. It was not so much that they wished to mesmerise society into forgetting the awkward circumstances of Hal's proposal. It was more that they took for granted the fact that the polite world would accept, must accept that such unusual occurrences could not be questioned, were not in any sense a subject for gossip, simply because the Pendleburys decreed it so.

Her uncle had certainly been overborne by them. Cassandra had no means of knowing what bribes, threats, blackmail or other forms of coercion Hal, supported by Lord Carston – who was, she had learnt, his godfather – had brought to bear on him. But Mr Millington had agreed to the match without any further protest, had given up any claim on Cassandra's property, and meekly signed where he had been directed to ratify her marriage settlements. Her estate and her fortune had been clawed from his grasp, and if damage had been done to her property during his brief tenure, which she feared to be the case, Hal and his man of business assured her that it would all be repaired. Her uncle could never threaten her again. Delaney had disappeared, regretted, it seemed, by nobody; Hal had had word that he had gone to France, the traditional refuge of disgraced Englishmen, now available for that useful purpose once more since the wars were over. She knew that he had never cared for her, but only for her money, and since that was now quite out of his reach she would endeavour to put him from her mind, as if his part in her life had been a bad dream.

The Pendleburys had closed ranks around her. All of Hal's siblings, over Lady Louisa's strenuous objections, had been summoned to Brighton to attend the wedding, along with their aunt, Mrs Winterton. She was a rather harassed grey-haired lady, who had greeted Cassandra in a friendly if slightly distracted fashion, but there had not been time to get to know her better. The presence of the younger boys had meant a house in constant uproar. There had been no frogs in her bed – perhaps amphibians were not easy to come by in fashionable resorts – but Hal had been tried to the limit of his endurance, and she had seen little of him. She retained a confused impression of four dark-haired youths, smaller editions of Hal: the twins, identical, deceptively angelic, eyes twinkling with constant mischief; Fred, voice wavering disconcertingly between high boyish tones and a booming baritone, full of tales of school; and Bastian, quieter and more reflective than his brothers, visibly proud to serve as his brother's best man, heartbreakingly handsome. They had all treated her with careless, teasing friendliness, much as they did Georgiana, and seemed to accept her without question, all of them, she supposed because of their great and very obvious affection for their eldest brother. He wanted her as his wife, and that was enough for them. If they were unaware of the unusual circumstances of Hal's proposal, they did not mention it to her, and she had, of course, no means of knowing what might have been said amongst the siblings in private.

She had had no opportunity for private speech with any of them, except for one brief moment when Bastian had drawn her aside a little before dinner one evening and said, smiling ruefully, 'I am sorry that there should be such a bustle always, and no chance to converse like sensible people. I hope to know you better presently, and call you sister. We are all delighted for Hal, you know, even the twins. He has spent far too much time worrying about all of us, and I for one am excessively glad that he has a chance to know some happiness of his own at last.'

These kind words from one who was a virtual stranger to her brought a sudden lump to her throat, but Cassandra was not obliged to find a reply, for Georgie imperiously claimed her brother's attention at that moment, and he moved away with a droll look and a murmur of, 'You see how it is with us always?' *A family*, she thought; *I shall be part of a family again. It seems I already am.*

Hal had returned her pearls – she had been wearing them that evening when Bastian had spoken to her – and she had been unable to protest; now that she was to be his wife, she could make no objection to his outlaying money on her behalf. But he had also bought her far grander jewels as a wedding gift – a set of beautiful emeralds, to match her eyes, he said – and had passed the Pendlebury family treasures into her care; nobody had worn them, he scarcely needed to tell her, since his mother's death. It was overwhelming, and she could not help but wonder how he felt, how any of them felt for that matter, at the thought of her, Cassandra Hazeldon from Yorkshire, taking their dead mother's place as Countess. She did not feel she could ask. She was not sure, after all, that she wanted to hear a truthful answer, however welcoming they all appeared to be.

She had spent most of her time with Georgiana and Lady Louisa; when they were not receiving visits of courtesy from the fashionable set, they were attending fittings at the modiste's. Cassandra had thought herself already well provided with all a young lady needed, but once she was betrothed to a peer she discovered that she had been mistaken.

She was wearing one of her new gowns this evening. Georgiana had cheerfully expressed herself jealous of the freedom that her married state would give her in matters of dress, and Cassandra, dazed, enveloped in a whirl of lace, velvet, gauze and muslin, of bonnets and pelisses, shawls and cloaks and spencers, had not fully apprehended her meaning until now. Kitty had laid out her gown for her and she had stepped into it and looked at herself in the cheval glass. She had gasped at what she saw, at the stranger who stared back at her, but there had been no time to protest. Had she tried this garment on, stood while it had been fitted to her? She must have done. She had no recollection of it.

It was green silk, like the gown she had worn to Lady Louisa's party, but it was very much lower cut than anything she had worn, had dreamt of wearing, before her marriage. The sleeves were tiny, and skimmed the edge of her shoulders; the bodice cupped her breasts lovingly, and the skirt was draped in such a way, it seemed to her, as to reveal rather than conceal every line of her body below her short stays. It clung to her belly, her thighs, her legs, her bottom . . . When Hal had seen her in it before dinner, his eyes had darkened and his voice had been husky when he addressed her. It would be foolish to wonder if it pleased him, when it was obvious that it did.

They had dined in a small room frescoed in a curious antique style in dark red and blue and ochre, copying, he told her, the decorations found at Pompeii, which his grandfather had visited on the Grand Tour and which had made a great impression upon him. Cassandra had been shy at first, overawed by the size of the Castle and the sheer number of servants brought out to greet her, but she was aware that Hal was exerting himself to ensure that she was not overwhelmed; he had firmly vetoed any suggestion that she should be conducted on a tour of the house upon their arrival. 'It'll take hours,' he had said frankly, 'and at the end of it you'll be no better off. It'll make your head spin. It's a terrible old labyrinth and it can wait until tomorrow. And I know you should interview the housekeeper and suchlike – don't look so nervous, Mrs Hodge is a treasure – but it doesn't have to be today.'

The room, and the Roman antiquities it contained, had furnished ample topics of conversation while they had eaten. Cassandra discovered that, like her, Hal had always longed to travel abroad and had never had the opportunity to do so, and they had found themselves debating the merits of various destinations, and idly planning a honeymoon journey that would surely take a year or more if they were to see all they wished to see.

It had all been remarkably easy, and pleasant, but underneath it all a current of tension: sparks of blue fire in his eyes as he looked at her, tingles of sensation when her eyes met his, goosebumps shivering across the bare skin of her arms, shoulders and décolletage. She was wearing the Pendlebury family diamonds tonight; she had been told that Pendlebury brides traditionally always did so on the evening of their wedding. They were heavy and cold against her skin, which was hot, almost feverish by contrast. She felt light-headed, intensely aware of her body inside her clothes – of her stays confining her, and the way they offered up her breasts to his intent gaze, of her chemise and petticoats, where they clung to her, of her stockings and her garters, tight around her thighs, and most of all of the core of her, naked under her skirts.

She shivered a little again now, and started from her thoughts when she heard a concerned voice behind her. 'I was afraid you would be cold,' he said. 'I'm sorry to have kept you waiting.' She turned, and Hal was there, close by, tall and handsome in his dark evening clothes and snowy-white linen. His face was serious, his eyes fixed upon her.

She did not know why she always felt this impulse to be honest with him, to reveal more than she should. Something about the circumstances of their meeting, perhaps, meant she could not hide the least thing from him. 'I'm not cold,' she said.

He moved closer and his hands were warm on her bare arms, above her gloves, below her exiguous sleeves. 'You're trembling.'

'I know. But I'm not cold.'

'Ah,' he said, his voice very deep. He pulled her close, and buried his face in her curls, and held her. His hands moved to her back, and she nestled close to him. It felt natural to be there, but his proximity did not cure her shaking. Quite the reverse.

He said, his lips brushing her hair, 'I would like to take you to see the little temple by the lake, but the grass is wet from the rain earlier, and your pretty slippers would be ruined. Will you let me carry you?'

CHAPTER THIRTY

He had carried her over the threshold here, to the cheers of his assembled household, but that had been a public act; this would be different.

'No,' she said. 'I have a better idea. Shall we go?'

She lifted her skirt and trod lightly down the old stone steps that led from the terrace to the lawn, careful where she set her feet. When she reached the bottom, she sat down upon the low wall that edged the flowerbed and untied her satin sandals. 'Will I need my shoes, in the temple?' she asked.

He had followed her down directly, and said, his voice amused, low, 'You know, Cassandra, I don't believe you will.'

'Then I shall leave them here.' She set them down on the wall beside her, and held up her skirts an inch or two to save them from the wet grass.

'Wait,' he said. 'Your stockings will be ruined.'

'I cannot pull up my skirts and untie my garters in front of you!' It was ridiculous, but she could not.

He grinned. 'Can't you? I could tell you I wouldn't look, but I fear that would be a lie. Well, then . . .' He was kneeling at her feet before she thought to stop him, turning up the hem of her gown and petticoat as he had done once before. But then he had stopped, and now he did not, lifting the folds and smoothing them back over her thighs. And now his fingers were exploring under the folds of thin fabric, finding the top of her stocking, finding the tie fastening of her garter and undoing it. The tips of his fingers caressed the smooth skin of her inner thigh for a tantalising second, and she bit her lip to stifle the whimper that threatened to escape her. Then with infinite care he rolled down her silken stocking to her ankle, pulled it carefully from her foot, and set it and the garter aside on the wall, on top of her shoes. Then his fingers found the other garter, the other stocking, and did the same. This time the brief, intimate caress lasted a little longer, drifted a little higher, but by no means long enough, or high enough. She wanted him to . . . she scarcely knew what she wanted. Shocking things. He held her naked foot in his hand, and bent his head, and pressed a swift kiss to the arch. She gasped at the touch of his lips.

She could not speak, but gazed at him on his knees before her. And then he rose to his feet, dusting off the knees of his black silk breeches, and held out his hand to pull her upright. She took it, but then released it and stepped off the path, onto the damp grass. Her skin was on fire; perhaps this would cure it. The cool wetness was delicious between her bare toes, tickling the soles of her feet, and she laughed at the sensation. It was familiar, and she had not realised until now how much she had missed it. She had been living in cities for too long.

She held her skirts high in each hand, pulled clear of the grass, and ran. She had not run since she left Yorkshire – ladies did not run – and it was exhilarating to do so after so long. She could hear him following her, laughing too and cursing as he slipped in his smooth-soled leather shoes, but he could not catch her, barefoot as she was, and she reached the steps of the temple ahead of him, and raced up them in triumph.

At the top, seeing what lay before her, she halted and looked back at him questioningly. He climbed to join her, and she said wonderingly, 'I thought it was just a folly.'

'My father created it for my mother. Sometimes all that' – he waved his hand in the direction of the sprawling building behind him, its terraces and courtyards and tall towers – 'can be too much. My grandfather had the building put up, as a sort of copy of the Temple of Fortuna Virilis in Rome, but it was just an empty shell – my father made it comfortable. I thought you might like it.'

'It's lovely,' she said softly. There was a verandah behind the four imposing Ionic columns, with tables and comfortable chairs set here and there so that one could sit at ease and admire the view of the serene woods across the lake. Behind the furniture, though, the tall space had unexpectedly been filled with large panes of glass set in wooden frames, and in the centre these opened into French doors. Inside there was a good-sized room, with a marble fireplace in which a fire blazed cheerfully. There were candles set in sconces and candelabra upon small tables, and the floor was covered with layered Persian carpets, upon which sat high-backed sofas, bookcases and large leather armchairs piled with bright cushions.

And a bed. A large four-poster bed, made up with faded red coverlets and hung with ancient tapestries. The covers were turned back invitingly to reveal crisp white linens.

'Come in,' he said. 'I'm sorry I left you before – I was making sure that everything was in order here to receive you.'

Her feet left wet prints across the stone floor of the verandah, but they were dry by the time she reached the carpet inside, and she shook her head when he offered her a towel. He shut the door behind him, and they turned to face each other. It was very quiet here, just the crackling of the flames in the fireplace and the little sounds of the logs as they shifted and settled.

'Cassandra . . .' he whispered. 'My Snow White!'

CHAPTER THIRTY-ONE

Once again she was in his arms, with little idea of how she had got there. His hands ran down her back and lifted her buttocks, pulling her tight against him, exactly where she longed to be. She wanted to touch him too, but she was still wearing her gloves, as she had put them back on after dinner, unsure in that moment of what she should do in such a grand house. She made a small noise of frustration now. He seemed to understand, for he murmured in her ear, 'Cassandra, we are both wearing altogether too many clothes, I'm sure you will agree. Will you let me undress you, and help me to disrobe?'

She held out her gloved arm to him in silence, and he said, smiling wolfishly, 'Oh, yes, indeed . . . it will be my pleasure, I assure you.'

With deliberate, teasing slowness, he began to unbutton her glove, and when he had done so fully he peeled it away from her arm and then from each finger in turn. Her bared skin tingled at his touch, and the fine down on her arm rose as he stroked it. When he had finished, he kissed each finger in turn, murmuring, 'I've dreamt of this moment, Cassandra. And the moments that will follow it.'

A low whisper, barely loud enough for him to hear. 'So have I. Oh, so have I.'

Her second glove followed the first, the fine kid leather slipping over her skin, and this time when he reached her fingers he took each of them into his mouth in turn and sucked on it until she gasped, and at last pressed a hot kiss into her palm. A jolt shot through her at the touch of his lips on the sensitised flesh. 'Now it's your turn,' he said, his eyes glittering.

She put both her hands on his broad chest, and then raised them to his lapels, and began to push the black evening coat from his shoulders and down his arms; it was cut tight on his body, and he had to help her to free him from it. Then her fingers fumbled impatiently with his cravat, and at last succeeded in untying it, ripping it from his neck and throwing it aside. Next she attacked his waistcoat buttons, and once she had undone them all he shrugged himself free of it.

She was very close to him, enveloped in the warm spicy scent of him, and she pressed her lips to his bared throat, while her hands tugged greedily at his shirt, pulling it free of his breeches so that she could reach inside it and touch his skin at last. She ran her hands up the corded muscles of his back, and with a muttered exclamation he lifted her from her feet so that he could kiss her.

Their mouths were wide open, hungry, their tongues twining, exploring, but it was not enough. They were united in the sense of urgency they shared. 'Still too many clothes,' he panted against her cheek. One hand held her clamped against his body, but the other released her to drag his shirt clumsily over his head, her eager hands helping him. His chest was bare now, and her hands were on it, tangling in the soft whorls of hair that covered it, moving down to explore the hard, ridged muscles of his abdomen. He groaned. 'That's a most becoming gown, Cassandra, but I will have you out of it. Give me your back.'

Reluctantly she trailed her hands from his body and moved away from him a little, the least possible distance, turning her back on him as he had instructed. The bodice of her gown was low at the rear too, and he dropped tiny kisses on her neck and bare shoulders – they made her shiver anew – as his fingers busied themselves with the delicate buttons. He found the little curls at the base of her neck and kissed them, murmuring that they drove him to distraction, as he unbuttoned her. Soon he was able to push the gown from her shoulders and down her arms, and it freed her breasts and slipped down to pool at her feet.

The room was almost silent still, with no sound but the spit and crackle of the fire and their heightened breathing. She turned in his arms, and he found the tie of her petticoat, tugging at it and pushing the straps down over her shoulders, and the flimsy garment slid over her hips to the floor.

Her short stays were of the kind that laced at the front, and his urgent fingers were on the bow, pulling the laces free, untying the shoulder fastenings, tossing the garment away from her body. She stood in her chemise, one of the delicate, near-transparent lace-edged garments that formed part of her trousseau. She knew that it revealed as much as it concealed: the curls at the junction of her thighs, the curve of her small breasts, and her nipples pink and hard against the flimsy fabric. She had been shy in her gown, earlier, but she was past that now; now she welcomed his scorching gaze, it made her heart beat faster, but she wanted more, longing for him to touch her everywhere. Hal gazed down at her and said, his voice husky, 'That's very pretty too, tantalisingly so, but I believe I will have it gone along with the rest. Must I pull it over your head?'

'There's a simple tie at the back,' she said unsteadily. 'It will slip off, if you undo it.'

'How excellent – almost as if it were designed for my purpose.'

'I think it was.'

He fumbled with the ribbon to free it, and then in sudden impatience pushed the tiny puff sleeves from her shoulders and dragged the lacy garment down her body. She stood naked before him, wearing only the heavy diamonds that flashed fire in the candlelight, not attempting to cover herself, her nipples taut and erect, and his eyes devoured her body, but still he did not touch her. 'I'm sorry if you find me rough, Cassandra,' he murmured. 'I am trying not to be, but if I followed my own inclination I would have ripped the thing from neck to hem.'

'I would not have objected.' It was true.

'Let's go to bed,' he said.

CHAPTER THIRTY-TWO

He picked her up and crossed the room in three long strides; setting her down gently on the bed and sitting beside her, his hands fell to wrestling with his buttons. He struggled out of his breeches, drawers and stockings, flung them aside, and came to lie close beside her on the crisp linen. 'I am torn, wife,' he said, striving for a conversational tone and not finding it, 'between wanting every inch of your body pressed to mine, between wanting your tongue in my mouth and mine in yours, and simply looking at you. You are so very beautiful, you see, and I have never seen you naked before, though I have imagined it often enough. I want to remember.'

His gaze was like a caress, moving down over her jewelled throat, her breasts and belly, to the red curls where her thighs met. 'I've never thought myself beautiful,' she said, 'but you are.' He was. His evening attire had not been cut to flatter him; his shoulders were broad, his hips narrow, his legs long and powerful, like those of a Greek statue of some young god, and he was all hard muscles and urgent desire for her.

'You take my breath away, when you look at me and say just what is in your head.'

'If I said all that is in my head . . .'

'Tell me. Tell me where you would like me to touch you. Tell me what you want.'

It was her turn to feel breathless. 'I don't . . . I think perhaps my response to you has led you to think me more . . . more experienced than I am. It is true that I have been kissed before, before you kissed me, and . . . and caressed a little. But I have not . . .'

'I wasn't asking, truly I wasn't, Cassandra.'

She wanted to ask him if he was not jealous, for that would make him a very unusual man, but she feared he would interpret her words as coquetry, and it would be in poor taste, she thought, to lie here naked on their wedding night and speak or even think of other lovers they might have known.

'I didn't think you were. I just wanted to be open with you.'

He reached out and cupped her face, and her body leant into his touch, so that the tips of her breasts brushed his chest and his hardness leapt against her belly. He sighed. 'I must repay the compliment. Cassandra, I want to make love to you. I want to touch you and kiss you and give you pleasure and take pleasure from you. I want to be inside you. Every fibre of my body wants that, with no barriers between us. But I don't want a child. Not now, not soon.'

Her eyes sprang to his in surprise.

'Cassandra, I would rather be touching you than talking, God knows, but I have no alternative but to speak, I think. I know I should have opened my heart to you before we married, but I could never find a moment in which we could be sure of being alone to discuss such a delicate matter. It is impossible to be private with the boys in the house. I am sorry. If you are angry with me for breaking this to you now, I own you justified.'

She said slowly, 'I'm not angry, just surprised. I suppose I assumed, if I thought about it at all, that we would leave such things to nature, as most people do. That you would want an heir and I had no choice in the matter, as married women generally do not. That I had agreed to that, by marrying you, with no need for discussion. But that was foolish, wasn't it? Because you have heirs.'

'I have heirs aplenty. Cassandra, please don't misunderstand me. I don't want to deny you children, if you want them. If I had meant to be so selfish, I would in honour have told you, so you could refuse me. It is merely that I would like to wait a while. A year or two, perhaps. Or more, if you are happy to delay. You are young, and so am I, and I have had enough responsibility in my life these past few years to last me for a while. The boys are older now, and demand a little less of me than they did, and I would like to make use of that freedom.'

'To travel, as you said earlier?' Her voice was eager, and he smiled to hear it, and moved one long finger to caress her cheek, and trace a line across it to her parted lips.

'Yes, to see the world, now that the wars are over and we can do so at last. Would you like that, do you think?'

'I would like it very much. I have no great urge to become a mother very quickly, Hal. Remember that I have been locked in my bedchamber, or as good as, for this past age. And I led a sheltered enough life before that. I too would relish a taste of freedom.'

He chuckled, his face a picture of relief and a little wonder. 'Well, just now locking you in my bedchamber seems a mightily attractive notion. But it does not have to be in England, after all; I dare say one can travel all day and make love all night. I am sure others before us have done so.' His hand had moved from her face, and was tracing idle patterns on her neck, and across her shoulders. His other hand smoothed down her back, and found her buttock and cupped it possessively. She almost purred at the sensation. The feeling of his hands exploring her was delightful, and it seemed to Cassandra that the time for talking was almost done. But not quite.

'Am I to trust you, then, to manage it, so that we will not have a child? You must be aware that I am entirely ignorant of how to . . . to . . .' She could not complete her sentence; it was not just that she did not have the words, but his hands were moving on her still, stroking, caressing, and it was becoming impossible to formulate thought.

'Yes, you may trust me. I promise you, I will not ask you to do anything that might be distasteful to you. Christ knows your pleasure is my main object.'

If she had meant to answer him, she could not, for his mouth sought hers, hungry, demanding, impatient now, and he was pressing her back into the pillows, and when he released it she was past speech, for his head was suddenly at her breast. He was kissing her skin and murmuring endearments and then – God, how she had wanted this – he drew her taut nipple into his mouth and began sucking on it. She wound her fingers in his silky hair and held him there, urging him on, and his hand crept up to find her other nipple and tease it, rolling it between his fingers. She gasped at the fierce rightness of it all.

He murmured against her nipple, 'This . . . this is what I wanted to do to you when we kissed at the ball. If we had gone undisturbed for a minute longer, I would have had your bodice about your waist, pressed hard up against that door as we were, and I would have worshipped your delicious breasts with my mouth and my tongue. I could feel how it aroused you, just the merest touch of my fingers.'

She moaned, part assent, part encouragement, and he said, as his right hand left her breast and slid down her body, across her belly and lower, 'And then, then I would have pulled up your skirts and found a way to give you greater pleasure. Just as I wanted to outside, when I took off your stockings. Did you want me to touch you then?'

'You know I did,' she panted. 'You were teasing me, just as you are now. Would you have me beg for it?'

'I quite like the sound of that,' he said wickedly. His hand tangled in her curls, pausing there, and she gave a little indignant moan and pressed herself shamelessly against him. He laughed breathlessly, and his fingers found the notch that led to her lips, and slipped inside it, resting there as she quivered at his touch. 'Is this what you wanted?'

'My God, yes!' she whimpered. 'Please, Hal!'

'I am yours to command, my lady,' he murmured. He did not tantalise her with light caresses, but parted her lips, and sought her secret places between them. Her fingers tightened in his hair and wordlessly urged his mouth back to her breast, and she arched her back against him. He obeyed her direction, and sucked harder on her nipple as she writhed beneath him.

He began to stroke her, rubbing around and across her nub as it grew tauter at his caress. She was wet for him, and grew wetter as his touch grew firmer, his clever, responsive fingers learning what she liked. Her hands left his hair and ran down his back, wanting to touch more of him.

Pleasure was building inside her, demanding release, and she pressed herself against his fingers. His mouth left her breast and she moaned in protest, bereft for a second, but he was merely moving to the other, and the sudden fresh sensation of his lips upon her nipple, while his left hand found the other, slick and wet and tender from his mouth, and tweaked it, sent a jolt of pure sensation shooting through her, right to her core. She cried out and dug her fingers into his back, and his caress became more insistent, the pressure impossible to resist. She did not try to resist. She let the overwhelming, dizzying sensations break and remake her, clinging to him, drowning in waves of pleasure.

His fingers found her entrance, slipping inside it, prolonging her ecstasy, and she moaned wordlessly as she convulsed against him. His mouth captured hers as he still touched her, and she tangled her tongue with his, greedy for yet more contact, more of him.

When he released her, she lay gasping, dizzy, while he sat on the edge of the bed, reaching for and removing something that lay in a small bowl on the side table. He returned to her a moment or two later, and sought her mouth again, and this time as they kissed their bodies were pressed together all along their length, her breasts crushed against his chest. 'Wrap your legs around me!' he gasped, and she did so, and a second later he was touching her in her most intimate place again, and then there was a little pain, a little confusion for a second or two, but she refused to let him stop, and then he was moving inside her, and they found a rhythm together. She discovered that like this she could reach his muscular buttocks and clasp them in her hands, and pull him even

221

closer. She could not see his face, he being so much taller than she, so she closed her eyes and buried her face in his shoulder and allowed herself to be carried off by sensation: the feel of him inside her, tight and unfamiliar but somehow perfect, her legs locked about his waist, their panting breath, his muscles clenching under her hands, their urgent fierce movements together. Her nostrils were filled with the heady scent of him, soap and spices and sweat, and suddenly she wanted to taste him too, and fastened her open mouth on the skin of his shoulder, licking his salty skin and then biting him as he thrust into her.

His thrusts intensified and in a moment he was crying out, convulsing into her, and she tightened her hold on him with legs and hands and teeth, and took him in and held him as he spent himself. Only afterwards was she conscious of his weight upon her, but just as she was beginning to feel uncomfortable he rolled them both over onto their sides. He moved away a fraction and slipped out of her – a sudden sense of loss – reaching down to untie and remove the sheath with which he had covered himself, then stretching out a long arm to return it to its place on the table.

She watched him, still held securely close to his body, drowsy with pleasure, and he smiled down at her and brushed her lips with a gentle kiss. 'Did you like that? It seemed to me, I am not being vain if I say, that you did.'

'How could you tell?' she teased. She should, she supposed, feel awkward, embarrassed, now that the frenzy of passion was over, at the intimacies they had shared, when a few short weeks ago they had not known each other. But she found she did not, perhaps because he seemed to feel no self-consciousness. If he did not, why should she? She was conscious chiefly of a great sense of physical well-being.

'How could I tell, minx? Let's see . . . There's the way you kissed me so eagerly, just as a beginning. I shall not mention how you ripped my clothes from me earlier. And then you moaned so deliciously when I touched you, and begged for more, and held me prisoner at your breast, and moved with me, and clung to me, and licked and bit me . . .'

'Oh, your poor shoulder!' she said remorsefully. 'You will have a bruise, I am sure, and marks besides.'

He chuckled. 'I shall wear the evidence of your passion proudly. And who shall see it but you?'

'Your valet?' She blushed at the thought.

'My very proper valet would no doubt notice how you have marked me, and be terribly shocked, though he would go to the stake sooner than utter a word on the subject. But he is away at present, visiting his sick mother, so Jem is taking his place. If he should happen to comment, I shall merely tell him not to be so damned impertinent.'

'Men are such strange creatures,' she said sleepily. 'I have observed before that you are only really rude to people you care a great deal for.'

'Nevertheless, I hope I will never be rude to you, my dearest.'

'You know that's not what I meant . . .' His words were, she thought foggily, somehow interesting, important, and would repay careful consideration, but after a long and tiring day and the sudden release of tension caused by passionate lovemaking, she found herself unable to concentrate. She nestled deeper into his arms, her head burrowing into his shoulder, and in a moment she fell deeply asleep in his embrace.

Hal pulled the covers up over their bodies, and she made a contented sound, and snuggled yet closer. *My wife*, he thought as he held her. *My God, my wife.*

CHAPTER THIRTY-THREE

Cassandra woke in the night, in desperate need of a water closet or at least a chamber pot, and inched herself from Hal's arms, anxious not to wake him. But he muttered something unintelligible and rolled away. The fire had died down and the candles were burning low, but there was enough light from the waxing moon coming in through the enormous windows to enable her to see her way. She was a little concerned that she would find nowhere to relieve herself, and did not relish the idea of going out into the darkness to squat naked and exposed behind a bush, starting at every rustle in the undergrowth. It hardly befitted a countess, she thought with a smothered giggle, that one of her first public actions should be, while wearing the famous family diamonds and nothing else, to urinate in the august grounds of her husband's castle. The ladies of the ton would surely be scandalised if they came to hear of it.

But she discovered when she explored the room that behind a screen there was a sort of rustic chamber with a simple necessary with a wooden plank seat, and, moreover, there were china washing bowls and pitchers of water, and piles of fresh linen towels. There was a round glazed window set high in the stone wall, enabling her to see what she was about. She made use of what was provided, and emptied the soiled water into the necessary when she was done.

She did not go back directly to bed, but went to stand naked by the window, looking out across the lake. It was a still, warm night, hardly a breath of wind, and the scene was tranquil. From where she stood, she could see nothing but the works of nature, or works of man that cunningly mimicked nature, and she drank them in.

She had noticed as she crossed the room that there were robes laid out across one of the sofas – Hal, or someone, perhaps Kitty, had thought of everything, and she was glad that they would not be obliged to struggle back into their evening clothes before they at last returned to the Castle, as she knew they would before morning. It was a beautiful building, rich in history, but it was intimidating, and she blessed the tact that had led Hal to decide that they should spend their first night together here. From here, she could not see the Castle, only the peaceful lake and the woods around it. She felt that this was no accident. The late Countess, with all her responsibilities, must have valued the time she spent here, whether alone or with her husband.

'You look glorious in the moonlight.' She turned to see Hal awake and watching her, the covers thrown back, his eyes glittering, but she did not attempt to cover herself. 'You like being naked, I think, Cassandra?'

'I suppose I do. I have never had the opportunity to be so before, or not in the last few years. In my uncle's house, I always felt I could scarcely be wearing enough clothes, and even then I was not comfortable.'

'But now you are? I am glad.' He hesitated, and then said with an oddly shy grin, 'Would you like to go for a swim? Do not feel obliged to say yes, if the idea horrifies you.'

'You mean that we should swim naked in the lake, this minute?'

'That is what I mean. The water is perfectly clean – it is fed by springs. And everyone in the Castle will be fast asleep by now, so no one will see us.'

'Oh, yes,' she said immediately. 'I would like that very much. Let us go immediately!'

An instant later he was at her side, naked and unashamed as she. He was smiling as he said, 'I think, my lady, that although in public you give every appearance of being a most correct young lady, you are a wild woman at heart. It is only today that I am truly beginning to perceive it.'

'It may be so. I was not brought up to be a correct

young lady, really. I grew up in the country, you know, running free, not in the city.'

'So did I!' he said. 'Come!'

He did not stop to pick up a robe, but led her out through the glass doors. There was a pile of towels lying ready on a table outside – he often swam here early in the morning when he stayed at the Castle, he told her – and he seized a couple, and hand in hand they ran down through the wet grass to the water. The night air was cooler than it had been inside, but not unpleasantly so, and she savoured its caress on her bare skin. It felt like freedom, and she had not imagined that her marriage would bring her such a sensation.

'The bottom's a little muddy here, but better once you are deeper in. Oh – can you swim? I forgot to ask.'

'Of course I can swim, sir!' He had put her on her mettle, and she was resolved to show no reluctance or hesitation. Dropping his hand, she marched straight into the water in a determined fashion, mud squelching between her toes, refusing the temptation to lower herself in gently because she knew he was watching; she could feel his eyes on her. She gasped in shock as the first chill of the water struck her, but she was determined not to let him see it. She continued bravely on, and once she was deep enough she struck out across the lake.

When she reached the middle, glorying in the silky feel of the cold liquid on every inch of her naked body and the exhilarating sense of liberty it gave her, she stopped to tread water and look back at the towers and battlements of the Castle, etched dark against the starry sky. There was not a light showing in any of the dozens of windows. The moon seemed to sit enthroned on the crenellations of the highest tower, as if the goddess Selene was resting from her nightly labours for a moment. 'It's lovely, seeing it from here,' she said softly as he swam to her side with rapid, powerful strokes that barely disturbed the slick surface of the water. 'It does not look quite real – more like an engraving from a novel.'

'Like you,' he replied. 'I must be the luckiest man alive, I think. I can hardly believe you are real either. You look like a nymph from a Greek tale, or a goddess, diamonds at your throat, coming out of an enchanted pool with moonlight in her eyes to meet her mortal lover. Will you kiss me, Cassandra, and convince me you are flesh and blood?'

She wound her arms about his neck. 'Oh, I am all flesh and blood,' she said as she raised her lips to his and tasted him. She was not able to stand upright here, but he still could, and as their kiss deepened she wrapped her legs around his waist again and pressed her slippery body to his. His big hands were on her back and her bottom, pulling her close, and her nipples, almost painfully erect, rubbed against his chest and sent frissons of delicious sensation shooting through her. She pulled him yet nearer, climbing his body a short way and tightening the grip of her thighs about his waist so that she could offer him her throat to kiss. Perhaps it was the darkness, the water, the silvery light, or him, but in that moment she felt as he had described her: powerful, magical, wild, in control. She tipped back her head, let her hands drop to trail in the water, and gazed up at the starry sky in a kind of wide-eyed trance as his lips explored her, his body supported her weight, and she pressed the hot core of herself against his belly. She tingled at the intimate touch, and as for him, he was hard against her, nudging against her soft, pliant flesh. She wriggled closer and felt him stir in instant reaction. If she was a goddess, and had power to gain anything she desired, she knew exactly what she wanted: him.

'My God,' he whispered against her skin, 'you *are* real. It is everything else that is not.'

CHAPTER THIRTY-FOUR

Cassandra, clad in demure pale green muslin, sat sedately eating toast and quince jelly with her husband late the next morning in an elegant breakfast room with a large Tudor bay window overlooking the lake. A busy week lay ahead: the tour of the great rooms of the Castle that she had been spared yesterday, a meeting with the housekeeper and a visit to her own particular domain, and rides about the extensive estate to see and be seen by the tenants. Soon enough, she could also expect ceremonial bride visits from the local gentry, and in due course invitations to take tea and to dine. They would host an open day, Hal had told her; it would be expected.

All these activities, she told herself firmly, differed only in scale from those she had been brought up to. Courtesy visits were usually dull affairs, but they were the social glue that held country life together, and she did not mean to shirk them. What was new was the contrast between the decorous formality of such a daily routine – Cassandra smiled thanks at the liveried footman as he sprang to pour her a fresh cup of coffee – and the wild passions that she and Hal had explored the night before. It was almost impossible to believe that such things had passed between them, as they sat here taking breakfast like a picture of a lady and gentleman in a newspaper advertisement. But then Hal looked up from his correspondence and smiled at her with such a wicked glint in his eye that she knew it was all true. 'I hope this room pleases you, Cassandra,' he said blandly. 'I have myself always enjoyed breaking my fast with this fine view of the lake and temple to enjoy. Do you not find it so?'

It was a fine, breezy morning, and little ripples hurried across the water below, while fast-scudding clouds laid down patterns of light and shadow that were constantly changing. A sodden white towel lay discarded, forgotten, on the grass that led up to the steps of the folly. They must have let it drop while he was carrying her back from the lake, on his way to lay her down on the bed and worship her most intimate places with his lips and his tongue; something that had shocked her enormously, and that she hoped he would do again very soon. 'Oh, I am sorry,' she said, 'did you say something? I was looking out at this lovely scene and not attending. I'm afraid I was quite lost in my thoughts for a moment.'

232

'It does not matter in the least,' he said gravely. 'I hope they were pleasant thoughts, though, my dear.'

'Oh yes!' she replied, and drank coffee. 'I am excessively fond of scenes of natural beauty. I find them so . . . so invigorating.'

'As do I,' he said. 'The estate has many more natural wonders, and I shall enjoy showing them all to you later. But I wonder if our tame southern landscapes can possibly be said to compare with the wild sublimity to be found in Yorkshire. The magnificent peaks, the secret wooded valleys, the mysterious caves in which a traveller might lose himself . . .'

'Yorkshire,' she said repressively, her lips quivering, 'is not especially famous for the grandeur and size of its mountains. We have them, of course, and they are fine enough, but the Lake District, for example, has many higher, as does Scotland, of course. And as for caverns, Derbyshire is the place for those.'

'I do not say the delightful peaks and secret places of Yorkshire are well known, or that they have yet received the attention they deserve,' he answered blandly. 'Only that they are beautiful, and I am sure they would reward further study. Time spent in nature is never wasted, do you not agree, Lady Irlam?'

If they had been alone, Cassandra would have crossed the room in that moment and set aside His Lordship's coffee cup, straddling his lap and assisting him in his exploration of the summits and secret places of Yorkshire, which he had not yet seen by daylight, but they were not, and so she merely coloured and bit her lip, and wished the footmen gone, while Hal grinned at her and ate a Bath bun very slowly in a manner not at all conducive to her peace of mind.

That first day set the pattern of the days to come: outward decorum, an observation of all the rules and strictures of society, and underneath it all a simmering tension between them, smouldering embers that could be set leaping into roaring flame by a glance or a seemingly innocent, fleeting touch. And when at last they were alone, guests received, welcomed and sent on their way, servants interviewed and dismissed, meals eaten, duties done, they fell on each other, eager to find new ways to give and receive pleasure. Because they were always careful not to risk conception, it was impossible for Hal to lift Cassandra up onto the dining table, push the plates and glasses aside and ravish her as he wished, and similarly when they rode out with a picnic one day, she could not pull up the skirts and petticoats of her riding habit and straddle him without preparation. But there were compensations. The manner of their love-making meant that Hal – perhaps he would have done so in any case, Cassandra had no means of knowing – paid intense attention to his wife's pleasure, rather than merely dwelling selfishly on his own. The sheaths he used had to be soaked in liquid for a while in order to fulfil their function, and there were always delightful ways in which the time required could be spent. And, although it offered him no immediate physical release, Hal appeared to derive a great deal of satisfaction from bringing Cassandra to the point of ecstasy and far beyond it.

One evening, not long before their honeymoon was set to end, the Earl and Countess attended a ball at the country house of the nearest noble family to Castle Irlam. Cassandra wore her clinging sea-green silk gown again, this time with the magnificent emeralds that had been Hal's wedding gift to her. As a bride, it fell to her to lead out the ball with her host, an elderly viscount with courtly, old-fashioned manners, while Hal, the handsomest man in the room in his immaculate black evening attire, took out the lady of the house. When it was at last their turn to dance together, Cassandra was conscious of all eyes on them, and told Hal so in a low voice. 'Of course,' he said, his face impassive. 'We cannot fail to be an object of curiosity to our neighbours, some of whom had not had the opportunity to lay eyes on you before this. And you are so very lovely, you know – the ladies are admiring your gown, one presumes, while many of the gentlemen . . . perhaps it is best if we do not dwell on what the gentlemen are admiring.'

'I care nothing for their admiration. There are other things I would much prefer to be doing,' she said frankly. It was a warm, still evening, and she could not help thinking how the lake water would feel on her naked skin, and more besides. There were better ways of spending such a glorious night than in a stuffy ballroom, especially when they would soon be back in Brighton, where their lives would be more constrained by social convention. There would be no more running barefoot in the grass there, nor making love in the dining room. It was not even as though she could dance with Hal more than twice tonight, and to dance with other men held no charms for her.

'Oh, God knows I agree with you,' he replied, his eyes glittering as they moved through the figure of the dance. 'But we will not stay late; we have a fair distance to travel, and I am sure that our hosts will look indulgently on us when we make our excuses. Old Foulkes cut a fine dash in his day, for all it was forty years ago – I'm sure he would have nothing but sympathy for what a newly married fellow might devise to please his bride on a carriage journey on a late summer night.'

Suddenly the ballroom was very hot, and her stays constricted her breathing. 'What might that be, my lord?' she asked. And he told her, in a whisper and in exquisite detail that brought her near to swooning, as they moved together, paced and twirled and parted. And people watching them, Lord Irlam's finely sculpted, slightly smiling lips close to her ear, his dark head bent close to her red one as he addressed her, her cheeks flushed pink and her green eyes shining like stars, thought them a very fine young couple.

It seemed an eternity until they were able to take their leave, with many congratulations and expressions of esteem. Cassandra sat facing the horses, and Hal sprawled on the seat opposite her as the carriage began to move. 'Now,' he said, 'you must consider this a pleasure too long deferred, for what I contemplate is precisely what I longed to do that night when Louisa and Georgie were most inconveniently present in the carriage. Would Miss Hazeldon have been shocked?'

'Yes. Shocked and . . . intrigued, despite herself. Miss Hazeldon had lately been incompletely ravished against a door, after all, and was in a pitiful state of frustration, poor creature.'

'And is Lady Irlam shocked?'

'Lady Irlam wonders why you are not yet on your knees and about your business, sir!'

He chuckled. 'A good question, sweet impatience. Pull up your skirts, then. Be for me the fierce wanton that I know you keep hidden from everyone else.'

She smiled at him, her eyes glittering in the light that spilt in from outside the carriage, and took hold of the hem of her silk gown and of her petticoat beneath it, raising them by slow degrees, to show her calves, her knees, and higher. Her breath was coming short and her nipples were hard against the fabric of her chemise. Her stockings were pale green, with darker clocks running up them, and her garters, once exposed, were a shocking red against the pale froth of white cambric. Her curls too were red, and she revealed them to him fearlessly. There was something unexpectedly arousing about the fact that she was fully dressed, gloved, constrained in her stays, with only her most intimate parts bare to him. She was wet for him already and he had not so much as touched her. Every part of her tingled in anticipation at the naked hunger and appreciation she saw in his eyes. 'Oh, yes,' he said. 'I have been longing for this all evening. I think you should hold on to the straps, madam.' As he spoke, he tugged down the blinds on each side of the carriage, not before time, and sank gracefully to his knees at her feet.

He settled himself between her spread legs, and Cassandra clung to the leather straps and hung on breathlessly as he reached out and caressed the arch of her foot. It was entirely dark now in the carriage and she could not see him. The world shrank down to the firm touch of his hands, slipping higher, higher, and then his lips were warm on her inner thigh. She gripped the carriage straps tighter, and spread wider, and he tantalised her with tiny kisses, his evening stubble rasping across her tender skin, somewhere in the debatable land between pain and pleasure. He nipped her soft flesh with his teeth. She moaned. His hands slipped under her buttocks and she raised herself slightly to accommodate them, and then his mouth was on her where she needed it to be. She bucked against the straps at the first contact, crying out and writhing in the warm darkness, and he clasped the globes of her bottom tighter and buried his face hungrily in her.

It was the most intense experience she had ever known – the blanketing darkness, his tongue exploring her wetness while his fingers held her tightly and she braced herself against the unpredictable motion of the carriage. There would be jolts, which drove his tongue deeper or jerked him tantalisingly away, and she longed to let go of the carriage straps and touch him, hold him to her, but she dared not, for fear they would both fall. For a while their only points of contact were his hands, kneading her bottom, stretching her taut, holding her captive, and his mouth, his tongue, worshipping her, driving her out of her mind. By instinct she raised her legs and draped them over his shoulders, her thighs enveloping him completely, and now he could taste her more deeply. His wicked tongue slid between her nub and her entrance, slipping in her wetness and his own, ruthlessly seeking her climax, demanding she come for him. He was devouring her mercilessly and yet he was imprisoned between her legs, at her command, dedicated only to the service of her pleasure. The waves of pure sensation crashed over her and carried her away.

CHAPTER THIRTY-FIVE

Hal tapped softly at the door of his wife's chamber, and heard her reply, allowing him entrance. He found her in bed, smothered in quilts, her face pale and woebegone. A novel lay on the counterpane, but she did not appear to be reading it. 'My poor Cassandra!' he said, crossing the room to her side. 'May I sit with you?'

She smiled at him wanly and indicated the pillows to her left. 'I'm sorry I did not feel well enough to attend the party. Do go without me, please. I am sure you would enjoy seeing your friends again now we are back in Brighton.'

He slipped off his evening shoes so that he could lie beside her on the bed. 'I don't want to, to be honest, Cassandra. There's no pleasure in such an event without you; if you're not there to dance and talk with me, I shall merely spend the evening watching Georgie flirt with every wastrel in a red coat, while Lamington looks on in complacency and I stifle the urge to shake him until his teeth rattle. I shudder to think what mischief she has been up to in our absence.'

She chuckled at the picture he painted, but said, 'Are you sure you're not just being polite? You need not feel obliged to keep me company, you know. I'm not really unwell, it's just my . . . my courses.'

'Believe me, I am sure. I'm only sorry you suffer so with them. My mama did too. I used to become so distressed when she was ill – this must have been not long after Bastian was born – that my father was obliged to explain to me what the matter was, so that I would not agitate myself. She used to drink some foul-smelling brew that Mrs Hodge made for her. Although I was never sure whether she took it because it truly eased her discomfort or merely so as not to offend Mrs Hodge.'

'I know – she made me some to bring away before we left the Castle. It is very nasty. Although I'm sure she hoped I would never have need of it!'

He grimaced in acknowledgement of the truth of her words. 'Does it relieve the pain, at least?'

'I don't think it does, much. But it was kind of her to think of giving it to me.'

He put his arm about her and she leant back against his shoulder. It was pleasant somehow to think that he still sought her company when there was no possibility of intimacy between them. She had every reason to know that he desired her; their passion was mutual, and far stronger than she could ever have imagined. Things had passed between them that she would never forget as long as she lived. Beyond that, he always treated her with consideration and could be described – so far – as a model husband. She thought – hoped – that he enjoyed her company even when there was no question of passionate exchanges. But she could not claim to know him. She did not even know if he would be faithful to her, she realised suddenly. He had made her no such promise outside the formal words the Church demanded. He had proposed to her so very publicly because he had no other option, and because he was an honourable gentleman, concerned only to save her reputation, even when this meant the sacrifice of his own freedom and any other plans he might have cherished. He was young; he certainly had no need for an heir, since he had explicitly said as much, and that could only signify that, as Lady Louisa had hinted once, he had had no immediate plans to marry. She had, she thought with a sudden sharp pang of conscience, very possibly ruined his life to save her own. She was not sure that the unbridled passion she found herself able to offer him, to share with him, could ever be adequate recompense for such a sacrifice. He might after all easily have sought and found passion elsewhere, without the chains of marriage, unbreakable as they were. What had she done to him? She shuddered involuntarily.

His arm tightened about her. 'My poor girl, I hate to see you like this. I wish I could help you.'

'Perhaps you can.' She found herself on the brink of tears. Maybe it was her courses, which always made her emotional; maybe she was being irrational in her fears. She could not tell. She was very tired, and her head ached abominably, quite apart from the dragging pain in her abdomen. She did not know what would become of them. She did not even know what she wanted to become of them. All she knew was that he was here, and she needed comfort, and he seemed to be willing to provide it. He had always been so good to her. She took his hand and placed it on her belly. It was large and warm and it seemed to her that it did soothe the cramping pain slightly. She sighed and relaxed against him. So tired. She felt waves of oblivion threatening to overpower her, and she welcomed them. At least she could rest in his arms, even if the intimacy they provided was illusory.

There did not seem to be any immediate need for further speech. After a few moments, Hal felt her slip into sleep, her tense body uncurling against him. He kissed the top of her head very softly, and settled himself more comfortably, his hand still on her belly.

A short while later, there was a light tap from the passage outside and Georgiana, resplendent in full evening dress, peeped cautiously around the door. Hal waved his free hand at her a trifle impatiently. Seeing Cassandra slumbering peacefully, she said nothing, merely smiling impishly at him as she withdrew very quietly and left them alone.

It grew dark, and Cassandra slept on, nestled against Hal's shoulder. He dared not move for fear of waking her, and besides, he did not want to. He was perfectly comfortable as he was.

Hal was glad he had avoided attending the party. He presumed that Georgie would make his and Cassandra's excuses to the hostess, whoever she was, for he could not quite recall the lady's name just now. An unwelcome thought occurred to him, though: if his sister was indiscreet enough to say that the new Lady Irlam was indisposed, that would start the usual speculation that swirled around young ladies who had recently married. That hideous phrase, 'an interesting condition', would be employed as ladies whispered behind their fans.

Brooding on it now, he expected moreover that soon enough he would in any case have to endure comments of varying degrees of indelicacy from gentlemen of his acquaintance (though not, he hoped, his close friends). New husbands were always teased in such a fashion; he had heard it a hundred times, and thought nothing of it. Wagers were offered – the young bucks of the ton would bet on anything – and dates laid claim to, odds offered on the outcome: a boy, a girl, twins? (Jesus: twins.) But now, of course, it was his most intimate life that would be the focus of such conjecture, rather than another's. He was not sure how he felt about that, nor what answer he would make to such remarks. Presumably, too, such impertinent interrogations would become more frequent and more pressing as time passed without his wife showing any sign of increasing. Devil take the chattering fools! Could they not mind their own business and leave others alone?

He remained firmly resolved not to become a father just at present, but he would not wish anyone to think for a second that he couldn't, that they couldn't, if they wished to; still less would he like it if Cassandra should be subjected to any disagreeable gossip. She had been an angel about the whole thing, seeming genuinely to share his desire for a time of freedom. Imagine if instead she had shown him a shocked face at the very suggestion of delaying parenthood; what would he have done? Made love to her anyway and damn the consequences, he thought now as he held her and listened to her soft breathing. Abstinence would have been entirely out of the question. One was not made of stone. And then she might already be with child, not lying here suffering with her woman's troubles. God knows their lovemaking had been frequent enough. Of course, it could still have taken them by surprise, in any case; he knew that accidents could happen, however careful one was. It was odd, but the idea did not fill him with the horror that it surely ought. And yet nothing at all had changed in his life save that he was married. What was amiss with him? Something was.

It was all very confusing, Hal found, and his thoughts were in a sad turmoil. His feet had not touched the ground, it seemed, since he had stumbled into his library and found Cassandra sleeping there. Since then he had barely had a moment in which to stop and wonder what he felt about all these changes. His life in recent years – ever since his parents had died – had been too crowded with incident to encourage habits of self-reflection, and he struggled now to tease apart the tangled skein of his thoughts.

One thing was certain: he liked being married. He grinned to himself rather wolfishly in the darkness – of course he did! He had won for himself (although 'won' was scarcely the appropriate word) a beautiful, desirable woman, and one, moreover, with an edge of wildness that called to something alike in him. A woman who would pour tea, cool and correct in white muslin, and make polite conversation with the dullest of his neighbours, as any wife might, while shooting him a surreptitious glance under her long lashes that promised very different diversions later, when they were alone. The moment they were alone. The contrast, that was what excited him. He thought it excited her too. No – he knew it did.

He had known when he first kissed her that her nature was passionate. But he could not have anticipated that hidden streak of recklessness that she had revealed to him when she ran barefoot and laughing through the grass on their wedding night, when she had seized so eagerly the chance to swim naked in the moonlight.

There had been a dozen occasions since when they

had encouraged each other on to some outrageously naughty action: that evening in the carriage, wrapped between her legs in delicious captivity, was only the most recent. They had been naked together on the roof of the Castle, making love under the summer moon. He had eaten syllabub saved from dinner from her beautiful breasts on the grand dining table in the state dining room, and afterwards he had eaten her, right under the enigmatically smiling portrait of Queen Elizabeth, who had been entertained there by his ancestor, one presumed in a rather more sedate fashion. One evening at dinner, she – Cassandra, not the Virgin Queen – had slipped off her shoes and slid her bare foot into his lap, smiling at him innocently as the footmen served them poached asparagus and she rubbed herself against his throbbing erection. And when the servants at long last had left, she had risen from her chair and knelt at his feet and demanded he tell her exactly how she could please him with her mouth. A gentleman could only oblige. He was hard again now at the thought of it all. Once she was restored to health, he was confident he could say to her, *I want to have you in a bathing machine in the sea*, and she would say, *Let's go now, this instant*. A man could live his whole life without experiencing such intensity of sensation. A man might never know such violent delights and, never knowing, think himself happy.

But was he happy? He must be. He had all that, and besides he liked her. He much more than liked her. She was brave, and funny, and it was a pleasure to spend time with her, whatever they were doing. They would travel the world, and experience all its wonders for the first time together. Venice, Florence, Rome, Naples, and beyond. When they were bored with travel, when they were ready, they would one day have children together, he hoped. He would conquer his fears, and face the uncertainty that was an inevitable part of life. And he was surely better prepared for fatherhood than any man alive; he had served almost a seven-year apprenticeship in it already. The thought made him smile.

He was happy now, holding her as she slept. He would be happy when she woke and smiled at him. Her smile could pierce his chest. But he was not . . . She made an adorable soft noise, and buried her face in his armpit, her hand creeping up and resting on his shirt, just above his heart. He tensed, but she slept on.

He was not secure. The word popped into his head. He did not really know what she felt about him, and so he was not secure. She had not said. But then again, he had not said. Sometimes he had been tempted, in the aftermath of passion, when he had held her and she had looked at him so, her eyes shining, as though he had hung the moon and stars for her – he had been tempted to utter words he had never said to another person since he had grown to manhood. But it might have embarrassed her. It might have embarrassed him. He could not have borne it, could not bear it, if she had not . . . And the moment had passed. Several such moments had passed.

Was it folly, to fear saying such words – to one's own wife? Plenty of fellows seemed to have no trouble saying them to other people's wives, to any number of women. Plenty of women, he supposed, said them too, said them casually. But not Cassandra, with her incurable frankness. Not to him, at any rate. He would not, he thought, want her to say them casually.

And after all, despite everything, he scarcely knew her. He did not, for instance, know the depth of her feelings for the Welby youth. He recalled now that he had been anxious, the night of their accursed ball, to declare himself to her, before Welby or anyone else had the opportunity to do so. Well! He had certainly done that, and done it moreover in a public forum, in circumstances that made it entirely impossible for her to refuse him. What woman would reject a man who had just defended her honour in such a spectacularly unequivocal manner, and then proposed to her in front of the cream of the haut ton? And then, afterwards, there had been no time to think. Events had taken over. Louisa, everybody . . . He should have given Cassandra in private the opportunity to draw back, to retract an acceptance made under what was, effectively, duress. Duress caused by his precipitate action, however laudable his motives. But if he had done that, if he had offered her the chance to refuse him, she might have thought that *he* was reluctant and had only offered to save her honour. She might have felt obliged to end their engagement, even if she did not want to, because she thought he wanted to. But he didn't . . . he hadn't! His head hurt him, and all his previous feelings of contentment had vanished as if they had never existed.

He had never told her, he realised with a sinking sensation in his belly, that he had intended to ask for her hand that evening in any case. If he told her now, she would think it odd and she might not believe him. And it was altogether too late. He would never know if she would have accepted him. If he told her now and she said that of course she would have agreed to marry him, what would that prove? She must say as much, must she not? She was his wife. There was no undoing that. If in sober truth she had been horrified to hear him speak, if she would a thousand times have preferred Welby to offer for her, she would never reveal it now. He had made sure of that. He was feeling slightly feverish.

He suddenly remembered her telling him that she had been kissed, caressed – he ground his teeth, quietly, at the thought – before. Perhaps it had been Welby. Probably it had. Perhaps when she welcomed his, Hal's, attentions, she was thinking of that cursed puppy all the time. Because her former lover was now irrevocably lost to her, and she had no choice but to make the best of her situation. Women, he supposed, felt frustrated too. Surely they did. They could feel lust. This he knew. She was a passionate woman, she was his wife, and he was, he flattered himself, not entirely unskilled as a lover. She had given herself to him with an abandon that could not be feigned. But in her secret heart, in the throes of passion, she might long for another. He would never know. They might spend forty years together in apparent harmony, and he would never know. One could not read another person's thoughts, even if one was married. Especially, perhaps, if one was married. She might be dreaming now, dreaming of a man's embraces – but whose?

As he lay beside her in the darkness, his imaginings grew darker and darker. Maybe she did not think Welby lost to her at all. Why should he be, in these modern times? Maybe she intended to take him as a lover – later, once she had given him, Hal, a child or two. The requisite son. Or even sooner, since she now knew precisely how to avoid unwanted complications, thanks to him. It was common enough in high society, the society in which they moved, for a married lady to take a lover. It was even fashionable. Maybe she thought he would not mind. He would mind. He would mind excessively. Maybe she thought he intended to do the same. He did not. The thought had not even occurred to him before this moment, and filled him with revulsion. He realised now that he had not so much as looked at another woman since the day he had met her. He wanted nobody but her. And he had not the slightest idea if she felt the same. It was not as if he could say to her now, in the course of some light conversation, *I may be a member of fashionable society, I may be the godson of the notorious Duchess of Devonshire, but my parents loved each other dearly and were faithful till they died; I will never betray you and I cannot endure if you were to betray me. I feel as though it would kill me.*

He groaned, softly. That way madness lay. He sighed, and closed his eyes, and tried to join Cassandra in sleep. Blessed oblivion was very long in coming.

CHAPTER THIRTY-SIX

The new Countess of Irlam was acknowledged by the members of the haut ton to be the sensation of the summer. The circumstances of her engagement were dramatic, and highly romantic, and the ranks of those who claimed to have witnessed, with their own eyes, His Lordship's delightful proposal had now swelled to preposterous numbers, more than even a nobleman's house could in reality hold. She was widely, and understandably, considered to be an object of envy: young, beautiful, rich and newly married to a handsome, besotted husband. If her life was not perfect, then whose was?

Undoubtedly there were ladies who were jealous of her sudden elevation, and would have been glad to see her suffer a reversal of fortune; perhaps indeed they had cherished dreams of winning Lord Irlam's favour for themselves, or for their marriageable daughters. But that was unreasonable, because the gentleman had raised no hopes; he had always, before the thrilling events of this summer, shown his disinclination to marry quite plainly, and had avoided debutantes and their matchmaking mamas with a determination that could almost be described as comical. If he had flirted, he had done so with ladies who were safely married, but it did not seem that he had gone any further than that, though undoubtedly he could have done so had he wished. There were many ladies in the very highest ranks of society who were famously accommodating, but none of them could claim him as her cicisbeo and be believed. Lady Lavinia Trumpington showed a disposition to pout, and consider herself slighted, but it was widely considered that she was only giving herself airs to be interesting, and she soon left off when she perceived that she was making herself ridiculous. Though it was to be presumed that Irlam had paid homage at the altar of Venus since he had grown to manhood, he had done so discretely. He had not, like others of his age and class, set up a highflyer as his light-of-love and paraded about the town with her to set tongues wagging.

In the absence of a jilted mistress, the chief object of interest must always be the bride, especially a bride won in such delightfully public a fashion. Miss Hazeldon had been atrociously treated by her uncle and his disreputable crony, everyone acknowledged, and it was greatly to

Irlam's credit that he had rescued her and claimed her like a parfait, gentil knight. The greater part of the ton was not, in truth, excessively interested in the welfare of young women and the injustices they suffered, both in secret and under the indifferent gaze of others every day of the week; but a young and lovely heiress, that was different, naturally.

Cassandra herself was aware that she was very lucky, despite the fears that sometimes tormented her, and would have admitted as much if anybody had asked her. Two months ago she had been in truly desperate straits: horribly lonely, cut off from her friends and anyone who had ever cared about her, at the mercy of her uncle and his co-conspirator and facing a future that she could only contemplate with fear and revulsion. Everything was so different now. She was no longer a prisoner, she no longer had to dread being at the mercy of a cruel, lecherous fortune-hunter, but instead she had a new, affectionate family, friends about her, and a husband with whom she shared a physical passion that she could scarcely have imagined.

And the travel that she had always so longed for was almost within her grasp now. In a few short weeks they would take ship for Italy. As soon as she had become betrothed to Lord Irlam, she had written as a matter of urgency to Mrs Thoroughgood, and Lord Carston had been able to expedite her letters by mysterious diplomatic means. As a result, the older lady had most fortunately received Cassandra's second and much more reassuring missive just as she had been about to set off post-haste to England on a rescue mission. The Pendleburys planned to rendezvous with her later in the year in the Kingdom of Naples. All that was delaying them was the issue of where Georgiana should pass the autumn – whether she should accompany them abroad, as Lord Irlam wished, or return to the care of Mrs Winterton at the Castle, or whether her engagement to Lord Lamington should at last be announced, and the wedding plans drawn up. Long engagements were not the fashion in high society; if there was nothing to prevent a couple from plighting their troth, a matter of weeks would suffice. The Irlam family had so recently arranged a wedding, and could very easily do so again, though Lady Louisa shuddered at the thought, and began to talk longingly of the comforts of her home in Richmond, from which she had been absent far too long, and to which Miss Spry was now safely returned.

It was impossible to say which of these three schemes Lady Georgiana herself favoured. At times it seemed she was tempted by the prospect of seeing Italy; at times, she admitted, she swayed towards the attractions of the Castle. Cassandra could not help but notice that the prospect of marriage, and of taking up residence in the staid Lamington household, did not appear at any time to hold any great allure for her. She recollected the evening of the Windleshams' ball, and Georgie's flushed, hectic face when they had encountered each other outside the ballroom, both of them, surely, nursing some guilty secret, some memory of illicit passion. She wondered if she ought to tell Hal of it, but still she did not do so. After all, she knew nothing for certain – she had no gentleman's name to offer him, and she was not by any means sure if she would give such a name up if she did know it. Georgiana had been so very kind to her – not on that occasion, perhaps, where she could be argued to have been acting out of mere self-interest, but when she had taken her into her home without question, and welcomed her into the family in a similar generous spirit. Cassandra was hardly in a position to moralise – Hal had been a virtual stranger when she had first flung herself into his embrace and had allowed him all kinds of shocking liberties. She did not, could not, know for certain that her sister-in-law had done something similar, and to tell tales on her would be rank betrayal.

She was worried about Georgie – as the time drew near where she would be forced to make a decision regarding her future, it seemed to Cassandra that her sister-in-law's habitual gaiety was forced and artificial, her eyes noticeably heavy and her cheeks either pale or flushed with a colour that hardly seemed healthy. Again she contemplated and discarded the notion of sharing her worries with Hal, or with Lady Louisa. It seemed presumptuous – as if she were saying that she knew Georgie better than they did themselves, they who had known her and had care of her all her life. If they saw nothing amiss, then it must be her imagination. And so she said nothing, but she remained uneasy.

She also considered and immediately discarded the idea of initiating with her sister-in-law a discussion about the intimate duties – 'duties' was a terrible word, a word that gave entirely the wrong impression, but she shied away from anything more accurate – of a lady within marriage. The very idea made her blush hotly. She did not think that it was the prospect of conjugal intimacy with Lord Lamington that made Georgie hesitate so – she did not give in the least the impression of a young lady who was scared of anything, certainly not of her prospective husband. If something was preying on her mind, Cassandra did not think it was that. Again it seemed presumptuous on her part to think that any reassurance was needed, and Cassandra thought that she would walk over hot coals before she would say to anyone, *A gentlemen does this on his wedding night, a lady does that*. Not only would she inevitably be discussing Georgie's own brother, and their most secret shared moments, but if by some chance Georgie should laugh at her – she could imagine it – and reveal a knowledge that she, as an unmarried lady, had no right to possess, what should she, Cassandra, do then? She had brought herself back to the concept of betrayal, and not just betrayal of her sister-in-law. In such circumstances she would unquestionably be bound to reveal what she had discovered to Hal, or as his wife she would be betraying him. She could never be easy in her mind, keeping such knowledge to herself, and if she did reluctantly keep silent she would for ever afterwards be afraid that he would come to learn of what she had kept concealed, and censure her very severely, with justification.

She had no one with whom she could discuss such matters. Georgiana showed no disposition at all to confide in her, and to lay her own doubts and fears in Lady Louisa's lap would seem to her to be cowardice – a craven desire to put off responsibility on another because she was too weak to bear it herself. She had already decided that as things stood she could not confide her inchoate fears to Hal, and to tell Louisa and not expect her to tell Hal would be sheer folly. His aunt would go straight to him, and he would wonder with some justification why his wife had not simply told him directly.

It was not as though there was perfect communion between them, or anything like it, so that she could seriously contemplate discussing her worries with him. It was very odd, Cassandra thought, that one could share so much with a person and yet still have no idea what he was thinking. There was not an inch of her body that he had not explored. He had been bolder than she could ever have anticipated, and so had she. She had learnt that she could reduce him to a state of helpless desire with a gesture, a smile, a movement, an unspoken reference to their passion. At times it was a torment to them both to wait until they could be alone and come together instantly with a hunger that seemed to grow rather than to abate. But they did not talk; no, that was a lie, they talked all the time, they laughed together and discussed their plans, they spoke of their childhoods, their likes and dislikes, but there was still somehow an invisible barrier between them. Or, to better express how she felt, it was as if they were swimming together in the sea, and the surface was shot with sunlight, but the water beneath them was deep and dark, and she had no idea what might lurk there, and when it might emerge from the murky depths and drag them both to disaster.

Cassandra had obtained her old friend and teacher Kate Moreton's direction not long after her arrival in Brighton, and had written to her, and received a prompt and delighted response. They had quickly established a regular correspondence, since they had a great deal to tell each other. Now that Kate was a married woman and a mother, and a stepmother too, she might be the one person in the world to whom Cassandra could open her heart. She had considered and rejected pouring out her worries to Polly, who had written to her several times from Leeds. Her old nurse had been delighted at the news of her charge's marriage to the handsome young gentleman who had come so gallantly to her rescue, and Cassandra felt reluctant to shatter her innocent pleasure and tell her that all was not perfect in her new life. But Kate had known heartbreak, before her current happiness; if she were to tell anyone, it could only be her. Yet it was surprisingly difficult, she found, to do so on paper. She started to write as frankly as she wished a dozen times, but then tore the letters up. There was no point seeking advice from Kate, or from anyone, if she were not prepared to be entirely honest with her correspondent, and this would involve, Cassandra knew, being entirely honest with herself. It was not at all that she did not trust her friend; she might tell her anything and be confident that she would never reveal it to a soul. But once things had been set down in stark black ink, they must be faced.

It was perhaps natural, but, as things turned out, regrettable, that in such circumstances Cassandra should turn for comfort to the one person she saw in her daily life with whom her relations did not seem to be fraught with difficulty and unspoken reservations: her oldest friend, Matthew Welby.

CHAPTER THIRTY-SEVEN

It was a ridiculous way to tear your life apart, Hal thought later. A matter of timing – a moment's impulse that changed everything.

He spent the night in Cassandra's bed and their morning lovemaking, as they reached for each other instinctively while still almost half-asleep, was not frenzied and urgent, as it so often was, but tender. Afterwards he lay with his head pillowed between her lovely breasts as she idly stroked his tousled hair back from his brow, and he almost spoke then, almost blurted out his true feelings. But he was so drowsy, so thoroughly comfortable in her warm embrace, that he let the moment slip past. *No matter*, he thought.

He passed the rest of the morning buoyed up with optimism, and resolved – since it seemed to be impossible simply to tell his wife that he loved her in the course of casual conversation – that he would buy her a gift, and bring it to her, and then tell her. That was the plan; he would create a moment, and then take advantage of it. He had previously observed that Cassandra was not, unlike many women of his acquaintance – his spoilt little sister, for instance – accustomed to receiving gifts, and so the very fact of his presenting her with some well-chosen trifle would, at the outset mark, an occasion. It would, in a sense, be the first real present he had given her, since the emeralds that had been her bride-gift had been something public, expected. He had, of course, imagined her in emeralds very early in their acquaintance, and so the gift had a private meaning for him – but she did not know it, for he had not told her. There were, he thought now, too many things he had not told her, and he was resolved that today would be the day when all that changed.

It was not that he expected Cassandra to return his adoration through gratitude, or tell him that she loved him merely because he had bought her some bauble – that was not in the least what he wanted from her. She was incurably honest; it was part of why he loved her. He did not think that she would say it if she did not mean it. But he hoped, more than he could possibly express even to himself, that she shared his feelings, and would tell him so today; therefore he wanted the occasion to be significant. Memorable. And, he later thought grimly, so it proved.

Hal went out alone, whistling cheerfully to himself, and, after much deliberation, chose for his bride a golden pendant on an intricate chain. It was fashioned in the shape of a heart – somewhat obvious, perhaps, but was a man in love not permitted to be obvious? It was set with emeralds and sapphires, which, the sympathetic young woman in the jeweller's shop explained, symbolised love and fidelity. He told her, and felt himself colour unaccountably as he uttered the words, that he was seeking a gift for his new wife, and the assistant beamed at him indulgently and complimented him on his taste. No doubt it was her job to do so, but she was very good at it and made him feel a devil of a fine fellow, so that he returned home with a slight swagger, carrying his precious box carefully in one elegantly gloved hand.

On reaching the house, he ran lightly upstairs to Cassandra's private sitting room, and entered without knocking, eager to see her face light up when she opened his surprise, impatient to pour out his heart and set their relations on a secure footing at last.

The surprise, however, was to be his. He opened the door to find his wife locked in a close embrace with another man – with Matthew Welby. They sprang apart instantly, and Cassandra moved swiftly towards him with outstretched hands, an expression of horrified panic on her face and words of placation, of explanation tumbling from her lips, but he did not stay to hear them. Blindly he turned on his heel and left as swiftly as he had arrived, thundering down the stairs, dragging the front door of the mansion open before the startled footman had a chance to lay a hand on it, and slamming it behind him with a crash that shook the house from its cellars to its attics.

CHAPTER THIRTY-EIGHT

Of course, he had to return eventually. Hal, in his desperate hurt, had entertained the idea of leaving immediately, running for the Castle – for Town, for anywhere that was not here – but, at last, he could not bring himself to do so. The Castle would inevitably remind him of Cassandra; he would have to open up one of the disused suites of rooms in order to find a place that did not hold some tormenting recollection of her, and in order to do so he would have to give instructions and some sort of explanation. Most of his staff had known him since birth, and he had never wished to be the sort of autocrat who demanded instant, unquestioning obedience to his every whim. Even if they did not question him, they would look at him, and understand that something terrible had happened, and pity him. He felt he could not bear it.

And the house in Town would be no better – his library, where he had first seen her; his bedroom, where she had slept. If he was to be reminded of her at every turn, he might as well remain and face things like the man he was supposed to be.

He did not have to be sober when he did it, mind you. Just now the oblivion that the consumption of large quantities of alcohol brought was entirely to his taste, and, after wandering aimlessly about the streets of Brighton for he knew not how long, he sought out one of the superior taverns that the town offered. He would find company there, and brandy, and drink until he forgot everything.

He found both, but yet it did not answer. His friends were very happy to receive him – Tom Wainfleet was present, and others he had known for years, but the devil was that they had to begin by teasing him on his recent absence from their revels, and on the new sober mode of life that he had taken up since his marriage. He feared that soon enough they would begin to quiz him on why he had joined them now, today – had the lovebirds quarrelled? Had married life begun to lose its savour, and so soon? That too he could not bear, so after a short while he made some excuse and left them.

A fine state of affairs, when a man cannot even get drunk in peace, he reflected sadly as he dragged his reluctant footsteps homewards. Well, he damn well would – he would sit in his dining room and drink himself to oblivion and nobody – nobody – would stop him. Was he not master in his own house, even if he was a cuckold? By God, he was.

The mansion was eerily quiet when he entered it. Wilson, his face a mask of impassivity, informed him that Lady Georgiana and Lady Louisa had gone out an hour since on some social engagement. 'But not Her Ladyship?' he enquired with an effort at insouciance that, he was aware, fell painfully short. No, not Her Ladyship. Her Ladyship had the headache, and took dinner in her chamber. 'Ha!' ejaculated Hal. Well might she have the headache. Wilson, not unnaturally, made no response. 'Brandy,' said Hal. 'In the dining room. Immediately.' Wilson bowed.

Hal sat at the head of the dining table and threw back a bumper of brandy. It burnt his throat and set him coughing, and in that moment he was as perfectly miserable as a healthy, wealthy young gentleman well could be. The whole world seemed in league against him. He was coughing, his eyes were streaming, and as if that were not enough, he could not even sit comfortably in a blasted chair in his own confounded house. There was something hard in his pocket, digging into him. He rose and fumbled for it: a box, its wrapping slightly crumpled. The box. The gift that he had so foolishly bought for her that very day. The gift that he had meant to give her as prelude to his declaration of love for her. Her, his faithless bride of a month. The woman he had thought a paragon of honesty and bravery and everything that was good in the world. He must truly be the greatest fool who had ever lived. He let out a crack of mirthless laughter and hurled it violently from him into the furthest corner of the room.

The door opened. He raised his head, ready to blast the unfortunate Wilson with an entirely uncharacteristic tirade of abuse. But it was not Wilson; it was Cassandra.

Her face was pale and woebegone and she was wearing a dressing-gown and a nightcap tied under her chin. Somehow the cap was the last straw. She never wore a cap. He put his head in his hands so he did not have to look at her, and ground out two words: 'Go away.'

She closed the door behind her, and advanced further into the room. 'We need to talk.'

He raised his head and glared at her. 'I cannot imagine what there is to be said. I have asked you to leave, madam, and I would be grateful if you would do so.' Hal was aware as he uttered the words that he was sounding ridiculously pompous, like one of his stuffiest old uncles, relic of the previous century. The trouble was, he did not seem to have full control of himself. He felt as though his limbs were made of wood, and when he spoke his face seemed to hurt, and his mouth move unnaturally. He could either talk like a stiff-rumped old fellow in a play, or lay his head down on the table and howl like a baby. He knew which he preferred.

'I will not.' Cassandra crossed the room to his side, pulled out a chair and sank into it, wringing her hands. He had never seen her half so agitated before.

Earlier in the day, he had rehearsed a dozen speeches in which he had excoriated her for her betrayal, in which he had flayed her fluently with words and poured out his anger and hurt in base language that he had never thought to utter to a woman he cared for. But now that he saw her white, miserable little face, the curses died on his lips, and he could think of nothing to say. What was the point? She was plainly as unhappy as he. It was with an obvious effort that she spoke now, her voice unsteady. 'Hal, I swear there is nothing between Matthew and me. I will swear it on anything you like – on my life.'

'You were in his arms. Alone together, when everyone else was out. You took the first opportunity that presented itself to fling yourself into his embrace. If I had come back a bare five minutes later, what worse sight might I have seen then?' His voice cracked as he accused her, and he found himself perilously close to tears.

'You misunderstood what you saw.'

'I say I did not. Do you take me for a complete imbecile?'

She reached out her hand in entreaty to take his, but he snatched it away. 'Hal, Matthew was upset, and I was comforting him.' He snorted in derision, but she continued doggedly, 'He is my oldest friend, and when he came to me in distress I held him while he cried. I swear that was all it was. He has recently formed a romantic connection, which ended unhappily just before he came here. There is nothing between us but friendship. I have not the slightest interest in him in that way, and I promise you he has no interest in me. Even if he did, if anyone did, I would not betray you. What kind of monster of depravity do you think me, sir? We are barely a month married, you know I came to you a virgin, and you truly believe I would fall straight from your bed into another man's arms?' There were tears streaming unheeded down her face as she whispered, 'When I recall what passed between us just this morning, our tender lovemaking, I realise that you must think me a modern Messalina. Do you truly think I am deranged? For I could only be deranged, to behave as you believe I have.'

She spoke with such passionate sincerity that he was shaken, almost ready to believe her and to doubt the evidence of his own eyes. Almost, but not quite. 'Answer me this,' he said suddenly, desperate to be proved wrong, desperate to hear an explanation he could believe, desperate to have faith in her honesty again. 'When you told me on the night of our wedding that you had kissed and caressed before, was it Welby you were speaking of? Was he the man who first touched you, or was it some other?'

Her face crumpled. There was a fatal moment of hesitation, and then she said slowly, listlessly, 'Yes, it was him. I cannot deny it. But you do not understand—'

He cut her off. 'I did not understand before, but I do now. I apologise to you, madam, for accusing you of infidelity – you are a light-skirt, I see now, but the man you have betrayed is Welby, not me, for he was there first! I owe him a profound apology!'

As he spoke, he thrust back his chair and strode from the room, heedless of how it toppled to the floor behind him, and heedless of Cassandra, who sat pale and silent and watched him leave as her tears fell, and did not attempt to stop him. The bright little box with the gift in it, bought with such high hopes so few hours before, lay in the corner, unheeded.

CHAPTER THIRTY-NINE

Cassandra laid down her needlework, and sighed deeply. She had the headache; it seemed she always had the headache now, a kind of heavy fog that had wreathed itself around her brain and prevented her from thinking of a way out of her situation. A week had passed since the terrible day on which Hal had seen her and Matthew embracing, and she had not been alone with her husband since. He had made sure of that. She had found no fit opportunity to speak to him in private, and although she could quite easily have gone to his bedchamber in order to confront him, she dared not. Given what he apparently believed her to be, that was the very last place such a conversation should be held. She thought that if passion flared between them despite their estrangement, as it well might, if their hunger overwhelmed them and they lay together despite everything, she really would have proved herself in his eyes the whore he already thought her. Marital intimacy, she was coming painfully to learn, a complete union of bodies, solved nothing outside the bedroom. Or at least, it did not for her and for Hal. Perhaps others were more fortunate.

She needed to speak with Matthew, to seek his permission to tell her husband everything. She could not in conscience go ahead without it, not even to save herself. She was well aware that it was no small thing that she must ask of him. But Matthew no longer paid calls on her, understandably, and she dared not seek him out at any ball, assembly or soirée they both happened to attend – not with Hal's eyes cold and judgemental on her, watching her every move. She needed to write to her friend, but certainly she could not leave out a letter with Mr Welby's name and direction on it for Hal to frank in the normal manner. Surely he would not. He might open it; society would undoubtedly consider that he had every right as her husband to do so. She could ask a maid or footman to deliver a missive for her, she supposed, but she could not help but be aware that every servant in the house from Wilson downwards knew she and Hal had had some terrible falling-out, and that Matthew was the cause of it. If she set down what she needed from Matthew in plain words and someone opened it – disaster. She could not do that to him. And if she were cryptic, if she said, *I need your permission to tell my husband the secret that we share* – well, that would be near as bad, if anyone read it. They would assume the worst. She was stuck. And Matthew, similarly, was unable to communicate with her.

They both should consider themselves lucky, she supposed, that Hal had neither attacked Matthew when he walked in on them in that horrible moment, nor thought to challenge him to a duel afterwards. They were the two men she cared for most in the world, and to think of them facing each other with swords or pistols made her blood run cold. She knew they were both very good shots, and shuddered to think what might have transpired. She could imagine no scenario that would not rip her life apart for ever. At least they had been spared that horror, not to mention the inevitable scandal that would have followed, whatever the outcome.

She was thoroughly miserable. To know herself unjustly accused and be unable to set things right was bad enough. She found herself tossing and turning all night, and she missed Hal with an intensity that surprised her – not just his touch and the passionate exchanges they had shared, and shared no longer, but also his conversation, his smile, the life that they had been slowly building. But in addition to her own pain, she could feel Hal's agony. It pervaded the house. He had made no more scenes, slammed no more doors, and was always coldly polite to her in the presence of others, but it was very obvious to her that he was suffering. There was no more talk of travel, or of any manner of plans for the future; it was as if they were walking on very thin ice. She had no clue what the next weeks would bring; they would inevitably leave Brighton soon, the town was emptying out already, and some decision must be taken on where they should go. Whether they should go there together. Or – but anything else was unthinkable.

Georgiana and Louisa had both spoken to her, had both asked her what was wrong, and she had told them – she felt she had no choice – that Hal believed her unfaithful to him, and would not talk to her so that she could explain. They had each separately said to her, using almost identical words, and phrasing it not as a question but as a statement, *You have not betrayed him, of course*, and she had been grateful for their trust in her, so much greater than that of her own husband. Louisa had surprised her by also saying, 'He believes that you have played him false with young Welby, does he?' and when Cassandra had assented with a single miserable nod, she had had muttered, 'My nephew really can be a fool at times, can he not?' When Cassandra had stared, wondering what she might mean, Louisa had said merely, 'He should have more faith in you, and more faith in himself, for that matter. But there is no reasoning with him when he is like this.'

Even Kitty had tried by oblique questions to divine what was casting such a pall of misery over the whole house, and making both her master and her new mistress so unhappy. Cassandra knew an impulse to lay her head on her maid's ample bosom and sob out her pain and

276

distress, but she did not do so. It would be shockingly undignified to seek comfort from a servant, and she felt that she had little at present but her fragile shreds of dignity to sustain her. She was a countess, and could at least try to behave like one. She thought, too, that Kitty was so very fond of Hal that she would always take his part, and, ridiculously, she did not think she could endure to see his mistrust mirrored in the eyes of another, whoever she might be.

The thought that he could not trust her, that he believed the worst of her so easily, was a constant niggling pain to Cassandra, but she tried very hard to suppress it, for she was forced to acknowledge the plain fact that he did not trust her because he did not know her. And she did not know him; she did not even know why he was experiencing such torment. It might be because his feelings for her were deep – she hoped that it was so – but equally she must admit that it could merely be that his masculine pride was wounded, to think that the bride he had so chivalrously and so very publicly rescued might betray him with another man within a matter of weeks. No man, whatever emotions he might cherish towards his new wife, could enjoy being fitted for a cuckold's horns when he had barely returned from his honeymoon. She supposed that men might be particularly sensitive about anything that seemed to cast doubts upon their prowess in matters of the bedroom. And even if he felt nothing at all for her beyond lust, he might consider her his property. She did not think so; she thought better of him – but how could she know for sure? What were they, after all, but married strangers?

As the days passed, it began to seem to Cassandra that the gulf between them was widening. She became possessed of a fear that Hal might be planning to leave for the continent without her, and without telling her, and if he did that, she wondered how long it might be before he returned. It could be years. It could be for ever.

CHAPTER FORTY

It was impossible to know how long this sad state of affairs might have persisted if something had not occurred that precipitated a crisis. One afternoon, Cassandra, much against her will, attended a picnic on the Downs outside Brighton; her husband had expressed his disinclination to attend, which could hardly be a surprise to her, and equally it was not at all the sort of event that Lady Louisa could be expected to enjoy. There was, in any case, not the least need for Louisa to exert herself, since now that Cassandra was married she could act as Georgie's duenna with perfect propriety, and Georgiana had expressed a strong desire to go, so Cassandra felt obliged to accompany her.

The Countess's nerves were feeling the strain, and she might even have welcomed the release of a screaming match with her foolish, stubborn husband, during which she would have enjoyed pointing out that if he really considered her to be devoid of every shred of decency and capable of moving straight from one man's embrace to another, it was to say the least odd that he still apparently deemed her fit to chaperone his unmarried sister and guard her from harm. She would have liked to seize him by the shoulders and shake him until his teeth rattled, to use his own expression.

If Cassandra had not been so thoroughly weary and dispirited, she might have noticed that Georgiana was in a very odd mood that afternoon, alternating between gloomy silence and a sort of forced gaiety. But her sister-in-law was too preoccupied with her own affairs to pay much attention to her, and they conversed only in a desultory fashion.

The party, which was large and composed of both ladies and gentlemen, both married and unmarried, drove out together in open carriages to a site that had previously been appointed, where rug and picnic hampers had been laid out ready by toiling servants under the shade of a large oak tree. It was an oppressively warm day, and once the pies and sandwiches and fancy little cakes had been consumed, not to mention the chilled champagne and orgeat cup, an air of lassitude descended on the company.

Conversation faltered, and then died out altogether. Silence fell. Some of the older persons present were soon quite shamelessly snoozing under the spreading limbs of the tree, and the livelier members of the party took advantage of the licence this afforded to disappear. Georgie strolled away arm in arm with two of her closest female friends, and although Cassandra could find nothing to object to in this, she could not be quite easy in her mind, and decided to walk casually in the direction they had taken and see if they were still together in innocent conversation. She by no means wished to spy on her sister-in-law, but she did not wish either to give Hal any more reason to be angry with her if she could help it. She felt it would be all of a piece with her ill luck in the last week or so if she relaxed her vigilance today and something untoward did happen. Their marriage stood on so shaky a foundation now, she thought, that the least thing would see it collapse altogether. Perhaps there was a thunderstorm coming, perhaps it was merely a reflection of her emotional state, but she, not normally in the least fanciful, felt a heaviness in the air, as if some disaster was about to overtake her.

The ladies she was following had passed out of sight, and she was making her way along a hedge line down a shallow slope, glad to be active and relishing, even in her downcast state, the chance to be alone in the open air, when she heard voices. She stopped, realising that someone from her party, though invisible to her, must be just the other side of the hedge. If it should prove to be Georgie and her friends, then she might continue with a clear conscience, and enjoy the panorama of the sea that the cliff edge would provide. She could sit for a while on the short-cropped grass – perhaps there would be a cooling breeze – and see what the balm of nature could do to soothe her aching heart.

The voice that she could hear was plainly Georgie's, but the tones that answered her did not belong to any debutante; they were those of a man. A young man.

'Dammit, Georgiana,' he said explosively, 'a fellow can only stand so much! It's about bloody time you made up your mind if you mean to have me or not, or if you're all talk and never had any intention of coming to Gretna with me!'

'Hush, Adolphus!' was Georgiana's hissed response. 'Someone will hear if you talk so excessively loudly!'

Cassandra had stopped dead, and found herself creeping closer to the thorny hedge in an effort both to conceal her presence and to hear better. She thought the gentleman's voice vaguely familiar, but one thing she was quite certain of: it was not Lord Lamington. Lord Lamington was no Adolphus – he had been christened Jeremiah by his fond parents. Lady Lamington had told her so herself, and explained that it meant that he was a gift from God, to which Cassandra had felt able to respond only by murmuring, 'How lovely!'

The gentleman behind the hedge had sworn robustly, too, which seemed entirely unlike His Lordship, and Cassandra recalled now that Lord Lamington was not one of their party that afternoon – was not even in Brighton, in fact, as he had escorted his fond mama to London for a couple of days so that she might have a painful tooth drawn by the particular superior barber-surgeon she favoured. They would return later that day. This too Lady Lamington had told her at exhaustive length, and since Cassandra had not been listening particularly attentively, she was momentarily impressed that she had remembered, until such a ridiculous thought was driven from her mind by the gravity of what she was overhearing.

She swiftly cast aside any momentary qualms she might have had about eavesdropping. Georgiana was her responsibility today, and it seemed that she had quite deliberately crept off, presumably with the contrivance of her friends, to meet a man clandestinely. Cassandra might have no real right to censure her for that, but she had been brought up cold by the talk of elopement. To fly to Gretna to marry there over the anvil, if indeed she was seriously contemplating such a desperate course of action – and to do so, furthermore, while as good as betrothed to another man – would irreparably damage Georgiana's reputation. She needed to know what manner of suitor was urging such a thing, and why. Georgiana was, Cassandra knew, a considerable heiress in her own right, and she was only too well aware from her own bitter experience how easy it was for young women of fortune to fall prey to men with base designs on their money as well as their persons. It might be that Cassandra would later struggle internally over whether she reported what she'd heard to Hal, but what she could not do was abnegate responsibility and walk away without troubling to listen further, telling herself primly that it was none of her business. She was a

Pendlebury now, even if she was presently estranged from her lord; it was her business.

Cassandra was not obliged to overhear any exchange of sweet nothings, such as would have made her uneasy. On the contrary, the couple were arguing. The gentleman was urging the necessity of flight upon his reluctant sweetheart. She could no longer prevaricate, he told her – if she delayed any longer, she would find herself carried off by her family to the continent, quite out of his reach, or at the very least to the Castle, where it would be nigh on impossible for him to meet her. And that was not the worst thing that might happen, according to him, for it was clear that he knew of the understanding with Lamington, and feared that he might press for a public announcement of their impending marriage, and for a date to be set.

'You know I would never agree to that, dearest,' Georgiana said in low, conciliatory tones. 'It was never more than a ruse; you *know* I have not the least intention of marrying him. Indeed, my brother quite despises the poor man, which is why I felt it entirely safe to choose him rather than any other. Hal would never countenance me being rushed into wedlock with him, and for his part Lamington seems quite content to admire me from a distance. He has never so much as tried to kiss me.' Cassandra thought she sounded slightly regretful.

'I should hope not!' exclaimed her companion indignantly. 'I would want to knock the fellow down if he had. But really, Georgiana, I still can't see what the ruse served. Here we are months later, and no further on.'

'Did you not enjoy meeting me in secret and deceiving everyone – did you not find it exciting?'

'You know damn well I did, you little minx,' he said roughly, 'but I can't afford to stay in Brighton any longer dancing attendance on you. My pockets are entirely to let, and damned insolent tradesman are dunning me every time I set foot outside my lodging. Once we are married and can lay our hands on your inheritance, we can live where we please and how we please! Your brother will be bound to set us up handsomely, if we force his hand. As soon as there's a moon big enough to see by, which will be early next week, you must sneak out of the house and meet me, and we can be off to Scotland as fast as four horses can carry us!'

'It does sound thrilling,' said Georgiana wistfully. 'And it would be famous to have my own house, and no longer be watched over by fusty old chaperones, I do agree.'

Cassandra had heard enough. She thought that Georgiana was allowing herself to be persuaded into flight; not, it seemed, because she cared very greatly for the young gentleman, but because the idea of romantic adventure and what she perceived as freedom appealed to her. For her own part, Cassandra did not think that marriage to a man so very obviously concerned chiefly with getting his hands on a young lady's money would turn out to be anywhere near as enjoyable and liberating as her sister-in-law in her naiveté imagined. She was determined to put a stop to it. She would save Georgiana from herself.

CHAPTER FORTY-ONE

Hal had not dined at home, but spent the evening with friends, and the house was quiet when he returned, only slightly foxed, around midnight. He had refused Jem's assistance in undressing, having no wish to endure another of his lectures about the abject folly of his present behaviour. He was standing in his shirt, boots and breeches, gazing sightlessly in front of him, having entirely forgotten what he had intended to do next, when the door to his chamber opened silently, and his wife slipped inside, and closed it carefully behind her.

Despite everything, despite the anger and the hurt that still gnawed away at him and refused him a moment's peace, his wretched heart began to pound at the sight of her. She had not dressed to entice him; she was wearing the cursed nightcap again, and a thick dressing-gown belted tightly about her waist. But she was here.

He opened his mouth to speak, though he had no idea what he would say. *Get in my bed*, perhaps, pathetically; *I cannot bear to be without you*; *I need you*; *I do not care what you have done*. But she raised a small, resolute hand and said, 'Irlam, I have not come here to renew our quarrel, or to say a word about myself. I have been waiting up for your return. Please listen to me. You must know I would not come to you like this if it were not important.'

She sat down in the armchair beside his fireplace with an air of great determination, and it was clear that, short of him putting her over his shoulder and carrying her from the room, she would not budge until she had said her piece. It gave him a twisted kind of pleasure to see her here, to be alone with her as they had not been for so long. He wanted to throw her on the mattress and seek sweet oblivion in her body. He was not even deterred by the preposterous nightcap. He wanted to make her come, to bring her to such ecstasy that she would lose all of her precious self-control and cry his name as she did so. Just for a moment, he would drive all thoughts of her lover from her head. Or if he did not, at least he would not know it. He could not speak for wanting her. Hal sank down onto his bed, and gestured wordlessly to her to continue.

'I have been worried about Georgiana,' she said, her voice expressionless. He did not know what he had been expecting to hear, but it was not this. He looked at her intently as she continued, trying to focus, to force down his desire for her, wishing that he were completely sober. 'I have always thought that she had not the least real intention of marrying Lamington, and in recent weeks her mood has seemed erratic to me, as if she were faced with some decision, and unsure what to do. I imagined that she was debating whether to go through with the marriage, and I would have liked to speak with her and see if I could help, but I hesitated. I was not sure I had the right, or if she would repulse me. I was selfish, I am obliged to own, and caught up with my own worries. But today, at the picnic, she walked apart with two of her friends, and I was uneasy in my mind and followed after them; I scarcely know why.'

She swallowed, and her hands plucked nervously at the woollen fabric of her gown. 'Please believe me when I say that if I had seen them still together, the three of them, I would have turned back. Georgiana has always been very good to me, and I have no taste for sneaking around or spying or prying into the business of others. But as I walked along, I heard voices, from behind a hedge, and I realised it was her, with a man, though I could not see them.'

'Lamington?' he croaked, entirely at sea now. 'There is no great harm—'

'No. Lord Lamington has been away, and returned to Brighton only this afternoon, if you recall.' He did not recall it, in his present condition, but her voice rang with certainty. 'It was another man, a young man, though his voice was only vaguely familiar to me. Not someone I know well, or have met in this house. And he was . . . he was attempting to persuade her to elope with him. To Gretna Green.'

'Nonsense!' he said instinctively.

'It is not nonsense. They have been meeting in secret, but he told her he could no longer afford to stay in Brighton dancing attendance on her. He said they must flee in a few days' time, and marry in Scotland. Then, he said, you would be forced to allow her access to her fortune. Hal, whoever he is, I think, I fear he is a fortune-hunter.'

He sat staring at her, his mind whirling, the fumes of brandy dissipating as he struggled to master the situation. 'Did she agree to go?' he said at last. He supposed it was the only question that should matter just now.

'I do not know; I did not stay to hear. I don't think she is in love with him – maybe I am wrong, but it seemed to me from what she said that she has been enjoying the excitement of their clandestine meetings, and that the idea of being married and free from chaperonage is attractive to her. Nothing more than that. But I could not . . . I know too much of fortune-hunters from my own experience. I did not think an honourable man would urge her as he did. I felt obliged to tell you, so that you can talk to her, and stop her. Make her realise that she will ruin her life if she does this.'

Hal did not answer her immediately. He did not think

to insult her by asking if she was quite sure that no other construction could possibly be placed on what she had heard. If she said that this had happened, he believed her without question. And it was odd, more than odd, that he believed her now, and believed that she had no other motive than concern for Georgie's future and her reputation, and yet when she had tried to plead for herself he had refused to listen to her, had assumed she was lying.

He had no time to puzzle this out now. He had to deal with Georgie, and then perhaps he would have leisure to consider his own desperate situation. That was how it had always been for him, these past six years – he had always put the children first.

But he could see that Cassandra was distressed, and that it had cost her something to come to him, after everything that had passed between them, and after they had barely spoken in days. Whatever she was – he did not know what she was – she had courage. But he had always known that, had he not, since their very first meeting?

He rose, and she stood too. He could not interpret the expression on her face. He moved closer to her, and took her cold hand, and raised it to his lips. Suddenly he felt very tired, and very sad, and despite all that he still wanted her as desperately as he ever had. More, in fact. *Let the world burn*, he thought wildly, *let Welby have her tomorrow and for ever, if I can only have her now.* 'Thank you, Cassandra,' he said, his voice very low. 'You did not have to do this – it would have been easier for you to say nothing. You might have thought all this not your concern. Never think I am not sensible of it.'

She achieved a tremulous smile, and pulled her hand from his. He thought he could manage to let her go, despite his overwhelming need for her, but as she moved towards the door, her back straight, he suddenly heard himself say hoarsely, almost against his will, 'Don't go. Stay with me, Cassie. Stay, just for tonight.'

She turned back towards him, her face white and set, and there was a world of sadness in her voice when she spoke. 'How can you say that to me now, after all the terrible things you have said before? When you have made it very clear exactly what you think of me?'

He crossed the room in two long strides and took her gently by the shoulders. He was almost pleading when he said, 'I know what I have said. I know what I saw, and I cannot unsee it, however much I try, and heaven knows I have tried. But tonight I don't care. I want you, Cassie, so much I feel I could die of it. Look me full in the face and tell me honestly you don't want me in the same way, and I will let you go and never trouble you again, I promise.'

Cassandra, whose fate it was to tell the truth and not be believed, found herself incapable of lying now, though a large part of her longed to do so. Not all of her, however. She raised her chin and met his gaze, and there were tears in her own eyes when she said, 'I do still want you. I wish I didn't, but I do. I won't deny it.'

He laughed a little sadly. 'Cassie, please don't cry, or I fear I will too. Take off that ridiculous cap for me.'

She untied it and let it drop to the floor, and faced him bravely. There was an aching hunger along with the sorrow in his eyes. It called out to her, and, despite the pain he had caused her and all the sleepless nights she had endured, a treacherous spark of excitement ignited deep inside her. It was wrong, it was wrong in so many different ways, but suddenly all thoughts of right and wrong were nothing to her. He was still her husband, was he not? And if he had not been, she still would have wanted him. Perhaps it would be the last time, in which case she must savour every second, or perhaps somehow it was still not too late.

She forced herself to say, 'If I do this, Hal, will you turn on me afterwards and cut me to pieces with your cruel words? Is this a trap you have set for me? Will you tell me I've proved you right by falling into your arms after all you have accused me of?'

'I promise I will not,' he groaned. 'No accusations. No more words tonight at all. Undress for me, Cassandra, so that I know without a shadow of a doubt you are offering me your body this last time of your own free will. But don't speak. And I won't. Not to reproach you any more, not to say a single word.'

She knew she should walk away and leave him; she knew she should at least hate herself for even considering staying. But she did not. God help her, she wanted this. Her fingers fumbled with the belt and buttons of her heavy robe, but at last she undid them all and let it slip from her shoulders. She stood before him in her thin nightgown and her nipples pebbled under his intense gaze. They were in dangerous territory, she thought, as if, wild as their lovemaking had often been before, some essential layers of civilisation had been stripped away now. She was desperately hurt still, and she knew he felt the same, mistaken as he was. Raising her hands to the tiny buttons at the front of her gown, she very deliberately undid them, and shrugged the flimsy garment from her shoulders, standing naked and exposed before him. But she did not speak. She too was tired of words.

He was very fast. Before she had become aware that he was moving, he had picked her up in his strong arms and set her down upon the bed. There had been laughter, often, when they had made love, but there was no laughter now. He lay close beside her and touched her hair with an unsteady hand. He was breathing hard.

He must have removed his coat, waistcoat and neckcloth before she entered the room, but was still wearing his buckskin breeches, his top-boots and his fine lawn shirt. Perhaps he felt somehow safer that way, less vulnerable, while she, uncovered, could not hide from him. But she thought they were past such distinctions now. As long as he was here with her, the power she had over him would still be undeniable. *Tomorrow*, she thought, *he will regret this more than I do, because of what he thinks I have done. He will be ashamed, and very likely turn from me for ever, and I do not know what I will do. Tonight, though . . .*

The room was very quiet, save for their rapid breathing. He did not kiss her. He reached out and began slowly to trace the curves and hollows of her body with infinitely careful fingers. It was almost as if he were trying to map her, to impress every inch of her upon his memory. *Surely*, she thought, *surely he cares for me, even if he will never say so now.* It was unbearably arousing, for he had studied her these last weeks and knew exactly how to provoke the most intense reactions from her body, and close on unbearable. The tenderness in his wordless touch almost broke her heart, but she would not think of that now. He was cupping her face, caressing its lines, and she turned her mouth to his hand, the tip of her tongue seeking his skin. If she could not kiss him, if he would not kiss her, at least she could taste him. She found his palm, and licked it, the familiar salt taste of him, and she felt him shiver at the touch. Good. It was still so good, despite everything.

She closed her eyes. She did not need to see him. She did not want to see him. She sucked a finger into her mouth, and felt him gasp. And then his body was on her, crushing her, and while his finger remained in her mouth, running around the moist, achingly sensitive flesh inside her lower lip, his mouth was on her breast at last. She arched her back against him and locked her fingers in his hair, clasping him to her while she still could, welcoming the closeness and heat of him even if it was all an illusion. Over the singing of the blood in her ears, over the pounding of her heart, she thought he moaned.

And then he was gone, his fingers from her face, his lips from her breast, his weight no longer pressing her into the bed. She gave a soft, involuntary cry of frustration. She dared not open her eyes, for fear of seeing along with his desire an expression on his face that would destroy her. Was he going to leave her now, like this?

But no. He was still close by. Very close. He kissed her briefly, his tongue claiming her mouth for a tantalising moment, and then he took her hand in his, and drew it down her body until it rested on her mound, and left it there. She felt the mattress shift, felt his warmth. He was kneeling between her legs, the leather of his boots suddenly cold against her ankles. He must be watching, waiting. She thought she could feel his eyes on her skin.

She bit her lip, and slid her fingers into the damp curls at the meeting of her thighs. She was wet, and she sighed a little and moved upon herself, her eyes still tightly closed. Her other hand found her breast, and stroked it. If he would not give her ease, she would take her own pleasure and he would watch her as she did, and surely it would be seared on his memory. How much more exposed and vulnerable to him could she be? But she did not think – while she still had the power to think – that it would come to that in the end. She could hear, attuned to him as she was, that his breathing was growing more ragged, and she knew instinctively that any moment he would break, and feel compelled to lose himself in her. If she refused to look, she could not know when he might do it. She hoped it would be soon.

Another of his swift, unexpected movements; he was holding her and positioning her in accordance with his desire, and she, unresisting, found herself on her side. Now his hand was on her left hand, guiding it to his buttons, and those buttons were very close to her face. She smiled unseen against the soft buckskin leather of his breeches, and undid him eagerly, and he sprang free, fully aroused. She would not see, but she could feel, she could taste, with her fingers and her lips, his skin, his silky softness and his warm hardness. It was all hers, for this brief moment. She made a small noise of animal satisfaction, and took him deep in her mouth, and lost herself in pleasuring him, and pleasuring herself.

He was close, she could feel that he was almost there, and so was she, when his hands tangled in her hair and brought her to a stop, holding her still. She moaned involuntarily against him – she had so wanted him to spend himself helplessly inside her, but he would not. He withdrew from her and they both lay panting for a moment, then he was moving again, moving her too, and now she found herself on her back, spread wide to him, and at last he was lifting her legs, and she was aiding him, opening herself to him. He slid inside her wetness with a sudden dizzying rush that made them both cry aloud. She reached out to touch him, to cling to him, any part of him that she could find, digging her fingers into his back, his muscular buttocks. And he was thrusting into her wildly with no barrier between them, as he never had before, but almost before she could register the difference, before she could think what it might mean, he was pulling out of her with a groan almost of pain, and spilling himself over her belly.

Her eyes were open now, and as the fierce urgency leached from his face her gaze pleaded with him to break down, to understand that two people who could share such intense moments could surely struggle their way to some sort of understanding, if they both cared enough. But if he read anything there, it seemed to her that he refused to acknowledge it. And still he did not speak.

And she could not speak if she had wanted to, because he turned her and positioned her again, and buried his face between her legs, and with his lips and tongue ruthlessly set about bringing her to the edge and over the edge, and when the waves subsided he took her there again, and yet again, until she saw coloured lights exploding behind her eyelids, felt herself break into a thousand pieces, and she thought perhaps she cried out his name, she did not know, and did not care. And if she was still angry with him, or he with her, she could not remember why. But the hurt and loss remained. She was weeping as she came.

Perhaps they slept, exhausted, spent, and perhaps

they held each other as they slept, but when Cassandra awoke to see Hal sprawled beside her, half-dressed, his face turned away from her, she rose carefully and covered herself, and slipped from the room, leaving him to wake alone. Because, after all, nothing had changed.

CHAPTER FORTY-TWO

When Hal woke and found himself abandoned, he was scarcely surprised. He thought he might even be glad. What could they say to each other? It seemed he would always want her, and she would always want him – he refused to believe that she was dissembling in that; no, he knew in every fibre of his body that she was not – but what good did it do, after all, and where did it take them? The gulf between them was as wide as ever, despite the intense connection they had always found in their lovemaking. And it was if anything too intense, too raw and elemental. He had so nearly lost control, so nearly and so unforgivably come inside her. There could have been a child from last night, and then he would be tied to her for ever. And he simply could not contemplate that, for the sake of his own sanity. And hers. He had seen her last night with her eyes firmly closed even in the throes of passion, refusing to look at him for reasons he dared not imagine, and then when at last she had met his gaze there had been such agony there that he had scarcely been able to bear it. He must put an end to all this.

He was glad when it was time to rise and dress and think about something else, even though the conversation he would have with Georgie today was not one any sane man could anticipate with anything other than dread. His sister was not an early riser, and so he went for a ride, losing himself in the physical activity as best he could, and still she had not appeared when he returned. It was nearly noon when he – sitting in his study with the door open a crack – heard light footsteps on the stairs, and his sister's voice, saying something to one of the footmen. Of Louisa and Cassandra there was no sign, and he knew he must take advantage of this moment. He rose from his chair, and went to the door. 'Georgie?' he said.

She turned, and as he studied her face he saw that Cassandra was right: she was unhappy. There were dark circles under her blue eyes, and the bright smile she donned to greet him was awry somehow. He realised now that he had been so preoccupied with his own affairs that he had neglected her. He should have noticed that there was something very wrong with her long since. 'Will you come and sit with me?' he said, trying and he thought probably failing to behave naturally in front of the servants in the hall.

She could hardly refuse him, and entered the room, her face closed and wary. He shut the door behind her, and leant against it, watching her intently. She pouted and said teasingly, 'Why, Hal, suddenly I feel as though I were a child again, and I have been summoned to account for some misbehaviour that my beast of a governess has reported to you. Whatever is the matter?' Her tone was deliberately casual, but her voice was not quite steady.

'Sit down,' he said. She did so, glancing up at him as he crossed the room to sit opposite her, and he thought for the first time there was fear in her eyes. It hurt him to see it there. 'Am I such an ogre?'

'Of course not!' she replied lightly. 'And I am no longer a child to be cowed by my big brother's stern face.'

'I don't think you ever were,' he said ruefully. 'Cowed, I mean. Not you, and God knows not the twins or Fred.'

A ghost of a mischievous grin flitted across her face. 'Do you remember the time when they—'

'Don't, Georgie,' he said wearily. 'I'm too tired to beat about the bush.'

She looked down at her clasped hands. 'I have not the least idea what you mean, Hal.'

He had spent hours this morning considering what he should say to her. He was determined to keep Cassandra out of it, not to reveal that she had overheard and come to him. It was ridiculous, he was aware, given what he had decided during his ride, but he still wanted to protect her, while she remained his wife. But as he sat contemplating his sister, all his careful phrases vanished completely from his mind. What was the point of it all? 'I'm sorry, Georgie,' he said simply.

'What are you sorry for?' she said uneasily.

'I'm sorry I made such a poor fist of looking after you – all of you, but especially you, I think. I tried, you know, I really did, but I was not old enough or wise enough.' His voice cracked a fraction as he said, 'I miss them, Georgie. I miss them every day. Most of all I miss Mama. I know you must, too.'

Her face crumpled, her lower lip trembled, and two fat tears slid down her face and vanished into the starched collar of her habit shirt. 'Oh, Hal!' she wailed. 'Yes, I do miss her! If only she were still with us, I think perhaps . . . But I have been so very, very stupid, and you will be furious with me, and I know you have every right to be!' She began to sob in earnest, and he handed her his handkerchief and waited.

When Georgiana's feelings had relieved themselves and she had wiped her face, she sniffed and said, 'It is I who should apologise to you. We have tried your patience beyond endurance, and no matter what terrible things the twins have ever done, this is worse, I think.'

'Are you with child, Georgie?' he said abruptly. This was what had occurred to him in his darkest, most desperate moments. Nothing that Cassandra had overheard had made this impossible, and the thought that his sister might be going through such trouble alone had pierced him to his core.

'Hal!' she said, in what appeared to be genuine shock. His squeezed heart relaxed a little. 'Of course I am not with child!'

'Then whatever it is, it cannot be so very terrible. Will you not tell me, and we will see if we can puzzle it out between us?'

She took a deep breath, and it all came spilling out of her in a jumbled mess of words. She had met Captain Hart in Bath, when she had been at school there, when she was about to turn seventeen. He had been so very handsome and dashing, and all the girls had mooned over him, but his fancy had alighted on her, and it had been intoxicating to be so chosen. For a long while they had not spoken, but had exchanged significant glances and smiles whenever they had encountered each other in public. The whole school had been agog with it.

Hal knew that he had to let Georgiana tell her story without interruption, but there were several moments, as she did so, when he found that he was digging his fingernails deep into his palms to prevent himself from blurting out his thoughts. There had been clandestine meetings in Bath – *What kind of man*, he wanted to cry, *entices a schoolgirl out to meet him in secret?*

It might have ended there, Georgiana told him; she had been quite prepared to forget the young officer's attentions in the excitement of her come-out. But he had followed her to London, in a highly flattering fashion, and renewed the acquaintance. Although the Captain's own regiment was not fashionable, he had many friends among the younger sons of noble houses – no doubt the disreputable younger sons, thought Hal grimly – and he was invited to all manner of balls and entertainments, though not, Georgie said naively, to dreary old Almack's. He had offered for her hand, as Hal himself must surely recall, in an honest and open manner, and Hal had refused him, making it horribly clear, Adolphus had told her afterwards, that he would never be considered a fit suitor. It was at this point that he presented her with the idea of elopement to Scotland.

'I was shocked, of course,' she said, sniffing dolefully, 'but it was quite exciting, too. I was not quite sure whether I should go through with it, though, so in order to buy some time I conceived the plan of pretending to accept Lamington.'

'Oh, good God,' said Hal involuntarily. 'Just for a moment in listening to you I had quite forgot Lamington. No, I'm sorry, I did not mean to interrupt you. Please continue.'

'Well, one does forget Lamington, doesn't one?' she said airily. 'He's always just . . . there. And I don't think he wants to marry me really – not truly – but of course he admires me.' *Of course he does*, thought Hal. 'And his mother would very much like us to be married, even though she disapproves of me so much, so I thought that he would probably offer for me, because he always does what she tells him to. And I know you think he's an idiot, so I thought you would say that we would have to have a very long engagement, and that would leave me free to decide what to do about Adolphus. And you did.'

There must be madness somewhere in our family, Hal groaned inwardly. 'That's insane, Georgie,' he said baldly. 'Why did you need to be engaged to Lamington in order to decide what to do? It's the craziest thing I ever heard in my life. And also, I am sorry to say, quite cruel.'

'It would be if he truly cared for me,' she said defensively, flushing and biting her lip. 'But I promise you he does not in the least. He thinks I am pretty, I dare say, but all the rest is his mother. I think . . .' Her voice grew small now, and she looked down into her lap and did not meet his eyes. 'I think my success went a little to my head, Hal. I was so very much admired, and so many gentlemen wanted to dance with me, and sent me flowers, and wrote poetry to me, even, and offered for my hand, and it all seemed unreal. It was like a game to me.'

'It's not a game, Georgie. It's people's lives. Your life.'

'I know that, I do.' She sniffed again, and twisted his handkerchief. 'And although it was very exciting to sneak off to meet Adolphus, and to have him kiss me, which I did like, I must be honest, and tell me that I was his whole world, I began to have doubts. It began to seem to me that he cared too much for my fortune. He was always speaking of it, and of how we would be able to live so well when we had it. And he realised I was wavering, and became more insistent, and my doubts grew stronger. I'm not sure I care for him, really, I think I probably don't, but I . . . I did not know how to pull back. And . . . and I thought that if I sent him away, even if he would go and not make an enormous scandal, I'd have to marry Lamington after all. Which I certainly didn't want to do. I realised quite recently that my Lamington plan, which I thought so clever, has some drawbacks. I have been,' she said resolutely, 'very, very silly. I do see that now.'

'I'm glad you see it,' Hal said a tad unsteadily. He suddenly found that he was suppressing a strong desire to laugh; he knew it would be fatal to do so, as he had frequently observed in the past that younger siblings, like cats, did not at all like to be considered objects of ridicule. He swallowed his mirth and said, 'I promise I will not read you a lecture like a prosy old bore, Georgie. I do not believe Papa would ever have done so, so I shall not. I only wish you had confided in me, or in Aunt Sophia, or Louisa. But I know we have all been preoccupied with our own affairs, and worn out with the boys and their constant chaos besides. I should have realised there was something wrong; I blame myself severely. But do you see now why I told you that you need not contemplate marriage in your first Season, because you are still too young?'

'I suppose I do,' she conceded reluctantly. 'Although,' she said, with a trace of her accustomed spirit, 'Cassandra is only a few months older than me, and has never had a proper Season at all, or been to any balls or parties – apart from provincial ones in Yorkshire, which I must think do not count in the least

– before she came here, and you did not think *her* too young to marry. I assume.'

'Perhaps I was wrong about that too, and should have listened to my own advice,' he said heavily, all trace of mirth vanished in an instant. He saw that she was about to speak, and shook his head. 'I cannot speak of my own affairs. Please don't ask me to, Georgie. We must resolve this tangle before I can think of them.'

'I'm sorry,' she said in a small voice. 'I really am, you know, Hal. Thank you for not being excessively angry with me. I know you have a right to be.'

'I expect Aunt Sophia will have plenty to say. Not to mention Louisa, for they both must know of it. And you will have to speak with Lamington, which will hardly be pleasant for you – you need not tell him all, you need not mention Hart, but you have no choice but to inform him face to face that you cannot marry him. You can surely see that you owe him that much.'

She nodded, grimacing, but did not think to argue, he was glad to observe. 'And . . . Adolphus?'

'I will deal with Captain Hart,' said Hal grimly.

'You will not challenge him to a duel, or hit him, or anything like that, will you, Hal? I do not want you, or even him, I suppose, hurt through my folly. I have done enough damage already.'

Perhaps there is hope for her yet, her brother thought. But all he said was, 'I shall certainly not challenge him to a duel, and I do not mean to plant him a facer, though I am sorely tempted and quite sure he richly deserves it.

You must realise that he has behaved like an absolute scoundrel, and a man who will meet a schoolgirl in secret and attempt to persuade her to elope with him will undoubtedly do so again, and perhaps succeed next time. I do not want scandal, for your sake, but I will impress on him the fact that he cannot treat women so with impunity.'

'I knew even when he was suggesting Gretna and I was entertaining the idea that it was wrong, and showed him in a very poor light. I wonder now if he ever cared for me in the slightest, or if it was all my fortune?' Georgie said sadly.

'I'm sure he cared for you, Georgie, as far as a man like that is able.' He was not sure of it at all, but he could not wound her further by saying so. He sighed. 'Not every man is a fortune-hunter. I had an endless procession of fellows asking for your hand, remember, and I am sure that almost all of them valued you for yourself. There is much to value, you know, my dear. But merely being attracted by someone's appearance, however powerful and overwhelming that feeling might be, is not enough, and none of them could be said to know you, or you them. And more and more I think that it is very perilous, to marry someone you scarcely know.'

Georgiana rose, and came around the desk, and put her arm about his shoulder, and leant her dark head against his. He closed his eyes and took a little comfort from her sisterly embrace. 'How are we ever supposed to get to know people,' she said reasonably, 'when men and women are never allowed to be alone together unchaperoned?'

He let out a crack of laughter. 'Really? You seem to have circumvented that convention of society easily enough, Georgie. And now here we are.'

'I suppose I deserved that. Thank you for not moralising at me about it.'

'I could hardly do so without being a rank hypocrite,' he said, thinking of the Windleshams' ball, when he had first kissed Cassandra, and would undoubtedly have gone on to do much more if they had not been interrupted.

'That would not stop most men,' his sister said. 'You're a good man and a good brother, you know, Hal, and we have all of us been a severe trial to you. I don't want to pry into your affairs, especially not when you have been so very forbearing with me, and heaven knows I have no right to preach, but if you think badly of Cassandra for some reason, I am sure you are mistaken. She is not by any means a silly, spoilt girl like me, you know. And I think she—'

'I told you I can't talk about it, Georgie, I'm sorry. It's not that I am ungrateful for your concern, but I need to speak with Cassandra privately. I know what I shall say to her now.'

'Don't say anything rash, Henry. If you do, I am sure you will regret it afterwards.'

He did not answer her, for he could not imagine any course of action that he could take now that would not lead to bitter regret. But still he must act, and act soon.

CHAPTER FORTY-THREE

Louisa and Cassandra joined Hal and Georgiana for a late nuncheon, which was a quiet meal, but perhaps a little less strained than had been the case in the house of late. When it was done, Hal rose with decision and said, 'Georgie and I are going to visit Lamington directly. You need not accompany us, Louisa.'

'I should think not,' his aunt said, her eyebrows raised. 'It is far too early to call on anyone, Hal – what can you be thinking?'

'I know it is,' he replied. 'But this is no visit of courtesy. Georgie will, I am sure, not mind me telling you both that she is today going to inform Lamington that she cannot marry him.'

'And I am going to apologise to him – and, I suppose, to his horrid old mother too, though it is hardly any of her business – for leading him such a dance over the past few months because I did not know my own mind,' said Georgiana resolutely. 'It will be nasty, I am sure, and she will reproach me at tedious length even if he does not, but it is quite my own fault, and I shall bear it without complaint.' She was not quite restored to her normal spirits, and her present demeanour was both chastened and somewhat self-consciously saintly. Hal supposed it would wear off in time, and the old mischievous Georgie would return.

'You will feel better when it is done, whatever she says to you,' he reassured her, as one might reassure an early Christian martyr about to enter the Colosseum that lions' teeth were said not to be too terribly sharp.

'Well,' said Louisa, 'good. It is not my affair, but I'm excessively glad you are not going to marry Lamington. It's bad enough that they're our cousins. You would both have been miserable within a twelve-month – or maybe he wouldn't have been, maybe he's too stupid to be miserable, but you are not, and he and that mother of his between them would have driven you to distraction, Georgie. And think, besides, of the deadly dull pink children you must have had with him, quite like a litter of piglets, I am sure. Not,' she said thoughtfully, 'the attractive kind of piglets, either.'

'It is a hideous picture that you paint, Louisa, and you are quite right in all you say,' said Hal, stifling a grin and trying without much success to banish the image from his mind.

'I know,' she said, 'I often am. Away with you both, then.'

'Yes, there is no sense in delaying. This meeting will not get any easier for being put off.' Georgiana grimaced, but rose, and they departed together, leaving their companions to gaze at each other in consternation.

Cassandra had not felt confident enough to contribute anything to the conversation – she could see that Hal and Georgiana had had a serious talk, and she must presume that they had discussed other matters than Lamington, but she could not be sure, nor could she know whether Hal had told his sister that she had spied on her. If he had and Georgie should be angry with her, and upbraid her, or go into the sulks, she would bear it; she was still sure that she had done the right thing. She thought that Hal had sought her eyes as he left, and even perhaps nodded slightly at her, as if to thank her again, but where he was concerned she no longer trusted her own judgement. She was dully aware that Louisa would not think to ask her if she knew what was in Hal's mind; she had to perceive that as matters stood between them he was not at all likely to confide in her, even though she was his wife. This knowledge stung, but she was glad at least to be spared the necessity of discussion, and of either telling Louisa exactly what she had overheard or dissembling. It was cowardly, she supposed, but while she did not know what Hal had revealed to Georgie she had better keep silent, for fear of causing more upset.

She had fallen into a brown study after Hal's

departure, and started when she felt a hand on her shoulder. Lady Louisa had risen from the table, entirely unnoticed by her, and stood by her chair, regarding her kindly. 'I wish I could help you, child,' she said with a warmth that brought tears to Cassandra's eyes. 'I have tried to speak to him, but he can be provokingly stubborn, like all men. You will have to work it out between you, and I hope you may. I am sure every union has its troubles from time to time, though they seem like the end of the world when one is experiencing them. I myself . . .' Whatever she had been intending to add, she thought better of it, and said no more.

Cassandra murmured some incoherent response, and could only be glad when Louisa left her alone. She spent the afternoon in her own sitting room, trying to read a novel and signally failing to take in as much as one word in twenty. She did not consider going out for as much as a second; she did not wish to see anybody and be forced to make polite conversation – she was on pins to know how Georgiana's predicament had been resolved, if in fact it had. Much more than that, she knew that she and Hal were at a crisis in their own affairs. They could not go on like this – the night they had spent together had solved precisely nothing – but she did not know what possible escape there could be from her situation if he still refused to listen to her. She had still not been able to have any communication at all with Matthew, and supposed that she had no choice but to at last risk giving Kitty a letter for him, and trusting that, despite her deep devotion to the Pendlebury family and to Hal in particular, she would not open it or take it straight to her master. If she could not rely even on Kitty, then the rest of the servants were entirely out of the question as emissaries, and she was lost.

She passed a tense couple of hours, alert for every sign of movement elsewhere in the house. She had told Wilson she was not at home to visitors, and so she did not fear interruption, but every time voices were heard in the hall she started up, only to sigh and subside back into her chair when she did not afterwards hear Hal's footsteps on the stairs; she would know his tread, she realised, among a thousand. She heard Georgiana return, her tones noticeably subdued as she greeted Wilson, but her sister-in-law went straight up to her bedchamber, and it seemed that Hal had not accompanied her home. She thought she heard Georgie come downstairs again a little while later, but she did not enter the room, and Cassandra was glad of it, distracted as she was.

She was beginning to wonder where Hal could possibly be, and if indeed her worst fears had been realised and he had left Brighton without telling her. She was summoning up her courage to find Georgiana and ask her if she knew where her brother was, when at last she heard his voice, and a few moments later her door opened and he stood regarding her. He entered, and closed the door carefully behind him. 'We must talk, Cassandra,' he said, and his flat tone sent a thrill of apprehension running down her spine.

CHAPTER FORTY-FOUR

'Is . . . all well with Georgiana?'

He subsided into a chair opposite hers, and stuck out his long legs, contemplating the tassels on his shiny hessians with an abstracted frown. 'Yes, and it is thanks to you alone. When I called her into my study this morning, she told me all before I said a word to her of what you had discovered. I never did so, in fact – I had not intended to speak of it, and there was no need. I think she was desperate to tell me, or perhaps to tell anyone – she merely needed someone to sit down with her and talk of something more than commonplaces.'

'Perhaps I should have spoken to her myself,' said Cassandra. 'I have been thinking that I am greatly at fault for not trying harder to gain her confidence.'

'It was my place to do so, not yours. You have only

known her for a few short weeks, after all. I have neglected her for a long time, I realise now. She poured it out to me – the business with Hart, for she told me unasked that he was the man, and her crazy misguided reasons, if you can call them reasons, for entangling herself with poor Lamington. I like to think that when it came to it she would never have taken the grave step of running away to Gretna, but I suppose now we will never know. Thank God that disaster has been averted.'

'Was Lord Lamington very distressed when she told him she would not marry him?'

'I left them alone to do it, so I did not see his immediate reaction, but she said he took it quietly enough, which was decent of him, poor fellow. She maintains that he never really cared for her, but was merely acting at his mother's behest. I do not know if she is right, or if it only suits her to think so. Her Ladyship, of course, was furious, though she cloaked it with a smile. She had herself on a tight rein; I think she believes that, if there is no open breach between the families, the thing may come off one day. In her eyes Lamington is such a great catch that she cannot really conceive that any sane woman could jilt him. She believes Georgie is a silly girl who will come to her senses given time. Let her think so. I do not care a jot. I have seen enough of the pair of them these past months to last me for years.'

'And Captain Hart? Will you allow her to see him again – does she even wish to do so?'

'I do not think she does. I think she had begun to

realise a while since that his chief object in wooing her was to gain control of her fortune. But she had gone so far with him that she did not know how to pull back. In a sense my intervention gave her the excuse she needed. And she will not have the opportunity to see him, for Captain Hart will be leaving Brighton no later than tomorrow. His creditors are hard on his heels, and he has no reason to linger now.'

'You have seen him?'

'Just now, at his lodging. What a ramshackle specimen he is – handsome enough, I suppose, but with not much else to recommend him. He blustered for a while, but as soon as he realised that I knew everything, he could see that his goose was cooked. He thought to try a little light blackmail, to extort money from me for keeping silent, but I made it quite clear that if he thought to damage my sister's reputation he could only do so by utterly destroying his own in the process. I heard myself threatening to horsewhip him if he slanders her, or approaches her, or if it comes to my attention that he has been trying to play out his tricks on some other young female. I won't, of course, but I think he believed me, and I can't have the fellow arrested, though I wish I could – I do not know what more I can do, in all conscience.'

'It is the second time you have threatened to horsewhip someone who thoroughly deserves it this summer,' said Cassandra with a swift, unhappy smile. 'You will be getting a name for it.'

'I know,' he said. 'I have felt for some time as though

I were living in a bad French melodrama and speaking lines written for me by an indifferent dramatist. I hardly recognise myself.' He sighed, and looked up at her, his face gaunt. 'We cannot continue on like this, Cassandra. It does no good to either of us.'

'I was thinking the same as I sat here waiting for you to return. But Hal, please—'

'My dear, there is no need to plead with me. Do not distress yourself further, but let me say my piece. This business with Georgie has made me come to my senses, and not before time. She said that part of the problem in life was that we are expected to choose whom we wish to marry when the ridiculous and unequal way our society is organised means that we scarcely have a chance to know them.'

'Georgiana really said that?' blurted out Cassandra, hardly knowing what she was saying. Hal's words were filling her with dread; she felt as though she had a stone in the pit of her stomach. What was he setting out to tell her?

'She might not have put it quite like that,' he said with a brief wintry gleam of a smile. 'But that is what she meant, and she was right, despite the fact that she has spent most of the last months very effectively evading any chaperonage. She is right where we are concerned, certainly. You must admit that we barely knew each other when we married, Cassandra.'

'You wish you had not married me, then? I suppose I cannot wonder at it,' she said in a low voice. If that was how he felt, she would try to feel the same. She had her pride. She would not fling herself at his feet and beg, no matter how much she might want to.

'Certainly I wish I had not proposed to you in such a preposterously public fashion, so that you had no option but to accept me. I do regret that very bitterly. I know the fault is mine, not yours. Nothing in that wretched situation can be laid at your door. I'm sorry too for all I said to you, the accusations I hurled. I was deeply wounded, but that is no excuse.' He rose to his feet, and came and knelt clumsily before her, taking her hands in his. 'I do know you have not been unfaithful to me. I only said so out of shock and pain. But I should know you well enough at least to realise that you would never do that. You are too good, too honest, and I should have believed you. Please forgive me for that, if you cannot for the rest.'

She shook her head in confusion. He believed her – that was happy news, surely? But he did not look at all relieved as he said it. 'But then why—?'

He went on as if he had not heard her, still clasping her hands tightly. 'I rushed you into marriage, when all along you loved another. I realise that Welby never had a chance to declare himself, and that you would have accepted him if he had. I am so sorry I have ruined everything for you. But I will try to set things right. Perhaps we can divorce, so you can be with him honourably. I do not know if it is possible, but I will consult lawyers, and I promise you I will do all I can to free you. If there is any blame to be apportioned, I will take it all. And if in the end we cannot be divorced, at least we can live apart, and Welby can be at your side. Thank God there will be no child. That folly at least I have not committed.'

She sat dazed under the torrent of words, trying to puzzle out his meaning, but still he had not done. 'I only wish I could have met you in other circumstances, Cassandra. Because I am a fool, a clumsy fool, and I have hurt you, but I do love you. I think I fell in love with you when I first met you, even though I was drunk and I did not know it. I told myself it was mere lust that I was experiencing, but I knew in my heart that it was much more than that from the start. I had been wanting to tell you that I loved you with all my heart, but I did not dare—'

'Hal, I need to tell you something! Please listen to me!'

'Hal!'

Cassandra turned, frustrated beyond measure at the interruption, which could not possibly have come at a more awkward moment. Her husband lurched to his feet as the door was flung open. Lady Louisa surged through it, slammed it violently behind her, and stood regarding them with a most peculiar expression, her splendid bosom heaving, her normally pale countenance flushed. Cassandra had never seen her half so agitated before.

Clearly Hal was of the same mind, because he said sharply, 'Louisa! What is the matter? Is it news of one of the children—?'

She shook her head. 'It's Georgiana,' she said, sinking into a chair. 'She's gone!'

CHAPTER FORTY-FIVE

They stared at her in mute incomprehension. Cassandra found her wits first, and said, 'What do you mean, gone? She came back alone a while ago – I heard her . . .'

'So did I,' replied Louisa grimly. 'And five minutes since I thought I should go to her and see how she did, foolish girl that she is. And when I went to her room, I found this.'

She had a crumpled sheet of paper clutched in her hand, and as she spoke she thrust it at her nephew. 'Read it!' she commanded.

Hal took the paper over to the window and scanned it wordlessly, and then passed it to Cassandra. 'I must go after her,' he said, but he stood and waited, tapping his booted foot impatiently, while she read.

It was a brief note, in a hand worse even than Georgie's habitual hasty scrawl, and it had plainly been written by a young lady in a state of considerable agitation.

Dear Aunt Louisa,

it began primly enough,

> *I am very sorry for the trouble I have caused you all, and I do not mean to cause you more, but on reflection I do not think it right that I leave Hal to deal with Adolphus alone. I must see him myself, and make him understand that I shall not marry him. Perhaps he never truly cared for me very much, if at all –* there was a blot here, as from a tear – *but he deserves that much, if Lamington does, and I was obliged to speak to Lamington myself, after all. I will visit Adolphus at his inn, and of course I shall be discreet. I will be back soon, do not fret.*

> *Your penitent niece,*
> *Georgiana.*

'Good God!' Cassandra blurted. 'She must not! Oh, Hal, we must go to her immediately!'

'"Discreet"!' Hal said heavily. 'She was never discreet in her life.'

'Nor was she penitent!' snapped his aunt. 'I will go and order the closed carriage put to – it may better serve your purpose. Take Cassandra with you; you may be in dire need of a chaperone before this business is done with. Get your bonnet, Cassandra, swiftly!' And she whisked out of the room; Cassandra had not known her capable of such urgency.

A bare few minutes later, Cassandra was sitting beside Hal in the luxurious travelling carriage, moving at what seemed to her an agonisingly slow place through the streets of Brighton. The summer was over, and the town was not as jammed with people and vehicles as it had latterly been, but there was still traffic enough.

'You do not surely think,' Cassandra said, as the tense silence in the carriage began to wear on her nerves, 'that Georgiana has been duplicitous with you today, and intends to run away with the Captain despite everything?'

'I do not want to think it!' he ground out. But then, in a slightly easier tone, he added, 'No. No, I cannot believe that of her. She was deeply sorry, I believe, and realised how foolish she had been. But the thought that Hart did not care for her, but only for her money, has wounded her deeply, and I suppose she wants to look him in the face and see if it is true, or if he ever did have tender feelings for her. I am not anxious over what *she* might do now, Cassandra – I am tormented by him. He is a gazetted fortune-hunter, deep in debt, he thought she had slipped from his grasp, and if she in all innocence has put herself in his power . . .'

'You think he may try to take her to Gretna after all,

even against her will? To kidnap her? Can he really be so rash?'

'I think he need not travel so far, or even trouble himself to leave Brighton. I think he may believe that he need only compromise her irrevocably and I must agree to their union.'

'You would not!' She felt she knew him well enough by now to be sure of it.

'No, I would not. Most other men in my position would, I think, but I will not consent to tie my little sister – she will always be that – to a rogue who cares nothing for her, and put her happiness, her future, her very life in his control, all for the sake of a piece of paper that says they are respectably married. If we can get her free of him, I care very little for her reputation, or mine, for that matter. But if he has hurt her . . .'

It was a horrifying thought. Cassandra's hand flew to her mouth, and Hal smiled grimly. 'Yes,' he said. 'More melodrama. I suppose if it came to that I could let them marry and then shoot him immediately after, but I would hang for it, of course, and then scandal would hardly be averted. I hope she is unharmed, my dear. I hope we can extricate ourselves from the coil that she has created. You at least do not deserve to be dragged down with us. I will do everything in my power to prevent that.'

The carriage halted. They had arrived at their destination; there was no time to reply.

CHAPTER FORTY-SIX

It was a tumbledown little inn on the outskirts of the town, its ancient, decayed timbers apparently crumbling by slow degrees into the muddy grass around it, and the proprietor recognised Lord Irlam – he could hardly do otherwise, as he had only left the place an hour earlier – and bowed them to Captain Hart's private parlour. They were not, the innkeeper said, accustomed to entertaining the Quality, and certainly not ladies. Cassandra could well believe it. At least, she thought, Georgiana was unlikely to have encountered anyone she knew here, or have been seen entering by an acquaintance.

The door was locked from the inside. Hal drew the host away, and spoke to him, low and persuasive. Money changed hands, and a key, and the man scurried away, anxious, it seemed, not to encounter Captain

Hart's wrath or to witness what next transpired between the Captain and the furious gentleman with the icy cold blue eyes.

Just as the man vanished down the dark passage, an inarticulate cry of pain was heard from inside the room, and hard upon it a loud crash, as of something heavy falling to the floor. Hal let out a strangled cry and sprang to the door, fitting the heavy old key into the lock with trembling hands and forcing it open. Cassandra did not know what she most feared to see in the dark, low-beamed parlour when she entered at Hal's heels, but in any event she did not expect the sight that met her eyes: her sister-in-law, flushed and furious like some wild heroine of antiquity, standing over her prostrate victim, who must surely be Captain Hart, who was lying groaning at her feet, clutching his bloody head, bereft of the power of speech. Georgiana was brandishing a stout rustic poker in one elegantly gloved hand, and as they watched in horrified fascination she kicked the fallen man smartly with one little booted foot, where it was sure to do him most harm. Cassandra could not help but feel a strong flash of déjà vu, though she did not think that she had looked so triumphant when she had struck Sir Jasper down in similar circumstances. She had not stayed to inflict further damage, nor to gloat over his well-deserved injuries; she had been too busy making her escape.

They rushed to Georgie's side and assured themselves that she was not harmed. 'Oh, but he meant to,' said the

Amazon in muslin and silks, panting slightly. 'Do not doubt it. I have been most thoroughly disillusioned, I assure you.' She appeared to reflect for a moment, and then went in for another well-aimed kick. Neither of her companions felt the least inclination to try to stop her. 'Apart from anything else,' she said, 'I would not have thought him so excessively stupid. It was plain as soon as I set foot in this horrid place not ten minutes since – for I was obliged to walk here, you know, and it took an age – when he ran to lock the door behind me so eagerly and put the key in his pocket that he meant to molest me in the most frightful way. He did not even trouble to attempt to win me over with sweet words and caresses. Not that he would have succeeded, naturally, but he did not even try. He thought, I suppose, if he compromised me thoroughly I must marry him, and my revulsion would be of no account at all once he had me secured.'

'I would not have had you marry him, whatever he had done to you, Georgie,' said her brother. 'I would not leave you at the mercy of such a creature for any consideration in the world. I think you should probably stop kicking him now, though, much as it pains me to say it.'

'I suppose so,' she conceded regretfully, looking down, her foot twitching. 'But what are we going to do with him?'

'I will not allow Hal to shoot him and hang for it, I know that much,' cried Cassandra hotly.

'Why not? It would solve all your difficulties at a stroke,' said Hal with a ghost of an unhappy smile.

Cassandra was horrified that he should think such an appalling thing, and turned on him, her green eyes flashing fire. 'Good God, how could you? Of all the terrible things you have said to me, that is the stupidest and cruellest! I should ask Georgie to lend me her poker, if that is what it takes to make you stop talking wicked nonsense and listen to me for once in your life!'

They gazed at each other intently, and the electric silence stretched between them for a long moment, until Georgie broke it by saying in a matter-of-fact way, 'Unless you especially want to stay here all afternoon, and I can't imagine why you should, you can't possibly like it, I really think we should leave. He's bound to wake up properly sooner or later, and I can't help thinking it might be a trifle awkward. As long as you don't intend to challenge him to a duel, Hal, or tie him up and throw him in the sea . . . ?'

Hal admitted that, much as he might enjoy it, he didn't think that drowning Captain Hart was a sensible solution to their difficulties, and might – who could say? – lead to further complications. The more prosaic idea of summoning a constable, if such a creature should indeed exist in this benighted part of the town, could not be seriously considered, since first of all it would lead to the sort of scandal they were concerned to avoid, and secondly it might be hard or even impossible to convince an upholder of the King's Peace that the gentleman who was still lying stretched out, almost insensible, on the dirty floor, moaning and bleeding was, in fact, the real evil-doer in the situation. And so they left him there, and made their exit. More money was pressed upon the landlord before they departed, and Georgiana was persuaded to leave her poker behind.

CHAPTER FORTY-SEVEN

It was a weary party that made its way back to the house, where Louisa was waiting anxiously for them. After a glance at Hal's set face and Cassandra's stormy expression, she drew her niece away, telling her sternly that she had caused enough trouble for one day and should, in a better-regulated household, be sent to her bed with a bowl of gruel. 'I should like to see you try it, Louisa,' Georgiana was heard to say as their voices faded and the couple were left alone at last.

'Where were we?' Hal said with a sigh.

Cassandra sat down, her anger draining from her. She might as well be comfortable for yet another exhausting conversation. 'You were on your knees, Hal. You had just told me that you loved me, a thing you have never thought to say to me before, and that nonetheless you wanted to divorce me, or me to divorce you – that last part was not clear to me.'

He sank to his knees again at her feet, took her hands in his and said, 'Damn it all to hell, Cassie, I don't *want* to divorce you. I don't want to lose you at all. But—'

She took back one of her hands and placed a finger over his lips. 'Ssshhh!' she said. 'Please let me speak. You do not need to free me or divorce me. I am not in love with Matthew and he is not in love with me, though he is my oldest and dearest friend. We were embracing that day because he has had a sad disappointment in love, and I was comforting him. That was one of the reasons he came to Brighton, to get away from home and from his sad situation there. It was not just to see me. I tried to tell you, but you would not listen to me.'

'But you said that he was the man who . . . who you . . . Once I realised that, what else could I think?'

She blushed, but met his eyes and continued resolutely, 'Yes, it's true, we were curious, and we wondered what it would be like if we kissed and touched each other. I expect you did the same with some girl when you were young. I do not think that there is any shame in it, and nor, I think, do you, if you could consider it dispassionately for a moment. But it was very clear that it was not right. I don't mean morally. It was not right for me – awkward, uncomfortable – but most of all it was not right for Matthew. He did not feel what he should have felt if he indeed desired me.'

He looked at her intently, and she wondered if he had

yet grasped her meaning. He said slowly, 'Oh, you are saying . . . ?'

'I could not tell you – it was not my secret, and I could not find a way of asking Matthew's permission to share it, because if I had tried to communicate with him you would have suspected us all the more. I was trapped. I hope he will forgive me for telling you now, but after everything that has happened I feel that I must. Hal, do you understand me? It is a matter of life and death, and I would never forgive myself if Matthew suffered any hurt because I betrayed his trust in me. You truly know why you must keep this secret, never tell a soul, not even your family?' He did not seem to be profoundly shocked, as she had expected him to be, and she worried that he had not perfectly comprehended what she was trying to convey to him without unseemly bluntness.

'My dear, I understand you to be telling me that your friend is, er, a devotee of Greek love? I think I am obliged to say it plainly – there have been enough misunderstandings between us. Am I correct?'

'Yes! The person who has bruised his heart is another man. You see now why I hesitated to tell you for so long until I was all but forced to do so?'

Astonishingly, he laughed. 'It is very laudable that you should seek to protect your friend, and feared I would be horrified and want to tell the world and cause him grave trouble, but there was not the least need. My sweet innocent, you have met my brother, have you not?'

She wrinkled her brow. 'Bastian . . . ?'

'Bastian. My mother knew it; I realised much later. I could say that she made me swear to do all I can always to keep him safe, but in truth there was no need; he is my dear brother. My heir, too, as things stand, and I could not ask for a better.'

She looked down at him, her relief so great that she could have burst into hysterical laughter. He believed her, and she had not endangered her friend by revealing his secret; she knew now that he would never tell, for he was well accustomed to keeping such a dangerous confidence. But there was more to make clear before they could be done talking. 'Hal . . . those other things you said . . .'

He was still kneeling at her feet, still holding her hand. He pressed it with a convulsive grip then let it go, and said a trifle sadly, 'Dearest Cassandra, I did not mean to pour everything out to you, but once I had begun I found that I could not very well stop. It was a relief to me to be completely open with you at last. You need not regard my foolishness, you know, if it was unwelcome news. If you will only stay with me – if there is no one else who has a claim on your heart – you need not feel you must—'

She slid from the chair to kneel beside him, and took his face between her hands. 'Hal Pendlebury,' she said. 'You are a great fool. You said you were, and it is true. Why are you so determined that I could not possibly love you, when I am sure I have loved you longer than you have ever loved me?'

He gazed into her eyes, his face full of doubt and dawning wonder. 'You love me? Truly? Please do not tell me polite lies, Cassandra. I could not stand it. Not today.'

'Truly I do. Do you imagine that I would allow the liberties I have allowed to you to any gentleman I did not love to distraction, just because he happened to be my husband?'

He sat back on his heels, and gazed at her in astonishment. 'You love me, despite everything? Despite the fact that I am an idiot? Despite my ridiculous nose and chin?'

'You are my own dear idiot. I love your nose, and your chin. They're wonderful. Have I not kissed them a thousand times?'

'But why didn't you say something?'

'Why didn't you?'

'I was afraid,' he said simply, bending his head at last to brush her lips with his.

'So was I!' she said, and then their lips joined hungrily, and there was no longer any need for speech. It seemed much too long since they had touched each other, and their mouths and their hands were soon busy reacquainting themselves with what they had so missed.

Some while later, he whispered in her ear, still holding her tightly to him, 'Why are we kneeling on the floor, Cassandra?'

'I don't know,' she said, 'you began it. We could at least be lying on it.'

It was later still when Lady Louisa, made uneasy by the extreme quiet that had descended on the house since their return and worried that her warring relatives might either have run away or murdered each other, peered cautiously around the door of Cassandra's sitting room. What she saw there made her withdraw as rapidly as was compatible with the maintenance of complete silence, although in truth she thought she could have made a great deal of noise and still gone unnoticed. She was still shaking her head in amused disbelief when she intercepted her niece on the landing, and barred her way to the sitting-room door with one extended arm.

'I was just going to ask Cassandra if she thought—'

'Not now, Georgie,' she said with unusual decision. 'I believe they would appreciate a little privacy, and for that matter you don't need any more ideas put into your head.'

'Oh, famous!' cried Georgiana. 'Is Hal with her? Are they doing something terribly shocking? Does that mean he has come to his senses at last and they are reconciled?'

Louisa said drily, 'I believe they might be. If they are not, I must say that they have chosen a *very* odd way of continuing an argument. And,' she said, 'while I think of it, now that all these family matters are settled, it is time and past time for me to return home.'

'To Richmond, and Miss Spry?' asked Georgie absently.

'Yes, indeed!' said her aunt with great decision, a curious gleam in her eye.

335

EPILOGUE

TWO MONTHS LATER

Midnight on the bay of Naples. Church bells counted out the hour, and then ceased. It was a warm evening, though it was late autumn, and Cassandra was standing on the balcony of her bedchamber, looking out over the sea. The moon had laid a broad, glittering trail across the water, over towards the island of Capri. The air was heavy with the scent of flowers, both familiar and unfamiliar, and it was very quiet, apart from the faint buzz of soft male voices, speaking English, laughing a little, from the lower terrace close by.

Hal came and stood behind her, and folded his arms about her, nestling her body into his. She sighed, and leant back against him, and he bent and kissed her neck. 'Is it all you hoped, my love?'

She chuckled, and arched her back against him, pressing the length of her body to his. 'Italy, or married life?'

'Well, I meant Italy, but . . .'

Cassandra turned in his arms, and pulled his head down for a long, deep kiss, answering him without words. He was loosely wrapped in a decadent silk dressing-gown, beneath which he was naked, and she wore nothing save a lace peignoir of scandalous Italian design. Her hands slipped under the silk and explored his warm, bare chest; he pushed the loose robe from her shoulders and returned her kiss with growing passion.

They had travelled out by boat to Genoa, accompanied by Bastian and Georgiana. Louisa had been invited to come with them, but had declined with evident horror, saying that no matter how much she loved them all she had seen more than enough of them to last her till next year. She was determined to be fixed in Richmond for many months to come. If they caused a terrible scandal on the continent, she said, and she expected that between them they would very likely do so, they must set it right without her help.

It had seemed wise to put some distance between the Pendlebury family and the Lamingtons; there must be whispers in the ton about the sudden cessation of Georgiana's unofficial engagement and what had prompted it. Everyone agreed that it was best to let the rumours subside, until they were replaced by some other topic of scandal. It had been the right decision.

From Genoa they had journeyed on by slow stages to

Rome and all its decayed and melancholy glories. It had been everything that Cassandra had hoped it would be, and more; not just the ancient city itself, but the eerie catacombs beneath it, and the ruins that stood in romantic isolation out in the Campagna. After some weeks there, they had made their way to Naples, where they had met Cassandra's Cousin Thoroughgood at last for a joyful reunion, and where Matthew Welby had joined them unexpectedly. He and Bastian were much of an age, and soon became inseparable, spending most of their time together. Georgiana had providentially met a bosom bow from school, accompanied by her distinguished parents, soon after their arrival in the south, and had decided to desert the Pendlebury party and go on to Venice at their invitation, muttering something uncomplimentary about lovebirds being excessively dull company. They had let her go; she had been suitably chastened by her experiences of the summer, and Hal found to his surprise that he trusted her to behave with discretion now. Or, of course, to defend herself with a convenient weapon if she could not.

The party was now staying as paying guests with a delightful new acquaintance – a handsome though sadly impoverished Italian count of some fifty years. His ancient family home, half villa, half castle, clung to the cliffs above the sea among the lemon trees, and great urns of flowers and classical statues decorated every terrace and alcove. It was delicious to relax there, to gaze idly at the view while conversation ebbed and flowed, but tempting also to venture out to explore. The Count was a fount of knowledge of his native coast, and had guided them up Vesuvius, and to the excavations at Pompeii, and across the bay to Capri and Ischia, and around the sinister Phlegraean Fields. It was all that Cassandra had pictured it to be, and to share it with Hal was more delightful than she could have imagined.

They kissed hungrily, their breath coming short, their impatient hands pushing aside soft fabrics to find and caress each other's nakedness.

There was a sudden burst of masculine laughter from the terrace below, cut off by what sounded very much like a gasp, low and intimate. It was not a gasp that betokened an unpleasant surprise, but far otherwise, and it was hastily hushed amid more laughter. Then a door opened – lamplight spilt out – and was hurriedly closed, and silence fell. Cassandra smiled a little to herself, and as if he sensed what she was thinking Hal said softly against her neck, 'It seems we are not the only ones feeling amorous tonight.'

Cassandra murmured, 'I wasn't sure you knew, or that you would approve, love.'

His breath was warm on her skin. 'I am so very happy, my dearest Snow White, now that I have found you, that I can hardly grudge an equal share of happiness to my favourite brother. My mother would be so glad for him. Life would be harder for him, she told me just before she died, the way our society stands at present. I still remember all these years later how she gripped my hand with all her fragile strength as she made me promise to watch over him. Of course, I was an unobservant young idiot then, and thought she meant only that he feels things more deeply than the other children do, because he has a more serious nature, but later I realised what she had really been trying to tell me. He is in love, and it is requited. How can I be anything but delighted? And I like your Matthew – I liked him somehow even while I was hating and resenting him because I thought he was your paramour. He's a good fellow. He is part of the family too, is he not, since you love him, and Bastian does?'

His hands were busy all the while with the ribbon ties of her peignoir, and as he released the last of them the lacy robe slipped from her body and pooled at her feet, leaving her naked. About her neck, though, was the heart-shaped pendant set with emeralds and sapphires that Hal had bought for her once, and then not given her in their estrangement. He had presented it to her at last on the day they were reconciled, and she almost always wore it now. He drew her close, and kissed the pendant, and the skin of her throat, sliding his hands down her back to cup her buttocks. 'Mmm,' he said, 'that's better. Much as I appreciate the sight of you gleaming and glorious in the moonlight, goddess, let us follow their example and go to bed. There is some witchcraft in the air in this place, and not only for the young – did you not observe your aunt and the Count at dinner? His ardent glances, her blushes, her quick darting looks in response, shy and then bolder, his hand on hers? That occasion when she dropped her shawl – I would swear on purpose – and he draped it about her shoulders, so very, very carefully.'

Cassandra giggled and said, 'But I was otherwise occupied, my lord, in looking adoringly at you. Is it really so? Well, if it is, I hope they are together now, and giving each other a great deal of pleasure.'

'So do I,' he murmured. 'And now enough talk of others. They must all shift for themselves – I have your pleasure to attend to, wife. And my own.' He picked her up in one swift movement, carried her through the French windows, threw her down on the big white bed, and moved to join her. Her eager hands pulled him close.

A light breeze arose, and blew in from the sea, stirring the long pale curtains and sending the heady Mediterranean scents of lavender, jasmine and lemon creeping into the shadowed bedchambers. It was quiet in the rambling old house, but not quite silent; there were soft sounds when stubble rasped deliciously on stubble or on soft, delicate skin, when lips met other lips, when fingers found the perfect spot, and wordless gasps encouraged, *a little more*. Ardent moans, and whispered endearments, and then sleep, and silence at last. The moon moved across the sky, and only the marble gods and goddesses were there to see it.

ACKNOWLEDGEMENTS

I wrote my first novel in my kitchen in lockdown. I'd never have developed the confidence to do it without the encouragement of all the complete strangers who commented so positively on my Heyer fanfic on A03. But the real inspiration came from my good friends in the Georgette Heyer Readalong on Twitter. I'm particularly grateful to Bea Dutton, who spent many hours of her precious time setting up and running the readalongs. I can't possibly name everyone – there are too many of us – but thank you all, amazing dowagers, for your continuing support with this second novel and beyond it. We have brainstormed insane plot suggestions and I have cried with laughter.

Like many people in the writing, publishing and reading communities, I've loved Twitter. It's been this introvert's ideal place to socialise. So, I'd like to thank all my Twitter friends for the years of chat and mutual support, especially the very talented Katy Moran and the wonderfully kind and endlessly gracious legend among women that is Katie Fforde. Thanks too to all the other lovely authors who took the time to read my work when they have so many other demands on their time, and gave me reviews that made my day, month and year. And anyone writing romance owes a huge debt to the RNA for their tireless work in ensuring romantic fiction finally gets the respect and recognition it deserves.

I've been obsessed with Georgette Heyer's novels since I first read them when I was eleven. They have their faults, but they've provided solace and escape for millions of people in tough times, so thank you, Georgette, even though you would have absolutely hated this book.

Thanks also to my family for putting up with me while I wrote one novel and then another in quick succession. And then another one. Thanks for understanding when I just have to write another 127 words before lunch so I can stop on a nice round number.

My lovely work colleagues Amanda Preston, Louise Lamont, Hannah Schofield and Amy Strong have also been extremely supportive: thanks, Team LBA!

I am very lucky to have a superb agent in Diana Beaumont of Marjacq. She has believed in my writing from the first time she read it, and will always be my champion. Her editorial suggestions are brilliant, and she's just an all-round star. Thanks too to everyone else at Marjacq, including Catherine Pellegrino and Guy Herbert. I know better than most people how important the whole team at an agency is.

Many thanks to everyone at Allison & Busby, including Becca Allen for the fantastic copyediting, to Christina Griffiths for the lush *The Second Lady Silverwood* cover, and Libby Haddock for working tirelessly to get my books into people's hands. And, of course, grateful thanks to my wonderful editor Lesley Crooks. Lesley's inspired edits have made both my novels so much better, and it is a pleasure to be published by her. It's been a long journey to publication for me, and I can't express how much it means to me that Allison & Busby have given me this opportunity.

Finally, if you're reading this because you've bought the book, or my previous one: THANK YOU!

EMMA ORCHARD was born in Salford. She studied English Literature at the Universities of Edinburgh and York, before working behind the scenes in publishing and television for many years. Her first job was at Mills & Boon, where she met her husband in a classic enemies-to-lovers romance. She now lives in North London.

@EmmaOrchardB
@emmaorchardbooks

THE SECOND LADY SILVERWOOD

It is 1814 and she is the talk of the town . . .

Sir Benedict Silverwood needs a new wife.

Kate Moreton, an impoverished spinster and Italian teacher, is an outlandish suggestion, but one that grows on Benedict, alongside his attraction to Kate.

Kate has been hopelessly in love with him for years so the idea of marriage when he doesn't reciprocate her feelings is appalling, but so very tempting at the same time.

Sparks fly and passion flares after the wedding, but it becomes clear that incendiary secrets threaten Kate and Benedict's fragile new life together. The question is, will he be able to love and trust the second Lady Silverwood?